The Fungal Stain

W. H. pugmire

THE FUNGAL STAIN

AND OTHER DREAMS

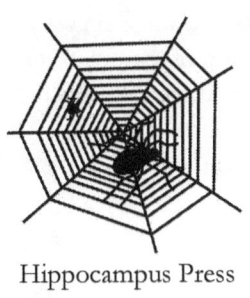

Hippocampus Press

New York

Acknowledgements

"The Hour of Their Appetite" originally appeared in *Dreams of Lovecraftian Horror* (Mythos Books, 1999). It has been utterly rewritten for this edition. Utterly.

"The Sign That Sets the Darkness Free" originally appeared in the chapbook *A Clicking in the Shadows and Others* (Undaunted Press, 2002).

"The Balm of Nepenthe" originally appeared in *Tales of Sesqua Valley* (Necropolitan Press, 1998). It has been substantially rewritten for this edition.

"The Darkest Star" originally appeared in *Tales of Lovecraftian Horror* #11 (Cryptic Publications, 1999). It has been substantially rewritten for this edition.

"The Phantom of Beguilement" originally appeared in *Tales of Love and Death* (Delirium Books, 2001). It has been slightly revised for this edition.

"Stupor Mundi" is an absolutely utter rewrite of an elder tale, "Graffito Flow." It is so utterly redone that it qualifies as original to this edition. (Anyway, I have lost ye original publication and have absolutely no memory of its title or publication date!)

"His Splintered Kiss" originally appeared in *The Urbanite* #10 (1998).

Published by Hippocampus Press
P.O. Box 641, New York, NY 10156.
http://www.hippocampuspress.com
Cover art and interior illustrations by Robert H. Knox. Cover design by Barbara Briggs Silbert.
Hippocampus Press logo designed by Anastasia Damianakos.
First Edition
1 3 5 7 9 8 6 4 2
ISBN 0977173437

This book is dedicated to Leslie and S. T. Joshi,
with so much eldritch love.

contents

An Eidolon of Nothing

Thank heaven! the crisis—
The danger is past,
And the lingering illness
Is over at last—
And the fever called "Living"
Is conquered at last.
—*Poe*

I.

"For pity's sake hold still, Simon," pleaded the artist. "And stop squinting like that."

His sitter slanted silver eyes until they were unpleasant slits. "I do not care for this artificial glare. Can you not work by candlelight?"

"Don't be stupid. I need to be able to see every outlandish detail of your unfathomable face. Simon, please, what are you doing?" Josiah Pope sighed in frustration as his subject rose and stretched.

"I'm going to devour another cup of your detestable brew, which you call coffee, and then I am going for a long walk. I have need of evening air." Taking hold of a soiled cup, he went to the coffee pot and poured out a portion of thick dark liquid. Grumbling, the artist extinguished the bright overhead lights, then smiled at the sound of his visitor's sigh of relief. He watched the tall lean fellow stalk around the large room that had been transformed into work room and storage space. The walls were covered with a plethora of paintings and hazy photographs, some portraits of unusual humans, others depicting scenes of strange, disquieting settings. Simon Gregory Williams stopped at one discarded stack of photographs and began to look through them.

"It would be much easier, Simon, if you'd just let me take your photograph and work from that."

"Pah. What a grotesquely modern idea. Anyway, I detest being photographed. No, I want my portrait conveyed in the traditional manner, or not at all. I will say that some of these scenic snaps are quite good. They have a kind of hazy quality that reminds me of Coburn's frontispieces for the New York Edition of James. Some of these scenes are quite exquisite in their weirdness. This one is particularly eerie."

"Which one?" asked the artist as he absent-mindedly began to put away various artistic tools. Simon brought a large photograph to him, at which Josiah momentarily glanced. "Hmm. Yeah, that is a weird one."

Simon waited for more, then frowned as he was ignored. "Is it a local site?"

The artist shrugged. "I guess so."

"You guess so? Come, now, surely you remember where you found so picturesque a place."

Josiah stopped momentarily to think. "Nope."

Deeply frowning, Simon turned the still over. "Don't you usually date and label these things on the reverse? This one is completely blank."

"Must have forgotten. Listen, are you coming with me to Sybil's gathering? It might amuse you."

The other slowly walked to his friend and shoved the photograph before his face. "Where is this place?"

"Dude, I can't remember. What the hell has you so hot about some stupid photograph?" Yet even as he protested, he began to gaze at the captured image, and suddenly a chill claimed his flesh. He took hold of the still and intently stared at it. "Dang, it is a weird one. Funny, now that you show it to me, I seem to remember having the oddest dreams about it. Where was it?" Josiah stared at the photograph and thought hard. Simon watched him with especial interest, his arcane instincts on high alert. "You know, I think I was walking home from Sybil's place and I came on this gate by accident. Man, why is it so indistinct in my memory? I mean, it's such a cool setting. Yeah, I found an alley that was paved with really old cobblestones, and that caught my attention. The more I study this thing, the more I remember. There was a hazy kind of fog or mist, and I was walking down the alleyway, because I love those old places that reek of the forgotten past. And just when you'd think the alley would end, there was this archway and wrought iron gate."

"The sculpted clock face is most interesting, despite its damage."

"No. I seem to remember that the crack down its middle is intentional, a part of the design."

"And beyond the gate?"

Josiah shrugged. "I wasn't interested. It was the archway and its cool design that intrigued me, plus the play of light against the shadows and mist."

"And you say it is near to the place where your friend's fête is to be held tonight?"

"Oh, it won't be lavish enough to be called that. Just a little gathering. Will you come?"

"Yes, but first we will visit this place in the photograph."

The artist studied the image in the still. "Well, if I can find it. It's in the industrial part of town. Let me put on some clean clothes, and we'll scoot."

After a little wait, they climbed into Josiah's small car and were off. Their destination was a part of town that Josiah had often visited, usually in daylight when the abandoned factories were easily photographed. Most of the old brick warehouses dated to the beginning of the last century, and the artist was particularly fond of a towering smokestack whose surface had been bleached by decades of sunlight. He parked the car and began to roam the sidewalk, followed by his tall companion. Finally, they came upon a cobblestone alleyway.

"Yeah, this is it. And look, there's that damn mist mid-way into the alley, just like last time. Look at these wonderful cobblestones, dude," he said, kneeling so as to touch the stony ground. "Don't they just reek of the past? Hey, wait up!" But Simon ignored him, fueled by an almost frantic curiosity. Josiah silently cursed, then softly chuckled at the sight of Simon fading into the mist. They had met at a showing of his photography that had been titled "The Forgotten Past," and his eye for the unusual had been quick to seize upon this character who dressed in outdated fashion, whose bestial face reminded him at times of a wolf, and other times of a toad. Simon had introduced himself as a foe of the modern age, and said that he felt instinctively that Josiah was a kindred spirit. "Why, even your name is archaic!" Simon had declaimed. They became friends and constant companions. Indeed, it had been peculiar, the way that Josiah's eyes had been opened to a sense of the past that he had not hitherto experienced. It was as if his befriending this unusual chap had awakened in him some kind of buried perception. He was looking at the world in a different way. Tonight was a typical example: he had completely forgotten about that atmospheric photograph and this hidden place until Simon's singular interest had reminded him of it.

He followed his friend into the narrow alleyway, past the mist-enshrouded walls of brick warehouses. Gradually it came into nebulous view, the blurred stone archway and wrought iron gate. He scanned the archway's sculpted frieze, at the center of which was the image of a cracked and handless clock, its Roman numerals dimly discerned. Simon was standing at the gate. "Most interesting," Simon whispered. "Without question a kind of threshold." Wrapping his long lean fingers around one bar, he pushed open one of the hinged barriers of extremely ancient iron.

"Simon, it's private property. I don't think . . ." But Simon ignored him utterly and entered a courtyard draped in heavy mist. Hesitantly, Josiah followed, shivering at the sudden increase of chilliness in the air. He breathed in fetid aether, and something in the taste and smell of it oppressed him. "Man, this place is creeping me out. Let's scat."

"Don't be skittish. This is a wonderful adventure." He turned to smile at Josiah, and his alabaster eyes gleamed with an uncanny perspicacity that was quite unnerving. "Let us explore this enchanting habitat. I admit it feels slightly diseased. I know of a distant place that exudes a similar sensation, what the *Book* of *Eibon* calls 'the *genius loci* of the spheres' and which most humans think of as an evil thing. In this other place, the region feels too deeply the shadow of a titanic twin-peaked mountain. It is a place where the soil, the vegetation, the impalpable oxygen sucked in is mutated and transformed. Oh, we must cherish such a clime. Doesn't it beguile you, the strangeness? Isn't that what lured you to it in the first place, that inspired you to photograph it? Didn't it speak to you with rare aesthetic language?"

"Perhaps it did, but somehow I've absolutely forgotten about it," Josiah answered.

"In your waking world, yes; but, dear boy, *it made you dream*. That is telling."

"Dude, you're speaking riddles. Let's go, this chill is getting to me."

Simon slowly stepped toward Josiah and placed a large hand on the young man's head, as if he were about to confer upon him some unholy benediction. "Let your senses deeply drink, and tell me what you feel."

Wearily, the young man sighed, then shut his eyes and concentrated. "I feel death," he said, shuddering.

Simon shook his head. "You feel mortality, the heavy sludge that is your flesh, your bone. You have spoken more than once of your weariness with life, of the hateful drag of blood that courses through you and pumps your little heart. Oft times such talk in one so young is mere affection, but you are sincere. Perhaps it is such unfeigned and wholehearted zealousness that led you to the discovery of this haunted place. No, Josiah, we shall not flee until we have looked around a little longer."

"As you desire," the young man sighed, watching as Simon approached a fountain that was situated in the middle of the courtyard. Reluctantly, Josiah joined him, although there was something about the fountain's winged figure that utterly discomposed him. He shivered, but not from chilliness. His eyes fastened onto the sculpted figure that knelt on an atramentous dais. The figure's arms were outstretched, in a manner of beckoning or beseechment. Elemental time had erased most of the features of the upraised face, and he could but dimly see the black liquid that spilled from what remained of ears and nostrils. Josiah looked down into the fountain's murky ooze, seeing nothing but a mockery of his reflection, weirdly distorted.

He turned away and walked toward the gate, hoping that Simon would follow him; and then realised that this was not the threshold through which they had entered, but a smaller one, at a different section of the stone wall. His eyes had adjusted to darkness, and thus he could dimly make out the frieze that had been hewed into the archway above the gate. At the design's center there was the image of an hourglass which existed as a kind of oversized bas-relief. Its round containers were composed of opaque glass, and the bottom one was shattered at one point, spilling a replication of black sand.

Josiah walked to the gate and raised both hands to the bars of smooth dark wood. He pressed his face between two bars, scanning a depth of moving shadow, profuse and illimitable. He reached through the barrier into the blackness, and felt as though its velvet texture reached to him, wrapping around his hand as if it would pull him forward. And then he espied a deeper patch of darkness, an undulating shadow that seemed to beckon.

A heavy hand clasped his shoulder. "I want to show you something," said his friend, guiding him reluctantly away from the second gateway. Simon led Josiah to a place where the sod was indented so as to form a shallow pit, a concavity filled with ash. Simon fell to his knees before it, motioning for Josiah to follow suit. "Do you remember when I mentioned earlier the *Book of Eibon*? It is one of a very few special tomes of magick, myth, and legend. Another, that you might have heard of, is the *Necronomicon*. No? No matter. There is in these books a recurring formula relating to the resurrection of dead matter, of rare necromancy. Do you see the words that have been etched into this ash? They form a potent part of this spell of reawakening. Does any of this make sense to you? Does it remind you of anything perceived in these dreams you mentioned earlier?"

"No. You know I don't believe in any of that rot, although I have listened politely to some of your outlandish theories about my keen perception of the weird in art. I can only repeat that I like the weird aesthetic because I find normalcy extremely boring."

"Perhaps," Simon pronounced, as behind them a night-wind rose in force. Josiah touched the bed of ash that had been disfigured with strokes of etching, and as his fingers smoothed the symbols away, the wind grew in strength and seeped into the pit of ash, that substance which it began to toss until another shape appeared on the sooty surface, a shape that pushed up and opened its shifting mouth. Josiah screamed as his name was whispered beneath the sound of wind. Frantically, he rose to his feet and hobbled out of the courtyard. Simon had not moved, but kept his kneeling position as he studied the face of ash. Then he spoke a curious phrase, and with one sharp fingernail he etched a symbol into the forehead of the fuliginous face. He watched as it sank into formlessness. Then he slowly rose and went to find his friend.

II.

They stood as a small group before her, this odd assortment of human creatures. Her heart ached to look at them, and when at last she opened her mouth in song, the sound was laced with deep emotion. They listened, bewitched, as she performed Baudelaire's "Le Vin du solitaire" set to music of her own composition. The voice that issued from the gaping wound that served as mouth in the face that was not a face was beautiful. The moist eyes, deep-set within the spongy synthetic substance of what had once been human flesh, expressed an almost unbearable tenderness, and many in the crowd began to weep softly.

Two persons were escorted into the room by a servant, and when she saw the unexpected yet familiar face her voice momentarily faltered. Turning her eyes from the bestial countenance, she looked deeply into the half-circle of friends who smiled at her with adoration. Buoyed by their innocuous affection, Sybil sang with more emotional force, with crystal water shining in her violet eyes. When her song ended, the applause was rapturous. She walked into the assemblage of friends, returning the press of hands and lips. Josiah suddenly stood before her, and although his smile was broad his eyes looked oddly emotional.

"That was magnificent," he enthused. "I've never heard you sing like that, it was awesome!" She kissed his forehead, then turned and slightly bowed to his companion. "This is my friend, Simon Gregory Williams."

"Yes," Sybil acknowledged. "Actually, Mr. Williams and I have met before." Simon narrowed his eyes at her. "In Prague, at the establishment of Simon Orne." Subtly, she smiled. "He had just raised me up." Simon made a soft inhuman sound, and Josiah frowned in confusion. "How frightfully long ago it was."

Collecting himself, Simon smiled. "But of course. Ancient Prague, and ancient Simon, with his little castle beside the river. Gracious me, how extraordinary to meet you again. I have no recollection of your being so accomplished a chanteuse."

"A skill from my *other* life," she said with emphasis. "I have changed since those long-dead days. Well, one had to, after being in the hands of so unskilled a—physician. You see what he did to me."

"Yes, his sorcery was limited. Unlike his pride."

"There you have it. His pride was his undoing."

"Oh, is he undone, then?"

"Oh yes," she coldly intoned. "Quite undone." And with a petite curtsy, and smoothing Josiah's cheek with a gloved hand, she passed through them so as to join other admirers.

Simon grinned at Josiah's questioning eyes. "What a very remarkable woman. However did you meet her?"

"Sybil's a loyal patron of the arts, and I've encountered her at various gigs. Her at-homes are quite rare—I don't think she has much taste for the social thing. Always seems a bit nervous and awkward. It may have to do with her tenants."

"Tenants?"

"Yeah, haven't you noticed them? Most everyone here is youthful and arty, but there are those few who look a little out of place. The rumor is that they are homeless freaks whom Sybil has taken a liking to, inviting them to live with her. You know, a wealthy eccentric's way of dealing with loneliness. You'll be able to tell them by their manner, and a couple by their, uh, smell. But they're pleasant enough, for an evening at least." Josiah looked at a figure draped in shawls who entered through the French doors that opened onto an expansive garden. "Here comes one of them now," he lowly muttered. "Hi, Noughtia."

The small hunch-backed woman offered Josiah her hand, which he hesitantly kissed. "Very good to see you again, Josiah. We don't have enough meaty men visiting us." She turned to Simon, smiling. "Isn't he healthy? For an 'artistic' type. Look at those other blokes. Fah, one would think they exist on a diet of peas and water! Not that there's anything wrong with staying fit. Your friend here is quite lean, and yet he exudes amazing vitality. And look at those massive shoulders! But these skinny artists, their weightlessness has always seemed to me mere aesthetic affectation."

Simon slyly grinned, then reached for the woman's hand and brought it to his mouth. Noughtia watched his lingering kiss, the pressure of his tongue as he tasted her flesh, the sucking of his wolfish nostrils as he smelled her. Releasing her, he bowed and said his name. And then, from somewhere out of doors, the sound of baying filtered into the room, and Simon saw the fear that trembled in the woman's eyes. She quickly turned and fled to Sybil, with whom she nervously whispered.

Their hostess clapped her hands so as to summon the crowd. "Mesdames et Messieurs, the Dance of Rebirth." She motioned to a distant darkened corner as the overhead lights dimmed. On a small raised platform two figures stood beside a shapeless mound. One figure held a tom-tom, which he began to beat, and the other brought a reed-like instrument to his mouth. The air was pierced with a wailing sound that reminded Simon of a ritual he had witnessed in Damascus in the early 1800s. As the music spilled toward them, the crowd watched the huddled shape (which reminded a select portion of the onlookers of a grave mound) begin to writhe and rise as a blue light eerily illuminated the performance. Particles of sand or dust fell from the rising figure, forming a pool of fine blue granules on the ground. The performance was like something out of Stravinsky, movement that contained a primitive elegance.

And then the performance faltered, as the sound of another flute sounded from somewhere within the crowd. The performers watched as the stranger danced toward them, waving a hand that encouraged them to continue. Josiah gaped in astonishment as Simon jumped onto the slightly raised platform and began to move with the confused dancer. The audience watched as Simon took one hand from his flute and waved it over the pool of blue dust, stomping into the stuff in time to the rhythmic noise. Particles of dust rose in disturbance, then floated downward. Again Simon stomped his foot, and again. The dust rose, then seemed to gather in shaping as it floated just below Simon's crotch. The gathered onlookers shouted as that cloud of blue dust formed itself into a semblance of the nude dancer's face. It lasted but a few seconds, and then Simon bent low and pierced the cloudy visage with his thin black instrument, from which there emitted a sharp and shocking screech. The drifting countenance tore apart, its substance flying into the gawking face of the naked performer.

The music stopped, and heavy silence subdued the crowd for a few seconds, until finally they broke into wild applause. The house lights flickered on, and Simon jumped from the platform into the congregation of new admirers who suddenly surrounded him. Simon acted as if nothing spectacular had occurred, until Josiah pulled him from the clutching enthusiasts and to a table that was covered with food. Simon suspiciously frowned at the dishes of undercooked meats.

"What the hell is with you tonight and this trick of yours with conjuring faces? First in that weird courtyard and now this outlandish performance."

"You fool," Simon savagely replied. "The first had nothing whatsoever to do with me. The second was merely a bit of subtle sorcery with which to send a message to our hostess." As if speaking of her had conjured her forth, Sybil appeared before them. Josiah, wounded at his friend's gruff reply, walked away in a huff and joined some artistic friends, who surrounded him and plied him with questions about his mysterious mate. Before Sybil could speak, the naked fellow, now robed, thrust himself toward them.

"That was good," the fellow said, his face still covered with a light coating of chalky blue dust. "However did you manage it?"

"Ah, my good man, a wizard never reveals his secrets."

"Yes," said the other, regarding Simon's outlandish features and curious silver eyes. "You wear a wizard's face. We'll talk furthermore, but for now I need to dress." He bowed to them as Sybil linked her arm with Simon's and led him through the French doors, into the massive garden. Simon studied the garden fountain with especial interest as his hostess began to talk.

"You have everyone speculating on your performance. Was that wise?"

"Probably not. I seem to have triggered jealousy in that dancer of yours."

"Yes, Edmond can be dangerous. He refuses to partake of the baths, and thus he reeks of semi-death. But then so many artists seem adverse to bathing. I've never known a more malodorous clique. You remember, of course, the baths in Prague. They remain one of the few soothing experiences of this beastly situation."

"Is it really so horrible? Your face, of course, is unfortunate. It was your misfortune to be raised by one who had become careless and alcoholic. Nothing is more odious than sloppy necromancy."

"Oh, my face was no accident. I was, in my former life, a great beauty. I refused his advances, and so he had me murdered, then raised me with inferior salts. But we had our own revenge. We slew him, you see, and then we consumed him. There rises with us from our tombs a savage hunger for flesh. Most of us have learned to tame it, and my fortune is enough to keep us in supply until the end of time. But that is the other thing, and perhaps, sorcerer that you are, you can explain it to me. Why is our existence so prolonged?"

"I cannot say for certain. There is an element in the alchemy of threshold, in the calling forth of Yog-Sothoth, that alters the corporeal chemistry. Yog-Sothoth is not a force that one casually calls forth. It is wild and ruthless. And what of these others? One or two of them look familiar."

"You may have bathed with them in Prague. Others I found in my search for kindred victims. But there were many whom I could not help, creatures incomplete, devils with ravenous hunger. We destroyed many."

"But you cannot destroy yourself?"

She shook her head. "There is something defeatist and ignoble in self-destruction that quite revolts me, strong as is my desire for nothingness. I think of nothing else. I dream of it always, the peace of oblivion."

Simon was about to respond when the air was haunted by a distant baying. "And what, pray tell, is that?"

"A thing of Edmond's doing. He learned much from Simon before that fiend's destruction, and brought with him many of the tomes I would have otherwise destroyed. Somehow he has learned to combine human ash with animal. He has risen two such creatures. This thing that haunts the night is a vicious thing, and I think its creation has frightened Edmond. For a little while, at least."

"What a wonderfully mad situation. I adore it! Well, I am here to assist you."

"A child of Sesqua Valley can. Yes, I know whence you were born. I visited the valley some decades ago. It's always trying to coax me to forget that it exists, but while there I filled a journal with extensive notes and drawings. I often visit the valley in my deepest dreaming. Indeed, I felt, while sitting on a mountain ledge, that I had entered some outlandish dreamscape, a place that had been conjured forth by the collective dreaming of its shadow citizens. What do the new age poodles call it—sympathetic magic? But I believe in it."

"As well you should."

"Why?"

"I'll show you when your problem has been solved. I imagine you have a spare room where I can settle?"

"You alone. Josiah must not be a part of this. His muscular body arouses curious cravings among the household, if you take my meaning. I keep him away as much as possible, much as I personally adore him. Oh, what a sad young man he is beneath that healthy exterior. Has he told you of his suicide attempt?"

"No, but I have noticed the scarring on one wrist. We need not tell him of my becoming a temporary resident. Now, as to my appetite, I do not partake of flesh, and thus those heavy plates of moist and succulent meats will not do for me. But I see you have a healthy growth of vegetables."

She lightly laughed. "We try to rule our barbarous cravings, I assure you. Ugh, those nauseating feasts in Prague!"

"Yes, but then Orne himself had been one of the restless resurrected." It filtered once more through the night, something howling at pallid moonlight. Smiling, Simon leaned back his head and answered with uncanny ululation.

III.

The sound of terror and torment came from the wee bungalow just off the garden and adjacent to a plot of land that was reserved for the burial of those few souls who had, by their own hands or by other means, expired. Simon, who had been bending over fountain water dropping petals, straightened and casually strolled to the building's open door. Noughtia was on her knees, her hand covering the fresh cut that discolored her cheek with blood. Edmond stood above her, a dagger in one hand, a bottle in the other. Seeing Simon, the brute stepped away from his victim, who whimpered and rushed away.

"She is *mine*," Edmond drunkenly yelled. "I created her, and I will use her as I will. Begone, fiend."

"I think not, dear fellow. Your festivities have reached an end. And, yes, I am a fiend."

The knife flew toward Simon's face and pushed into his skin. Edmond watched the oddly textured blood that seeped into the strange wide mouth, and listened as that mouth sighed an ancient chant that Edmond knew from diabolic study. He watched the wound on Simon's face begin to mist, to fade with healing. "What the devil are you?" Edmond rasped as he drunkenly took another swing at Simon's visage.

Simon easily caught the hand that held the knife, bending the wrist until the bone snapped. Edmond howled as a hand entwined its fingers around his throat and dragged him from the shack onto the graveyard ground. With abnormal force, Edmond was pushed onto the ground until his mouth tasted mud. "I am a child of Sesqua Valley. Look at you, as repulsive as your master had become. Eat dirt, for you are the worm beneath my heel."

And then the stronghold ended, and Edmond, choking and cursing, pushed himself up onto his knees. "I'll be nobody's worm. I'm a sorcerer as well, and I can raise the dead who lie beneath this sod and have them rip you limb by limb."

"Do they lie here because of your mischief? There is one other who doesn't lie beneath this mud, one who hates and hunts. That amulet around your throat won't protect you forever." Simon hunkered and tore the small piece of jade from the chain that encircled Edmond's throat. He held the exquisite thing to moonlight, admiring the craft that had created so skillfully this image of a winged hound, or perhaps it was a sphinx with a semi-canine face. How strangely the expression on the thing's malevolent visage resembled Simon's own. Derisively, Simon chortled, then tossed back his head and howled unto the moon. His summons was followed by another baying, one that echoed very closely. Edmond's fevered heartbeat sounded in his ears as a shape appeared on a nearby hill. The thing's silhouette expanded as it clumsily raised itself on two distorted legs. Fueled by nameless appetite, it loped toward them. Simon winced at the smell of carnage that exuded from the creature's snout.

"Behold thy fiendish witchery, Edmond Wye. It hath come to claim thee."

The monstrous thing stretched its mouth with sardonic mirth.

"Hello, master," it choked, and then it was voraciously upon him, tearing out his throat before Edmond had time to scream or beg. A plash of crimson flew to Simon's mouth, and suddenly he joined in the fray, ripping, shredding, devouring.

And then it was over, and the beasts stretched upon the cold earth, panting and spitting. Turning onto his stomach, Simon curled his mouth distastefully at the remains that wetly littered the blood-soaked sod. Crawling to the mangled mess that had once been Edmond Wye, Simon clawed into the chilly earth, deeply digging. His companion joined him, snarling, until they knelt waist-high within a pit into which they dragged the corpse.

Simon, who had held onto the amulet all this time, offered the soiled relic to the monster beside him. "Take this, and know that rest is thine. Recline into this, thy final grave." The beast reached with hideous paw and took hold of the jade amulet. Its other hand touched Simon's mouth, that organ that spoke from memory the potent spell of saying down. The thing in moonlight raised its yellow eyes to the remote welkin and pulled back its snout, revealing fangs that were dyed with gore. Its howl lasted but a moment before its substance darkened and dropped as dust into the pit, mingling with the ashes of that other thing that had answered Simon's thaumaturgy.

In the mansion, in one section of the cavernous cellars, Sybil entered the great sunken pit that had been transformed into remedial pool. Others followed her, moaning in ecstasy as the water, treated by alchemical means, soothed their reeking flesh. Turning her head to investigate a sudden sound, Sybil watched as Simon entered through the doorway, his clothing torn and covered with indescribable filth. She had never seen such fury as that which smoldered in his silver eyes. Gasping at the fumes that rose from the pool, Simon tore off his clothing and rushed into the water, splashing his way to his hostess. She did not understand the emotion that trembled in his hands, those massive forepaws that reached beneath her breasts and pulled her to him.

Dipping his mouth into the pool, he sipped the analeptic liquid, felt it slide down his throat, that throat that was tainted with the taste of blood and death. The savagery of his feasting dissipated. Lifting his wizard's face before the woman he embraced, he cupped his hands into the water, brought the steaming stuff above her head, washed it over her ruined face. His heavy breath pushed toward her, sinking beneath her eyes, entering her disfigured pores. He smoothed his hands, so softly padded, over her ruined countenance, and the others shouted as they watched her features smooth and heal. The ugly wound that had been her mouth took on form and color. With tears stinging her eyes, she gazed at her reflection in the water, at the face that was healed and beautiful.

And then he noticed her, the distant figure draped in a length of heavy white cloth, who cowered from the others as if in shame and exile. Sinking into the depths, he pushed toward her through the soothing water. Taking her hands, he pulled her toward the others.

"No, I can't. They don't accept me. I'm foul."

Bending to her, he kissed her weeping mouth. "Be not afraid." Unwinding the heavy robe with which she concealed her form, he let it sink beneath the water's surface. Noughtia continued to weep as he caressed the folded flesh that formed her bunched back. Simon gently pulled, and finally the woman relaxed and spread her fleshy wings, those wings that had been conjoined to her by the salts of the prehistoric reptile that Edmond had mingled with her own remains. Simon's phantom eyes flashed with wonder. Beautifully, he laughed. "You are *magnificent!*"

IV.

Josiah leaned against the wall of cool brick and stared at starlight. Walking for so long a time in such cold weather had triggered his asthma, and he pouted as he reached into his pocket for the inhaler. Sucking in the mist that helped him breathe, he cursed his fate. If something as simple, yet as fundamental, as breathing was so difficult at age twenty-eight, how arduous would it be at fifty? He hoped an early death would render the question moot. Why had he lasted as long as he had? What had he accomplished in those years? He hadn't any real ambition because he didn't really care about anything in life. Existence did not interest him, but rather the escape from modern reality. The century in which he found himself was a vulgar nightmare void, especially in America. Little wonder he escaped through art and dreaming into a past that was, for him, far more substantial. The past was real, it was the key to his art, his soul.

He deeply sighed, then watched the fog that floated from his mouth. It reminded him that he was looking for some place that he had recently visited with Simon, a place encased by heavy nubilation. The memory of such a place lurked in some dim pocket of memory that he could not conjure forth. He could almost see it, like the forgotten word that lingers on the tip of the tongue. Pushing away from the wall, he continued his aimless search for the forgotten place, but soon was lured by a cacophonous clamor of chaotic music. He saw the familiar doorway, passed through it, showed a young woman his ID, and advanced past the small round tables to the stage. A trio of wild young things ruled the stage, happily sneering now that someone was paying attention to their noise. He bobbed his head for a little while, then stumbled to the nearby wall that had been covered with shards of cloudy broken mirror. How he enjoyed peering into its reflected depths, into that other place of nebulous light and shifting shadow. Tilting his head and grimly smiling, he fingered one jagged edge of mirror, then sliced his fingertip on the mirror's filth-encrusted point.

A tingling in his hand shot through the rest of him as he watched a drop of blood materialize, one dark and fluid bead of his abhorrent mortality. Bringing his finger to his mouth, he poked it between numb lips and ran it over aching teeth. Josiah leered at his reflection, tasting blood, and saw the spectre just beyond his hazy image, an indistinct thing that beckoned him. Raising his wrist, he gently ran the old white scar against a dull edge of mirror, then violently banged his forehead against the glass and wept.

V.

Noughtia awoke to a sound of whispered words, words that she recognized from Edmond's ritual chanting. Were they coming from her lips? Had she been dreaming of him and his horrors? Would he never cease to torment her, even after his destruction? She brought her hand to a painful place on her throat, where something gritty soiled her flesh. Examining her hand, she saw upon it a thin coating of fine bluish-grey dust. There was a smell in the room that she did not like, and she sensed a semi-presence of something that had recently lingered in the room.

Rising from the mat on the floor that had served as her bed, Noughtia scanned the small collection of elder tomes that had been Edmond's dearest treasure. She felt certain of her course: she must build a fire and hurl those books into the flames

"Good afternoon." She looked at the bungalow's open doorway and smiled at Simon. "How have you rested?"

"Horribly. I've had vile dreams—of him. It's like an undying portion of him burns inside my brain and whispers those damning spells and rituals that so intoxicated his diseased mind."

"I have frequently wondered if the majority of humankind has ever paused to reflect upon the buried but tremendous significance of dreams. I was speaking of this to young Josiah not long ago. These nocturnal visions, born within the deepest caverns of our skullspace— how portentous they may be! Ah, the deep-buried knowledge, the secret ecstasy, the wonder of a world beyond wakefulness. Oh, the exquisite *dread*. You say that you heard the whispered rituals that Edmond used to perform?"

"I did," she assured him, rubbing that painful place on her neck. Simon knelt beside her and gently examined her odd and chalky bruise.

"Were you the whispering one, Noughtia? Did you utter the alchemy found in those moldy books?"

"But I don't know the spells. I never wanted to. I didn't share Edmond's mania for magick, I abhor it! It's because of those damned books that I can never rest. Help me destroy them, Simon."

He rose. "No, we'll do no such thing. I'll remove them from your little home. There is a place, where I come from, that will welcome such a library. And tonight, with your permission, I'll slumber here, in Edmond's bed."

"Yes, I'd like that. I feel safe with you, despite the fact that we've only recently met."

He smiled at her, then went and opened a curtain that covered a small window. For the first time in her memory, sunlight spilled into the room. Simon bathed in the warm celestial rays, then casually began to examine the window. He found what he expected to find, on the outside of a bottom pane of glass. Vacating the place, he went to the window and ran a finger along the sill and its thin coating of blue dust, dust that felt oddly moist. Sensing someone behind him, he turned. "Great Yuggoth, whatever have you done to yourself?"

Josiah tried to smile. "Nothing. I fell. Ow, don't touch it, it's still really sore."

Simon removed his talons from the bump on Josiah's forehead, then took the youngster by the arm and led him into the ballroom. Taking the young man's hand, it turned it over and saw the wrist's re-opened slit. "Silly child."

"Don't lecture me, Simon. Explain why you're here. I needed to find you, but you weren't home, and that was damn unusual. I'm feeling really weird. Fated. Things are going on that I don't understand. Life has become weird since you entered into mine. What is this . . . influence you carry with you?"

Before Simon could answer, a figure entered the room. Josiah stared at the lovely body encased in a gorgeous dress of golden silk. He identified the eyes that gleamed beneath the golden mask, but the mouth—the smooth and beautiful lips—baffled him. Going to her, he reached behind her head and unfastened the silk mask, letting it fall to the floor. "This cannot be," Josiah whispered.

"And yet it is," Sybil assured him. "No, do not frown and question and try to understand. Only rejoice. Now come with me and let me tend your ruined crown." The woman exchanged a look with Simon, then led Josiah from the room. Bending low, Simon clutched the golden mask and fastened it over his face. It was an awkward fit, and he laughed as he danced from the room, into the garden, to the place of buried death. Dropping to the ground, he pushed his fingers into the mound that formed the most recent grave, that mound that was stained with traces of blue ash.

"Well," Simon quietly told the mound, "you continue restless after all my art. You were certainly well-schooled by those tomes you stole from Prague. Was it not enough to evoke the formulae of the descending node? Must I summon the lurker at the threshold? It is not a choice I lightly make. However . . ."

Returning to the bungalow, where he found Noughtia sleeping in a pool of sunshine, he went to Edmond's library and took down a heavy volume. His eyes gleamed excitedly as he studied the charts, the diagrams, the unfamiliar alphabets. Yes, there was wisdom buried in these wormy pages. He studied until the darkness fell, and being too lazy to light a candle, he dozed. The language of the book spoke in his dreams, and hungrily he drank in its potency. Deeply entranced, he was unaware of the woman who rose from her bedmat and staggered into moonlight.

Noughtia walked in slumber, to a voice that called to her from a depth of darkness. It filtered through the mound of earth and rose as a cloud of ethereal dust. She held her arms to it, embraced it, smoothed its substance into her flesh. She listened as it coaxed her to climb the fountain and perch upon the base that rose at the structure's center. She listened to the ritual that spoke from someplace deep inside her brain, then quietly began to recite the words of sorcery, those words that would wed his essence with her own.

"Y'AI'NG'NGAH, IOG-SOTOT."

Noughtia shook herself awake at the sound of those awesome words. With blurred vision she indistinctly beheld the tall lean fellow whose outlandish face was a thing of rage. She listened as that face of fury spoke once more the terrible words. And then she choked as her body began to painfully heave. She tried to scream in torment, but her mouth was filled with bile, a substance that drooled as blue ash from her mouth, that seeped from her ears. The woman was unaware of the others who had been awakened by her torment, those others who watched the void of blackness in the aether just above her, that blackness that hungrily sucked into itself the substance that had once been Edmond Wye. And then they rushed to the fountain as Noughtia's spasmodic body fell from the base, into a depth of water. Above them, the madness beyond time and dimensional space fractured, then closed itself and was gone.

VI.

They awoke in a haze of bright morning light shooting into the room from a window at which the curtains had been left open. Josiah smoothed her soft face with his hand, then turned to watch Simon enter the room. The beast of Sesqua Valley sat next to them on the sumptuous bed and touched a talon to the young man's head. "Well, now it's your face that needs my healing touch."

Josiah fought his natural inclination to back away; for this was, he realised, the first time that he had observed Simon's face in full daylight, and this shimmering natural light revealed what had been until yesterday dimly concealed, the true aspect of the non-human assemblage of features that combined in the creation of Simon's bestial countenance. "What the hell are you, Simon? How in the name of God could you cure the ravages done to her face in a bomb explosion?"

"The name of a 'god' is precisely what I evoked," he said, his argent eyes twinkling. "Was that your story?"

The woman shrugged. "A bomb in Belfast blew away my features, and the inadequate reconstruction of clumsy modern surgery. Not only did it explain my face, it stopped further questioning, out of compassion to horror. I was, I confess, tempted more than once to try and heal myself by uttering that potent name; but something in the dark arts withheld my hand. I felt the lure of necromancy, how it can entice, enrapture and enslave. Thus I refused the lure of mad enthrallment and settled for an epicurean existence. I had no taste for the alchemy of those books and was glad to have left them behind in Prague. You can imagine my emotion to discover that Edmond had pilfered those tomes from Orne's library. I was indifferent about the situation until he raised Noughtia, and then we all became very much afraid when he raised that other thing. I think what made us especially nervous was that Edmond, too, was fearful of that thing, and ever watchful. He understood too well its appetite for flesh. I saw by his example that I had been wise in not uttering the name beyond the threshold. What is it the mad Arab warns, not to raise that which cannot be put down? But it *is* intoxicating, isn't it? The memory of the language of those books, even the touch upon the tongue of words I did not understand and probably mispronounced, stays with one. I've dreamed of those books, and their evocations have mumbled in my dreaming brain. Oft times I have awakened to the echo of those incantations in my mind, to the tingling touch of those words upon my mouth. More than once I have awakened to the whispered name of Yog-Sothoth." Josiah felt her shudder in his embrace, whether from ecstasy or terror he could not fathom.

Simon sagely nodded. "That would explain the wonderful thing." Reaching into the place between his jacket and shirt, he pulled out a glossy photograph and tossed it onto her lap. Before Sybil could take it, Josiah snatched it up and scowled at the other fellow.

"You took that from my studio. That's the place I was hunting for on the night of my—accident. We visited it. It's all coming back to me. I couldn't remember what it was, or where. Seeing it now, I remember exactly."

"Such is the nature of such realms," Simon sagely answered.

Sybil took the photograph and brought it close to her eyes, those orbs that brimmed with tears. "How can you have visited this place?" She gazed at Simon with an inexplicable expression working her lovely face. "This is the place of my entombment, across the sea."

Simon chuckled in delight. "Sorry, my loves, but I'm simply amused that you do not recognize the product of your dream-soaked longing. I confess that I cannot comprehend your craving for extinction—the world is so full of marvelous adventures! Be that as it may, the name of threshold has been uttered, and it will be satisfied. Your fate is inescapable. I pray that it will be everything you have dreamt it to be."

Sybil's smile was a forlorn thing. "Such rich irony. If this is indeed an answer to prayerful dreaming, it will be a thing of nothingness."

Simon rose from the bed and stretched. "Well, I must attend to my studies. I've absconded those delightful books of sorcery from Edmond's library. Noughtia was overjoyed to be rid of them. I've attended to her, by the way, and she is in recovery. Such a fascinating creature, and with such a simple soul. I am taking her with me when I return home. I leave you now, but I shall return anon, when darkness falls."

And so he did, guiding them from the mansion to a forgotten part of town. The evening was cool, and the long walk had exhausted Josiah, who was forced to use his inhaler. And yet how excited he felt when he began to recognize the place, the darksome alleyway en-shrouded in pale mauve mist. Sentient shadow stirred, sensing the scent of mortality that approached it, welcoming the ones for whom it had long awaited. Pausing before the archway of elder stone, Sybil gasped in amazement. It was the remembered place of her interment, yet some-how distorted, like a remembered place revisited in slumber's vision. She watched as Simon opened the gate, then took his proffered hand as he ushered her within the courtyard. All about her were images from places she had dwelt, yet oddly misplaced and malformed. She gawked at the fountain, at the winged figure that reached with beckoning hands unto the dark cosmos.

Josiah trembled beside her, feeling deeply the other, the unseen, in-habitant of the haunted place. Turning, he walked away from them and approached the time-worn wooden gateway. Peering into the blackness beyond, he became aware of that patch of deeper shadow, the beckoning idolum. Like some wan and pallid angel, Sybil floated to him and wrapped her arms around his waist. "What is this dismal place, Sybil?"

"There was a little plot of unconsecrated sod wherein the unhal-lowed souls of suicides and such were interred. The unwanted dead. As a child, visiting the cemetery with family, I was always drawn to that place. I felt a kinship with those nameless dead ones, for I have never felt wanted. And when Simon Orne raised me from my grave—hush, Josiah, do not weep and groan for what is past—I often returned to that neglected plot of graveyard ground. It was my prayer that should I ever be lucky enough to die once more, I would be buried with those other unwanted souls. I had been stained, you see, by Orne's necro-mancy, and like a victim of rape I felt absurdly guilty of the crime that had so violently abused me."

Simon came to them as Josiah tried to open the wooden gate. "You need to use the key, my dear fellow. Sybil, you have brought forth this wonderment by that same power that raised you up. You need only to utter the syllables that work the key. Your dreaming self knew them intimately. Do you recall them?"

The woman shut her eyes. Deeply, she inhaled the heavy air that wafted around her, that atmosphere that slipped into her mouth, her nose, and sank into the pit of her being. She began to dream, and with dreaming came the remembered words that issued as whispering from her trembling mouth.

"Y'AI'NG'NGAH, YOG-SOTHOTH."

Cold wind quavered beyond the gateway, a low moaning that vibrated before them like the release of long-held breath. Josiah gagged at the noisome air that pushed into his face, but Simon drank it in like some intoxicating bouquet. With this foetor there came an almost-sound, in which Sybil thought she heard her name pronounced. The wooden gates silently parted. Opening her eyes, the ancient woman peered into the seething darkness, this answer to her longing. From its depths, something summoned. Josiah's hand clasped her own. She wanted to grace him with a reassuring glance but found that she could not turn her eyes from that which lurked before her, that awesome and seductive depth of oblivion. Josiah reached for her chin and tugged at her face. Tasting with her psyche his fear and desire, she smiled at him with ataraxic eyes.

Simon had moved to the fountain, watching and whispering the provocative name that had served as symbol and summoned forth the madness beyond time and space. Something deep within him would have delighted joining them into that alien dimension. But he knew that such was not his destiny. Sesqua Valley awaited his return. And so he wistfully watched as the mortal lad and the immortal woman crossed the threshold and became one with the audient void. He watched as the gates closed behind them, as an outré mist began heavily to rise all around and enshroud the spectral dominion. Sighing, he turned away and walked past the archway of ancient stone, that stone that eerily dissolved as he swept his soul beneath and beyond it onto an alleyway of cobblestone. He paused momentarily, wondering what he would see should he turn around for one final look. But then he shrugged and smiled, and pressing his lips together, he filled the night with eldritch whistling.

Hour of Their Appetite

(For Christopher Heyerdahl)

I wait for God with gluttony.
—Rimbaud

I remember the stars in the galaxy, how they brightly gleamed on that evening of starvation. I remember with what frantic weariness I roamed the city streets, defeated by another day of desperately seeking (and failing to secure) employment. I was an actor out of work, and we are oft a desperate race. I remember wandering through an unfamiliar section of the elder city to which I was still a stranger, and as I walked down a dark and lonesome lane I fancied that the world became quiet, exquisitely hushed. I remember the haunted children who huddled among the shadows of one doorway with hands outstretched. I thought that they were beggars until I noticed the movement of those tiny hands, how the fingers daintily gestured to the sky. Their famished faces did not consider me as I passed them by.

Quickly, I walked, past silent buildings, until across one avenue I beheld a rather wonderful edifice. It was a movie theatre from a bygone era, and although the ornate façade near its top was cracked and stained, still it bespoke an aesthetic charm that seemed entirely absent in this dull unimaginative modern age. I remember that I looked past that topmost place, to the nighted sky beyond; and I remember that I was puzzled by the absolute lack of starlight in that patch of aether just above the theatre.

There was no person in the ticket booth, from whom I could extract (as was my plan) an employment form; and so I pushed through the heavy ornate doors and entered the vacated lobby. Immediately, I noticed the refreshment stand, and all other matter was wiped from my mind. Like some automaton I stumbled to the counter, and then behind it. Caring not who saw me, I slid open one glass panel of a refrig-

erated case, and found therein a pitcher of clean cold milk. In a slightly
heated case I found plates that were packed with a kind of pita bread,
and in a place behind me I saw a small bowl of honey. Taking the
pitcher and bowl and placing them atop the counter, I was reminded of
the production of a biblical play in which I had played Aaron, and one
of my lines (from Deuteronomy 26) came back to me. Grabbing a fist-
ful of bread and dipping one into the bowl of honey, I remembered the
funny finger-sign made by the children I had seen earlier; and so I imitated that signal as I spoke my remembered lines: "And he hath
brought us into this place . . . even a land of milk and honey." Starved
and slightly lunatic, I ate like an uncouth thing that could not contain
its abysmal hunger. I stuffed my mouth with such an amount of bread
that I began to choke, drooling bits of chewed substance onto the
counter. Greedily I crushed the pitcher against my mouth and gulped,
then choked again, coughing. As I tried to quiet my strangled breathing,
I heard from some distant place the metallic voice. It came from beyond the dark velvet curtains that were the entrance to the theatre.

Grabbing my inherited sustenance, I walked backward through the
heavy curtains, into a vacant place. Although the auditorium was dark,
my eyes quickly adjusted, and I saw around me what seemed like some
magnificent temple. Designs in bas-relief jutted from various corners,
and distorted gargoyles seemed to observe me sardonically as I went to
the third row and found a comfortable seat.

Upon the cinema screen was an image in black and white. The film
must have been ancient, judging from the tinny sound quality and many
scratches. A severe yet rather handsome gentleman sat before an oversized microphone, speaking in what I took to be a Norwegian tongue.
His manner was quietly intense, and although I could not understand
his language I sat entranced by his voice, by the occasional flashing of
his dark eyes. When he raised a pale hand and made the by now familiar
signal, I imitated him; and when his language altered, becoming guttural
in phrasing, I echoed the phrase that he repeated in a voice that was
hypnotic.

I suddenly awoke to the sensation of cold liquid drenching my
crotch. The bowl and plate of food lay broken on the dirty floor, and
the pitcher was nowhere to be seen, although its liquid was obviously
the source of my discomfort. I moaned, and something mocked my
sound. I gazed unto the screen. At first I could not see clearly the image

before me. It was a dark form, a figure that seemed born of the blackness around me. Its hooded head bent slightly forward.

It sniffed.

The absence of light made it impossible to see clearly the dim features of the wide and palsied face. I saw somber black eyes, a wide expanse of moving lips that clothed the churning mouth. I saw the nostrils that flattened and expanded with breathing.

It was joined by another of its kind. They watched in the lightless place, waiting silently; and then they sniffed the theatre air. I watched the bloated lips that began to part. From the opened mouths came a pulsing whispered sound of alien respiration. I could feel its vaporous rhythm deep within me, the airy beat that matched my body's pulse. The twin mouths blurred, became one awesome cavity. I felt myself impossibly pulled into that gaping void.

My frantic body tried to repulse the efforts of these beings who were no cinematic image. But there was no escape. I suddenly knew not where I was. I beheld shapes, indistinct and loathsome. I heard the deep chords of twin breathing. I remember the feeling of darkness and doom that seemed to seep into my soul. My flesh crawled, twisting among the wet padding of some alien surface. I was drenched with hot moisture, a heavy wetness. My sickened mind registered that portions of my body were being devoured, yet something in the numbing pain beguiled. I understood my fate, and acquiesced. Even now, with so many portions missing from me, I welcomed the ravaging hunger of the feasting beasts. For I am the foodstuff of Gods. Devoured by them I become one with their immortality, glistening in their ravenous and eternal glory, until I am utterly and absolutely consumed.

The Sign That Sets the Darkness Free

I sang with hands, to quiet music, while standing on the dark verandah. How sweetly it filtered through my ears, the soft music, as light as the drizzle that moistened my ecstatic face, my moving hands. The record had reached its end, and for a dull moment all was silent; and then it came flowing to me (indistinctly at first) from a distance deep below, the strains of strange melody.

I looked to the cobbled streets that zigzagged down the steep hill, those lanes that seemed to spill into a vortex of lost time. They were very dark, those narrow streets, and the tottering houses on either side seemed almost to lean and touch roofs. Past those huddled roofs I gazed, past the deep flowing canal, to the hoary mist-enshrouded steeple of St. Toad's.

Yes, it was from there that the threnodial dirge issued, the strains of which tugged at my brain and tautly pulled. I leaned, with reaching outstretched arms, as if to touch the sound; and stretching stupidly too far, I toppled over the verandah's ledge, to wet grass below. It was a fall of some eleven feet, and I am not a young man. Unable to curse loudly, I silently sobbed. Yet while the tears still stung my eyes, I struggled to my feet and followed the melodic resonance. Down the ancient hill I hobbled, beneath the unwholesome shadows of antique roofs, across the aged stone bridge, not ceasing until I stepped onto churchyard ground.

I turned (I know not why) to observe my home atop the hill. Past the sleeping shaded streets and sagging dwellings with which they were lined, up to the venerable centuried hotel and to my window where still a single candle flickered. Luna rose behind the building, her ghastly light filtering down so as to encase the hotel's outline with faint phosphorescence. I looked at the window of my little room, wherein I lived my small existence. A single moonbeam drifted to that window, feebly melded with the candle's amber flame. It beckoned unto me, this cold lunar light, as though to turn me from my present course.

I turned my back to light and sighed at the darkness before me. No moonlight tainted the church of stone, its cracked and fungi-smothered walls, its oddly-shaped stained glass windows, its black spire that pointed to a heartless heaven. I wondered at the peculiar absence of starlight in the patch of cosmic aether directly over St. Toad's.

Where was the music that had lured me? I heard only the rushing water in the channel just behind me. Scanning my caliginous surroundings, I dimly discerned the small creature that stood surreptitiously among the tombstones. Slowly, very slowly, it began to stir. I could just make out the fiddle that was raised to hairy chin, the bow that cautiously began to move.

Yah, those chords! More mournful than any hymn to death sung by Kentucky hillfolk. It brought me to my knees, and thus I crawled to the creature that played its fiddle. A woman, small and petite, with girlish frame; yet her face was as ancient as the town wherein I dwelt. I gazed at the milky patches that had once been eyes, at the head's weird tilt, at the strange and unsettling smile on dry lips. Hesitantly, I reached for the hem of her tattered garment and brought the fabric to my mouth.

Music ceased. Her visage faced my own. That strange smile became even more peculiar. Touching her bow to my face, she traced the outline of a mouth she could not see. Her own mouth opened wide in song.

"Touch my tones with heart and hand,
    When thy voice cannot be found;
    Music of the darkling land
    Hie thee unto shadow's bound."

The fiddle was raised, and once again she played. And as she performed, she danced. And as she pranced about me I imagined that shadow playfully followed at her heel, like some adoring familiar.

Once more she stood directly before me. The bow was directed toward heaven, where moonlight tried to reach us. It found, that lunar glare, only the scarred and blemished flesh that had once held liquid eyes. She played, raising a muddied foot that was pressed into my mouth. Her dry and dirty flesh vibrated with music's pulse.

"Oh, man of muteness, we have tasted your dreaming, your conjuration of desire. Like heartbeat, like brainwave, we have known your soul's tumult." Swiftly, the foot was pulled out of my mouth. She fell to her knees before me. The taste of her stained flesh was replaced by her tang of heaving breath. Her panting mouth was pressed against my eye. "The thing," she cooed, "will come to thee at three. Its beauty is terrible, its wonder inescapable. It is the awful answer to your morbid prayer."

The mouth upon my eye curved in mirth. Its kiss was dry. Stinging tears stained my eyes, whose lids I shut. Weird red shapes danced before those tiny flaps of flesh. I raised my hand so as to wipe away my salty tears. Opening my eyes, I saw that I was alone in the dark and silent place.

I sucked, tasting night's ambience. Digging into ground, I touched the past. I somehow knew that my secret longing, my desire to be released from this neoteric age, would come to pass. I arose, laughing at arthritic pain. My hands were raised in singing. Staggering among the silent stones I quit that place and tumbled onto the ancient bridge that crossed the filthy canal. Tottering into thick streetlamp light, I sneered at its detestable radiance. Bah, how searing was the light of hearth-glow that leaked through windows passed. With what mockery burned the detestable moon. I tried to shield my eyes but found my hand too pale, its flesh too bright.

Happily, I entered the blackness of my room. The candle at the opened window had mercifully extinguished. I pushed the candlestick out of the window and listened to its fall. I shut the window's shade and placed a hard wooden chair into the bleakest corner of the room, then sat facing the wall. I gently dozed. A delicious chill awakened me.

The window had been left open, and its frail lace curtains lightly moved. The breeze that breathed through the window was gentle and fragrant, yet contained a cosmic chilliness that sank beneath my pores and found my bones. The chilliness began to push at and lift my soul. Deftly, I drifted to the window, on feet that lightly touched the wooden floor. My nails ripped away the curtains.

The green window shade shot up like a startled beast. Shards of starlight stabbed the sky, yet dimly. The mauve moon seemed very far away. Its sunken glow shone directly over St. Toad's, an amphibian light. Within that light I saw the shadow of old stone and watched it oddly stretch. I saw it ooze in huge proportion across the churchyard ground, the rotting tombstones, the creature with a fiddle tucked beneath its chin.

St. Toad's chimes sounded three times. The bow moved across the fiddle and played the music of the spheres. I raised my hands in accompaniment. Gawd, how monstrous was the symphony of sound! How could such pandemonium issue forth from a single instrument? Whenceforth came those other, those outré chords?

All noise ceased. My hands stilled, yet remained hanging in mid-air. I watched as the distant woman thrust her bow into the sod. I saw her raise a hand to moonlight and move in genuflection. My own hand moved in imitation of her motion, and as our hands moved, so too did shadow. It fumbled about her, then floated forth from out the churchyard. It spindled and stemmed, branching blackly. It wormed up the ancient hill, and all other shadows clung unto it. It dragged, this darkness, toward the hotel. It rose and spread before me with sentience.

I felt the darkness flow onto my fevered brow. I saw it glove my moving hands. Heavily, it pressed against my eyelids, closing them. It shut my fingers into tight fists and echoed coldly in my ears. It seeped into my mouth.

Darkness ached within me. I wanted to sing, but my hands refused to open. Thus I opened my mouth, that organ blessed with cosmic shadow. My mouth, which had never uttered sound, began to sing as darkness dragged me skyward.

Jigsaw Boy

(To ye memory of Todd Frank Nelson)

His nodding head sat fitfully upon a clump of damp earth. Reaching with a nude arm, he clutched the crop of lice-infested hair. Indolently, he pulled the head to him and put it into place. Blinking slumber from dark pools that were eyes, he summoned his scattered and disjointed fragments of flesh. They moved, soundlessly, joined together, became one.

With smooth motion, he rose. Lifting the bleached, the bony limbs that were arms he watched them swim in moonlight. His tattered fingers fitted together, took on a semblance of wings, waved with gentle elegance in evening air. His somber silhouette cast its obscene shadow upon the weathered wall of an abandoned building that had been his habitat.

Cold wind gather around him, pressed against him, moaned remorselessly through the empty place of his missing piece. His sense of play evaporated. Placing a soiled hand on his breast, he fingered the hollow spot where once he had worn a heart. He scowled, tried once more to recall how that organ had been lost. But recollection evaded his hazy half-numb mind, and thus he began once more to search the night.

Filthy clothes were pulled over pale flesh. Picking up his staff of rough dark wood, he vacated the place of refuge. Wind rushed at him, coaxing him to follow it through the sleeping town.

He knew where it would lead him.

Pursing lips together, he whistled a melancholy tune.

He liked the bitter cold. It kept the humans in their hovels. It complimented the chill bitterness that iced his hungry soul. Ah, how weary and withered that little soul seemed now.

He passed the darkened church where the population prayed. How he loved the grim austere building, the angels that watched with bent heads and outstretched arms. Entering, he found the dark window of stained glass whereon the Christ was formed. He ran his fingers through the lines of glass that, soldered piece by piece, created this creature of divinity and grace. In wavering candlelight he saw the muted reflection of his face upon the breast of Christ. He could only just make out the dim dark eyes sunk inside a pasty face.

He bent to kiss the dark reflection. Just beneath his ugliness he thought there lingered a glimmer of grim beauty. With effort, he could be as magnificent and sensual as this effigy of the effete Christ. But he had chosen to cultivate misery, and misery was not pretty. Yet how could he be otherwise, heartless creature that he was? Twisting scornful lips, he spat at the image of the sacred bleeding heart.

He returned to wind and twilight. The sibilant air led him to his favorite place, the river beneath the willows. He looked at the movement of rushing water, at the mirrored moon. Night's swaying shadows were caught upon the water. How would it feel, he wondered, to flow so swiftly as the water before him? He closed his eyes and tried to imagine it, swayed to and fro in chilly darkness.

The ground was wet where he stood. Suddenly, he lost his footing. The wooden staff escaped his grasp. He watched it fall into the water and flow away. His hands, now free, found their way into the pockets of his coat. His fingers touched a smooth warm pulsing thing.

He cupped his hand around it. Brought it to his face.

Gazed in amazement at his missing piece. His parting lips hissed with mocking laughter.

He gazed at the trembling object. He kissed it. Tenderly, he fit it into place within his breast. He gasped, sighed, moaned softly to the darkness. Tears gathered in the shadows of his eyes. He felt, for the first time in nameless eons, what it meant to have a heart. Overwhelmed with sorrow and despair, he covered his weeping face with shaking hands.

Taunting wind kissed his shivering frame. It pushed him so that he leaned precipitously over the rushing water. Hugging his disjointed form, he gazed at his shimmering reflection. The song of the river soothed him. It beckoned.

He smiled, pressed his lips together, filled the night with airy music. Tilting toward dark water, he shut tight his eyes, sighed one final note of song, and fell in pieces.

The Fungal Stain

Grow to my lip, thou sacred kiss . . .
—*Thomas Moore*

I.

I was leaning against a window in a cramped bookstore, holding aloft a candlestick to scan a volume of Justin Geoffrey (drinking in his cosmic madness), when I noticed a figure hovering in the fog outside. Strange, isn't it, the play of shadow and light that dances in a pool of fog? I saw this person, this woman, and at first I thought my eyes were playing tricks. Her face seemed all wrong, more bestial than human. And the way she lifted her curious mouth so as to drink in the evening effluvium was most unnatural. She lowered her face and looked at my window, drawn perhaps to the glow of my candle's flame. Her lips curled to form an uncanny and esoteric smile, and as I watched the movement of her mouth the fog thickened and veiled her face. When again I saw that visage, it looked as usual as any I had ever seen, with nothing in it that would stir uneasy curiosity.

I returned to my book, listening, and heard the shop's door open. A sudden chill rushed past me, and entrails of mist vaguely mingled with surrounding shadow; and out of this she approached the place where I stood. Glancing sideways, I watched her pretend to study titles, then closed my book and reached to return it to its shelf. Her hand touched mine as she took the book from my grasp.

"This is rare," she said, smiling. "He had a wonderful sense of place, don't you think?"

Sardonically, I laughed. "My dear woman, he wrote of a landscape of nightmare!"

"Exquisitely so," she agreed, and then quoted from memory the following lines of verse:

"And in the village where it stands,
    That place where Time had shrugged and passed it by,
    I found deep-etched in sod and on black stone,
    My mortal name."

Nodding to her, I blew out my candle, took it to the dealer's desk, and stepped into misty night. The air had turned surprisingly chilly, and I pulled the collar of my coat closer to my naked neck. Then I stopped and smiled at myself. I had no idea where I wanted to go. I knew only that I wasn't in the mood for social chatter, especially with some tourist who was taking in the ancient charm of Kingsport. I stood for a while, watching a streetlamp glow in encircling fog, when I heard footsteps on the bookstore's porch. She stopped at the bottom step and looked around uncertainly, nodding as she noticed me standing in the hazy lamplight. I leaned awkwardly on one foot and then the other, then stopped at the noise of musical humming. Her odd song issued as mist from her unmoving mouth, and the thickening fog that encased her met and mingled with her exhalation. Something in her song beguiled me, and with an almost unconscious motion I began to creep toward her. I watched as I slowly walked, and saw the shadows of her face darken, distorting features. Soon there was nothing but her indistinct form, and the twin pin-pricks that were her diamond eyes. I thought they queerly smiled, those eyes, as finally the fog completely entombed her. I reached the place where she had stood, but I was alone.

I had decided, the next evening, to attend Poetry Night at the Pennywhistle Café, a truly bohemian establishment. Here one could find the loud rebels who hung their unruly art upon the walls and stood on chairs and tables so to declaim their bitter odes. Now and then, however, one could encounter that especially sensitive artist, those dreamers who souls seem as quaint and twisted as the eldest Kingsport lane. I liked to think of myself as such a bard, and I considered my vision quite singular. It had been some time since I had attended the weekly doings. I had, however, recently composed a new poem. Thus I braved the evening's chill and took a bus to that section of town known as The Hollow, then scuttled from the bus to the small building that housed the café. The turnout was okay, and I nodded to several casual acquaintances. Five makeshift rows had been formed with folding wooden chairs, and I took my usual place in the third row.

The evening's feature poet was a homeless woman whose appearance was quite pathetic. Yet one forgot her stained clothes and missing teeth when she began to recite her work. Unlike many of the poseurs who had more ego than talent, this woman's poetry came from some authentic place in her unhappy, lonely soul. She read for fifteen minutes, and then the café's owner, who always served as master of ceremonies, invited the rest of us to approach the podium and recite our immortal odes. I listened as two friends went forward and dramatically read new work, then I arose and stepped to the podium. My reading went well, even though I was somewhat startled to see a certain figure standing near the back. As I returned to my chair she came forward, book in hand, and stood before the podium.

"My name is Genevieve, and I am not a poet. But I love the craft and have been enchanted by what I have heard tonight. I would like to read a short piece by a poet who is now largely forgotten. Sadly, we now live in an age where, in this country, poetry is seldom bothered with. We cannot be forgotten, for we are utterly ignored." A murmur of agreement filtered through the room. "But none can deny us our voice. Here is the voice of authentic poetry; and although his vision is not quite as quixotic as the piece we've just heard from Mr. Christopher, it is its equal in extravagance."

"The impudent vixen," I angrily thought; then leaned back and frowned at her as she opened a book and began to read.

> "I kiss the cosmic wind that finds my face,
> This face that burns as if encased in flame,
> An ember glowing in an alien place,
> An ancient land that seems to call my name.
> I tell my name among the stones that stand
> As towers of black slate beneath black stars,
> Those stars that spill toward me like dark sand,
> Like sand that stains the mortal flesh it mars.
> New-made I rise, a pillar of dark stone,
> A nascent thing on Yuggoth's hoary sod,
> And feel the hunger of a howling wind
> That echoes laughter from a raving god."

I had closed my eyes as she began to read, and kept them shut as polite applause ushered her from the podium. In the darkness of my mind I could see the imagery from the poem, with which I was of course familiar. The sound of a gentleman's loud voice shook me out of reverie, and I casually looked around but did not see her in the room. Rising during applause, I made my way through the throng and stepped outside. She was leaning against the building and looking at the stars. I thought that she was waiting for me.

"Doesn't the fog smell rank, like an unwashed lover, sweet and sour? Can you smell the coming storm?"

"No," I bluntly replied, reaching for the pack of cigarettes in my shirt pocket, and hoping that smoking offended her. "Will you have one?"

"Certainly," she said, smiling. Placing a fag in my mouth, I lit it, took a drag, then held it to her. She brought the thin narcotic cylinder to her face and deeply inhaled its fumes. Her mouth never touched it. "I enjoyed your poem, Keith. One wouldn't think to look at you that you were such a romantic."

Sardonically, I blew smoke into the air. "If you found it romantic, you didn't understand the poem. It wasn't about a person, it was about a place."

"Places are far more worthy of romance, Keith. How can a hand-some face with sparkling eyes compare to the smell of some old deep-buried hideaway? That's why I like your town. It absolutely reeks of se-cret places, of displaced memories, of a past that refuses to die. Deli-cious." She came close and linked her arm with mine. "Will you walk with me?"

"If you insist." I was not fond of human contact, and women were a race I did not understand and with which I felt most uncomfortable. And this was no ordinary woman. From the moment I first laid eyes on her I had felt unsettled. She was like one of Wilde's alluring panthers, as dangerous as she was beguiling. I fancied that I could sense her bestial appetite as her hips moved against mine.

These alarming observations overwhelmed me until I heard the sound of distant music. Ah, how I smiled. We approached a sight that would stir her curiosity, and in her distraction I would slip away and make my escape. Nonchalantly, I led her toward the sound, to the over-grown and usually abandoned courtyard that was lit by one weak lamp-post. Beneath the dim light were two figures. The taller one, a bent old man, played a worn and weathered accordion, a slender tube-like in-strument from another century, with buttons rather than keyboard. He moved its pleated billows in a mechanical manner, as though oblivious to the heart-wrenching music he produced.

Beneath him knelt one of the oddest and most pathetic beings I had ever encountered. One knew instinctively that the diminutive thing was not a child, even though the monkey mask of flayed rubber covered most of the creature's face. From its dome, just above the mask, was a mess of mangled hair, coils of matted filth that resembled thick dead worms. Bent over the image that it drew on pavement with a piece of chalk, it was oblivious to our presence.

I looked at the woman and saw her watching the remnants of hands that clutched yellow chalk. The right hand was little more than a fist, for its flesh came to an end just above the knuckles. The left hand retained two middle digits, and they stopped their drawing as we got closer and the wee creature turned his head to look at us. How oddly his black eyes shined behind their monkey mask. His fingers dropped the chalk and began to move as if he were attempting some pathetic form of sign language. He then stood upon truncated legs and did a little dance; and as he danced, he bent his torso low and pushed his arms backward, so that his elbows seemed to form the tips of wings. Glancing at his chalk drawing, I saw that he had tried to depict some kind of malformed angel or succubus.

The music swelled, and with rakish glee I took Genevieve roughly into my arms and danced her closer to that pair of beings who stood like harbingers of doom. The old man lifted his fantastic face so as to watch our frolic, and I tried not to look at the growths of bumps and folded flesh that grotesquely disfigured his visage. His prancing familiar watched us with bent head and held out what remained of a palm. Pushing me from her, the woman went to him, bent low and kissed the open palm. I watched the small thing shuddered.

The music stopped, and the old man released one hand from his instrument and held it to her. She took the beckoning hand and lifted it to her face, smoothing her features against his cracked and ancient flesh. Her hands swam through air toward his white hair, into which her fingers wound. She bent closer to him, touching her mouth to his, then moving it to an ugly growth upon his cheek. Her kiss was a prolonged thing, and when at last she pulled away I was horrified to see the blood that oozed from the place on the old gent's face that had been eaten into. Sickened, I backed away, then turned to run as the ancient fellow reached out with shaky hands and pulled the woman's face once more to his.

II.

I wandered through the moist and stinking fog, that queer mist that had stayed now for two days. From the sound of bells and horns I knew that I had reached Harborside, and when I found myself on Water Street I calmed a little. Walking to a familiar address, I passed through gates that were supported by stone walls eight feet in height. The gnarled trees that surrounded the ancient dwelling were swathed in thick mist. From the wide covered porch I could discern a lantern's glow. I heard the faint humming of a drunken song. Winfield Scot watched me, smiling.

"Ah, brother poet, come and share my wine. Or try this kick-ass rum. It'll warm you from the coils of detested fog. You look like a fellow in need of fortification. What ails thee, son; what's her name?"

I took the proffered bottle of rum and gulped a generous portion. "She's a very devil."

"Aren't they all, god love them. Give me the hellish details, and steady on the rum. It's another week before my beloved government gives me another check of crazy money."

I babbled of my encounter, and as I told my tale Scot's eyes sobered. I think sometimes he plays at being more intoxicated than he actually is, as if it were expected of him to play the part of crazy town drunk. He carefully listened to my account.

"Hmmm," he said after a long pause, then brought a bottle of red wine to his mouth.

"What?"

"You say she appeared to you out of this damnable fog, as if she sought you? And you were reading from *People of the Monolith* at the time? Reading aloud?"

"I don't know. I sometimes read aloud. I like to feel the words on my lips. Why?"

"Justin Geoffrey—funny, he has two first names, just like you. I've cautioned you before about speaking certain esoteric verse aloud. Now, you know that fellow's history, of how he wrote the initial draft of his infamous poem in a state of rich madness while he sat near a tall monolith of cursed stone. A haunted place, a haunted mind, linked in lunacy. In such a state, believe me, humanity is open to unusual influence. You and I, son, as poets, know too well the weird stuff that leaks into our imaginations. From where?"

"I've heard all of this before, your theory of the universal madness of poets."

"Not all. And there are degrees of madness. I speak mainly of those of us who dig the weird cosmic stuff. You've written just a bit of it, but you read it always. This place, this old seaport, welcomes those of us who thrill to outside influence. We have felt the velvet kiss of the kind of madness that produces the poetry of *People of the Monolith* and *Al Azif*. We tap into a language that is fraught with energy, with power. The result is poetry that is truly *evocative*. We should use caution in speaking such words aloud."

"Okay, I know where you're going with this. You're saying that I summoned this witch woman by uttering the alchemical syllables of a mad poet's song."

"You catch on quick. Come on, I want to show you something interesting." Clumsily, he held out his hand. I took it and pulled him to his feet. He stumbled to the door of the ancient house and pushed it open.

"I don't think so, Winfield."

"Hand me that lantern and don't be a wuss. The trick is not to linger too long inside. Take my hand, child, if it makes you feel safer. Can you feel it? This, too, is a realm of madness." I walked close behind him, taking in the debris with which the shadowed room was cluttered. "The old lunatic who lived here until the end of his unnatural life, bless him, left the stigmata of craziness within these rotting walls. Man, the weird junk he picked up as he sailed around the world. This place is a trove of nameless loot. From the stories he told me, and from the bits he cautiously left out but hinted at, he was ruthless in his pursuit of plunder. Settle down, don't look so nervous. Ain't much can reach us here from Outside, not as long as those painted stones stand unmoved in the yard. Ah, here it is."

He took up a small box of polished black wood and set it on a nearby table. Undoing the latch, he opened the lid. I reached for the small obsidian dagger that nestled on black velvet. "What is this?"

"Feels creepy, don't it? You see, Justin Geoffrey wasn't the only lunatic to visit the black monolith of Stregoicavar. Over the decades foolhardy souls have taken ax and hammer to that stone, but they never did much damage. Around the base is a litter of shards, and from one good-sized piece our sea captain had this ritual weapon forged. God alone knows what he used it for."

"Let's get out of here," I said, closing the lid of the box. Winfield watched as I placed the weapon in my coat pocket, then followed me to the door and onto the porch that was his homeless residence.

"Listen, man. This old town ain't just a seaport. It's a portal. Things can be summoned from the other side. Wouldn't surprise me if that crazy old coot initially called up this woman, whatever she is. If she's linked to the Black Stone and Geoffrey's alchemic verse, carrying that thing with you is a bad idea."

"I want to study it. There's some symbols carved onto the handle that look familiar. I think I remember them from a book I saw in the library at Miskatonic. Maybe I can find some answers about this woman . . ."

"This avatar, you mean. You're fricking mad."

Calmly I smiled, then turned and walked into the fog.

III.

I walked past Water Street, toward the ocean, to the wharves. Dropping the façade of calm that I had faked so as to disguise my true emotional state from my inebriated friend, I walked the lonely place until I found the pathetic shanty that was my destination. Breathing deeply of the unwholesome fog, I pushed opened the crooked door of disjointed wood. He was sitting on a crate, eating fish that had been wrapped in newspaper. Flickering light from a single candle illuminated the place, and looking into one corner I saw the mound of blankets wherein his squat companion slept.

"Hello, Enoch."

He looked at me with rheumy eyes, a shred of fish hanging from one corner of his mouth. "Evening."

"Are you okay?"

His eyes blinked. "Never better." I watched his gnarled hand reach for a place on his face, which he thoughtfully scratched. From outside, I could hear a boat's forlorn howl, and as if in answer I heard another low moaning, which I took to be the wind on water. This latter sound increased, became a gale that shook the edifice of wood and metal and thick cardboard. I looked at one of the trembling cardboard walls, at what I took to be papier-mâché masks that had been glued to its surface. Stepping to the wall, I carefully touched one of the pale faces. Its thin membrane pushed inward at the force of my fingering.

"What are these, Enoch?"

"Oh, aspects of her and her kindred. They like their false faces, aye."

I reached to touch another of the ghastly things, gently poking a finger into the hollow eye socket. Hideous as they were, they were strangely seductive. So soft. Perhaps, if I was very careful, I could peel one of them from the wall and slip it onto my own visage.

The old man began to hum, as outside the wind blew roughly against the shack. Enoch's humming became a low chanting singing. "Across black gulfs toward us they dance, and mock our insignificance." From a corner of the room, fluted music accompanied the old man's singing.

I turned to glance at the malformed gnome. Still wrapped in many blankets, he glowered at me with glistening black orbs. A cracked flute was pressed against the mouth opening of the monkey mask. Something soft touched my shoulder, and I turned my face to hers. Her cool mouth pressed against my forehead, and her tongue—so oddly soft, so warm and heavy—fastened to my flesh. When she backed away, I knew that it had not been her tongue that had tickled me, for I could feel it still upon my flesh, the soft heavy thing. Reaching to my face, I touched the fungous growth upon it. Her diamond eyes beamed as shadows shifted the shape of her inhuman face. She bent to me a second time and touched her lips to mine. As we kissed, my hand went into my pocket and found the diminutive ritual dagger. Joyfully, I pushed the blade into the face to which I made love, just below one eye. How easily that visage tore, like mushroom. Sediments of her sardonic physiognomy spilled to me, onto my eyes and mouth and into my nostrils.

I pushed away from the creature and fled that haunted place. Wild tempest tore at my hair, my clothing; it had pushed away the noisome fog. Above, the dark sky was laced with silver starlight, and I shivered as those gems remorselessly winked at me. I watched the roiling storm clouds that gathered at the jutting edge of Kingsport Head. I listened to the waves that cruelly crashed against the ports of rotted wood. Behind me there came an odd scuttling sound, and turning I saw the assemblage of large leaves that followed me, pushed by wind along the ground.

No, not leaves. Rather, they were soft hollow faces moving toward me in the moaning wind. I groaned into that wind, as beneath its noise I heard that other sound. I saw them dimly in the distance, the two fig-

ures that had followed me from their shabby abode. One played an antique accordion. About his feet his masked companion frolicked, a flute
at its mouth. Behind them, in spreading darkness, she emerged, gliding
toward me. Windstorm whirled around her, lifting to her the scattered
faces in a column of spinning air. Reaching out, she took hold of one
face. How easily it covered her split countenance.

Mindlessly, I began to whisper some snatches of lunatic verse. The
bumps of substance that stained my mouth and forehead began to
slowly expand. From black heaven came initial drops of moisture, light
and soothing. Then the sky fractured, and heavy rain poured on me like
some unholy cosmic baptism. Thus claimed, I gazed one last time at the
creature who swam toward me through moist air; and then I shut my
eyes and awaited her final kiss.

Balm of Nepenthe

(For Samuel Loveman)

I had been feeling execrable that season, oppressed with an ocular tugging that had made reading impossible and existence a misery. And so I was unpleasant to be around when our small poetic group gathered for our monthly meeting. Simon Gregory Williams had just read one of his pretentious poems in imperial tone, and he smiled as the others applauded, then scowled at me. "Did you not enjoy it, Harley?"

I shrugged. "It was okay."

His silver eyes squinted with annoyance. "Is it? Well, let us hear your divine offering."

"I don't have anything. My eyes are bugging me again, and the damn hand cramps have returned. It's impossible to hold a pen for more than half an hour."

"Ah," Simon sighed. "Mortality can be such a burthen for you humans. Well, that explains your rudeness this evening."

Pushing out of my chair, I rose and faced the goblin. "Yes, it must be tiresome for someone as superior as yourself to have to bother with the likes of me. Almost as tiresome as your repetition of imagery in poem after poem. Why I bother with you fools is beyond me. I think I'd find better company among the shadowed woodland."

"I'm sure you're right," Simon sniffed. "You'll certainly find no sympathy here."

"A pox on your sympathy, Simon," I said, storming to the door and rushing into the cool night air. I gazed skyward, at the dazzling starlight. It had always seemed strange how bright the starlight was over Sesqua Valley, how close those cosmic gems appeared to be. I reached out my hand, as if to touch the shimmering light, and felt my fingers stiffen, then oddly spread. This was a cramping that I had not experienced. It was as though my hand were trying to form some signal to the distant sky. I brought that hand to my mouth and bathed it with moist lips, tasting my wretched mortality. How weary I was of existence.

This sense of disconsolateness had crouched within my remorseless heart for some little time, affecting appetite, keeping slumber away, bringing headache and fatigue. My bones felt heavy, encased in their prison of flesh. How I longed to free myself of humanness. How I longed to be as free as the sibilant wind that moved among the tree-tops.

I let that evening wind push me along the road, toward the center of town. Most of the buildings were dark, but I noticed the pale light that illuminated the ticket booth of Sesqua's dilapidated cinema house. Approaching it, I smiled at the young bespectacled man who sat within. "Hello, Howard," I said.

He started at the sound of my voice, looked up from the notebook into which he had been scribbling, and squinted at me through his eye-glasses. Then his stiff mouth, which rarely smiled, curved slightly in recognition. "Mr. Randolph, good evening. Did your group let out early?" I knew that Howard aspired to write poetry, and it was only the need to earn a living that kept him from our monthly meetings.

"What's that you're working on?" I asked, ignoring his question.

He smiled that anxious smile one sees on artists when they are provided a chance to discuss their work. "A strange thing, but mine own," he said, shrugging modestly. "I was wandering the old cemetery, and came upon that weird statue of the faceless angel. Do you know it? There's something about it that's quite unnerving. I felt the strangest compulsion to kneel before it. Have you ever closely examined the stick that it holds? At first I thought it was supposed to be a scythe, and that some vandals had knocked off the blade. But I went to study it in sunlight one afternoon, and it's not a stick but a piece of delicate bone, thin and long. It's certainly strange. I've been dreaming about it lately, and not being able to get it out of my mind, I decided to exorcise it with poetry."

"I often expel my daemons in such a way," I told him. "Let's hear your poem."

Lifting his notebook to the light, he read.

> "Half-lost, I wandered down the winding lane,
> Beneath the glow of streetlamps queerly dim,
> Until I saw the sober seraphim

Whose shadow spread before me like some stain
Of somber doom that would affect my brain
With words to utter as unholy hymn,
With language that is dangerous and grim,
With words one had forgotten, found again.
I slowly stepped before the faceless one.
The mist that issued from my mouth and nose
Formed as a cloud of furtive shape that rose
To kiss the thing of stone that I would shun.
My hand reached to chill starlight subdivine.
My fingers moved to form an elder sign."

How melancholy I suddenly felt. As my hand began to tingle and slowly spread, I shoved the stiffening thing into a pants pocket. I met Howard's eyes, and something in my expression must have bewildered him, judging from his expression. Quickly, I forced a smile. "Your poem is quite impressive."

Momentarily, he beamed. Then his face became quite serious.

"It needs work, of course. This is but a first draft." He stopped as I began to pull my out my wallet. "Good lord, are you actually coming in to support the student film festival?"

"I thought I might. Anything worthwhile?"

"A few interesting efforts, if slightly pretentious. The first intermission is just about to end." Thanking him, I walked into the lobby and made my way to the dusky auditorium. Seeing one familiar face, I entered a row and sat next to her.

"Harley," she uttered, looking bemused. "You've just missed the most boring bit of cinema. I was trying to decide if I should depart this place, but now that you're here to hold my hand, I think I'll abide."

"And such a pretty hand, Alexis." I assured her, taking it and bringing it to my lips. "Boring, eh?"

"This last one was a pseudo-factual farce about the Arkham witch trials, a dreary subject to begin with. When lack of imagination is coupled with a serious want of budget, the results are not happy." The house lights began to darken. "Ah, here we go. Hold on to your seat, dear heart."

An image began to flicker on the screen, and words began to form:

The Miskatonic Film Society Presents
A Film by Theobald Loe.

This faded, and the film's title appeared, in Greek, which I could not read. All became black. Slowly, one discernible image began to vaguely manifest itself, a depth of shadow within a flux of restless penumbra. I watched as two small spheres began to drift toward us out of this immortal night, spheres that opened and seemed to smile with supernal mockery. Other pinpricks of light began to flicker, then fell like grains of sand. No music sounded, but one could subtly hear a kind of humming, perhaps of wind. A moon hazily formed, gigantic and round, and silhouetted against it was a figure that wore a triple crown. The moon transformed into a disc of light that glared over a stretch of desert sand. The only color on the screen was an eerie sepia tone. The sound that might have been wind mutated and became an articulate buzzing, as if a thousand insects were trying to call a monstrous name.

Beside me, I thought that my friend was mumbling something to herself. But I could not take my eyes away from the robed figure on the screen, the crowned daemon that raised its claw and esoterically moved its talons as if in signal to the sky.

I watched that sky grow dark once more, until there was nothing but a void of which the mocking daemon was lord. Alexis let go of my hand and rose to her feet, walked out of our row and to the screen. Clumsily, like one who walks in slumber, she gracelessly surmounted the platform on which the screen had been built. Wobbling slightly, she raised herself to a standing position and placed one hand against the haunting image. I watched as the color of her clothes and flesh began to slowly fade into a dim sepia tone as the screen began to blacken.

Darkness fell, and for a while I sat unmoving, listening to the sound of dying buzzing. Then I pushed out of my seat, stumbled out of the auditorium and to the door that led outside. I scanned dark heaven, which was weirdly devoid of starlight, looking very like the image I had momentarily witnessed in the cinema. How wonderful that sky appeared to my weary soul, like some long, peaceful night of non-existence into which I could rest my bones.

I stood and listened to the hum of rising wind, then allowed that wind to push me where it would, like one lost in rich dream. I drifted to the aged necropolis wherein outsiders to Sesqua Valley were interred. Approaching the graven angel of which Howard had written in verse, I knelt before the tomb of which it was a part. The grave was very old, dating to one of the valley's founding fathers whose unhappy child had taken his own life. There was no special spot of unconsecrated ground wherein the humans of the valley were buried, for the rate of suicide among them was extremely high, and more than half of the souls buried in this place had ended their own lives. Although I was deeply unhappy, I was not suicidal. Yet I often found a kind of consolation when I came to mutter to the sad souls that were buried in this place. So many of them were ridiculously young, like the youth who laid beneath this mammoth monument. How absurd that one so young should have so easily escaped existence, while I was condemned to linger for so long.

I whistled to the wind, and as I did so I felt my hand begin to ache, to stretch its digits, those slender bits of bones clothed in flimsy flesh. The hell with it. I raised my hand to heaven and let it make its sign to whatever god or devil may perceive it. I whistled with more force, and the air before me began to quiver. From the rotting stone before which I knelt there rose a film of dust, and as I watched the stuff shaped itself into the semblance of a sad young man in centuried garments.

"Why have you awakened me?" it moaned.

Dishearteningly, I smiled. "You've slept for over one century, and—oh!—you were so young. This is not a place for one so youthful, so beautiful. Look at my tired eyes set deep within this weary face. Who best deserves eternal repose?"

The figure looked around and frowned. "I did not like the creeping shadows of this cursed valley. Father would not listen to my pleas. And so I walked into the dark lake, and I became one with shadow. I do not fear this place as once I did. I would happily walk it again."

Softly, I began to whistle. I raised my hands to him, and he floated to me, softly kissing the hand that moved in elder genuflection. He raised his phantom mouth to mine as I continued to whistle my aching tune. My hot living breath filled his insubstantial frame. The dead thing drank my life.

Now I rest within a depth of peaceful nothingness. At times I remember a hideous thing called life, but I push those memories from me. Sometimes, from some place far away, I hear a whistled song from the sad soul whose bed I have absconded, that soul who weeps and would return. But I ignore his mortal plea.

Some Darker Star

(To ye memory of Joseph Payne Brennan)

I.

Thoby Whateley sat at the old oak desk, took up the pen with long lean fingers, and began to write.

My dear Adrian:—

You have certainly missed out by not coming with me. This valley is as wondrous as our sisters have suggested; and we have more kin here than either of us have realised, from the distant Dunwich branch. We had some of them over for coffee two evenings gone—strange, furtive folk, so they are. They had a manner of gazing at one, with subtle inquisition, while asking questions pertaining to obscure family background. My utter ignorance of such matters seemed distinctly to dishearten them—oddly so.

The town is rural, with few paved roads or sidewalks. People seem to enjoy walking along the sides of dirt streets; and there are so few vehicles that this is not at all hazardous. The simplicity of life here is like nothing I've encountered elsewhere. Townsfolk are amiable but distant. Children are few, and thus the quiet is absolute. I've seen a minimum of canines, but everyone seems to own at least one feline.

I arrived by train, and it was a quaint experience. The "depot" is an absurd little shack. There is a much larger bus station, with frequent activity. I believe many of the residents work out of town, using the bus line to reach their place of employment.

One large and sturdy old building serves as post office, general store, motel, and lord knows what else. This is located on the main street, which is paved with a kind of black pitch. One particularly run-down building serves as cinema, and I noticed a bookshop and our younger sister's hair salon. On our walk (yes, *walk*) from town to our sister's spacious old Georgian residence, we passed a church; well, I think it was a church, although I could espy no cross. It had a steeple, ergo . . . The building is incredibly old, and Virginia informed me that it was built by one of Sesqua Valley's founding fathers. I mean to investigate it when I have some free time.

Vanessa's salon brings in, so it appears, enough capital for the two of them to subsist on in easy comfort, and thus Virginia is able to concentrate on her books of poetry, for which there is but a little audience. Ginnie is looking older, yet quite lovely still. She says that the valley is filled with writers, but lacks the egos and competition she experienced in Arkham. Actually, the valley seems to be a veritable nest of aesthetic activity of every kind. While strolling through the woods yesternight I came upon a number of rather odd statues, in the most unlikely of locations. This afternoon Nessa is to show me more of the local sights. I've asked about hiking up Mount Selta, but neither are thus inclined. It is a rather magnificent sight, this mountain of sparkling white stone. Situated northeast of town it rises some 4,000 feet. The white rock of which it is composed must contain some sort of crystal residue; to see it sparkle in the valley's misty light is quite bewitching. Most unique are its two peaks, narrow and curved, somewhat resembling wings folded on the back of some hunkering behemoth.

An enchanting place all told, dear boy, and very good for my poor old nerves. My condition seems not so bad as it was in Arkham. I understand why the school board felt it necessary to give me—how did they phrase it?—"an extended leave of absence," so as to take care of myself. I find my breakdown an embarrassment now, but at the time I simply could not control my emotional state.

Well, that's all for now. I miss our debates, and most especially my library, although Virginia's is as impressive as I predicted it would be. I miss you, dear boy, and hope your students are treating you with kindness and respect.

Thoby read over what he had written, signed the epistle and set it aside. When he entered the capacious dining room, he found his elder sister spooning soup into bowls.

"Ah, Thoby, I was just about to call you. Please, sit. Vanessa is tending to the casserole, which I think you'll find quite excellent." In a lower voice she confided, "I'm glad to have another literary soul here, I must admit. One cannot really talk books with Nessa." She smiled a comrade's smile, and he took in her appearance. Her tall, angular body moved with easy grace. Violet eyes twinkled above the aquiline nose. The dark hair, wound in a conservative bun, was beginning to gray.

What a contrast to his younger sister, who now sailed through the kitchen door carrying a casserole dish. Thoby took in her astonishing, almost youthful beauty. She wore a pretty dress, white with a design of yellow flowers; low cut, so that one could easily admire the milky smooth complexion of her dainty bosom. Her dark luxurious hair fell onto her shoulders, and it had been scented with some kind of lavender ointment. She wore a modicum of makeup, expertly applied.

"Do sit down, Thoby. You needn't play the gentleman here."

They ate slowly, rarely speaking as had been the family way. He liked being there, with them, liked the easy and familiar feeling of intimacy. They ate in a realm of shared memory, and the years of having been absent from each other melted away. When their repast was completed, the two younger siblings prepared for their walk.

October wind greeted them with the rich scent of the valley. Vanessa, draped within a hooded cloak, linked her arm with his. They stepped onto a wooded path, and the green shade felt cool and soothing on his eyes. He found that he was becoming accustomed to the valley's unusual air, which when he first arrived affected him oddly, seeming heavy and somewhat sweet. As they walked, he heard beating wings and saw shadows sail among the distant trees. He liked the patches of moss that spotted the thick trunks of towering trees. Now and then a slate-colored sky was seen above outstretched branches.

And then they came upon a sight that slightly startled him, a bust of what looked like Pan, sitting on a pedestal of black stone. "My dear great god, what pagan practices are here revealed?" Thoby lightly laughed, running thin fingers through thick dark hair.

"It's a custom of the valley, brother, to place creative pieces here and there. I can show you some rather curious creations. This is the work of a woman who went away. Rather wonderful, isn't it? There's a far more unusual piece in the clearing up ahead. It's rather grotesque, actually. Would you care to see it?"

"My curiosity is at fever pitch, Nessa darling. I'm only thankful not to be tramping these mystic woods alone."

"Come on," she said, laughing. Before long they came upon a

clearing that was encircled by pale willows. Thoby unlocked his arm from Vanessa's and slowly approached the unsettling object that knelt in the center of the clearing. Of what it was composed he could not ascertain; pigskin, perhaps, or bleached leather. Its worn and tattered feminine clothing moved in gentle wind. As Thoby examined the enigmatic creature he could not repress a shudder. The thing was entirely queer. The arms stretched skyward, as if reaching for the stratosphere. Upon the left palm was etched, in yellow thread, a curious symbol, one that was repeated, inlaid in gold, on a clasp of achromatic marble or some such material that had been fastened to the figure's blouse.

Most strange of all was the mask of yellow silk that veiled the figure's face, beneath which, with suggestive folds and hollows, appeared the semblance of a death's-head, with mouth stretched hideously open. He reached to touch the colorless clasp. How cold it was, with what an unearthly chilliness. Thoby kept his hand upon it, not wanting to take his fingers away. Oddly, there seemed to emanate from the kneeling figure a slow and subtle vibration, a pulsation that sounded in echo within his skull-space. And, how weird, that same vibration seemed to echo above him, in deep heaven. Thoby raised his eyes to the darkening firmament. How had it grown so quickly dark? Why did starlight move, encircling the smoldering sphere that drifted downward? He reached with shaky fingers to the sky.

"What?" Vanessa touched a comforting hand to his cheek. "What is it, Thoby?" she asked, perplexed by the expression in his cloudy eyes.

"That sphere. That star of flaming shadow. Oh, it hums my name. Its eyes, those myriad eyes, they summon the sign. Ah, it calls my name!" He reached for the clasp and tore it from the figure's blouse, pricking a finger on its pins. He raised the golden symbol to the seething sky as dark blood dribbled down his hand. Shaken and wild-eyed, his sister tilted toward him and clutched his arm.

"You *see* it?"

"It speaks my name with voice of storm," Thoby croaked, then fell heavily to the ground, his breath issuing as a torrent of gasping. When again he looked skyward, there was no star to be seen. The heavens were just beginning to shade with the blue-violet of early evening. His heaving exhalations eased as he shook his startled head. Spreading his hands over the sod on which he knelt, Thoby frowned. "What's this?"

"This?" Vanessa asked as she took a handkerchief from her pocket and began to dress his bleeding finger.

"Look. They seem to be prints, circling this work of diabolic art. Are they children's bare footprints? They appear almost human, don't they? And yet—not quite."

"They aren't the prints of anything, dear. They're a part of the piece, etched into the earth by the artist. Now hold still. Damn, look at the blood on my new dress."

He gazed oddly at her, then looked again into the sky. The first few stars were beginning to twinkle. "This is certainly a queer place to which you've lured me."

"Stop talking nonsense. Are you feeling better?"

He smiled at her and shrugged. "I haven't had a spell like that in ages. Must be this heady valley air." He deeply inhaled. "I can feel it so heavily in my lungs, floating here, just around my heart."

Vanessa lightly laughed. "I think you had too much supper. Come on, get up. It grows chilly, and I need to get this dress into cold water."

Clumsily, they rose, holding onto each other. Thoby hesitated. "Funny, I feel reluctant to leave, as though I were somehow rooted here." He tried to laugh, but the feeble effort failed. Looking into his sister's wary eyes, he noticed their strange expression. Slowly, Vanessa reached for the clasp held in her brother's hand. Leaning close, she pinned it to his coat lapel. Keeping her hands upon it, she deeply stared into Thoby's troubled eyes. Gently, he covered her hands with his. "You're trembling," he whispered.

"Yes," she uttered, moving from him. "It grows chilly. Come, let us go from this place. Ginnie will worry." She began to walk toward the spreading willow branches, those green and yellow vines that streamed toward the ground, moving sinuously in the evening wind. Pausing, she turned to her brother, who stood staring at the grotesque figure.

"What happened here?" he asked in a subdued tone.

Strolling to him, the woman smoothed her fingers through his thick dark hair. "Nothing, Thoby. Nothing happened here." She smiled a curious smile. "Let us go, dear heart." He sighed and shook his head, then took her hand. Together, they walked toward the trees, into the valley's sequestered shadow.

II.

Thoby laid his head upon the soft pillow and listened to the noises of the valley, those sounds of wind and calling beast that served as lullaby.

As he closed his eyes, this subtle and almost articulate sonance spilled into his dreaming mind. Unfathomably, he found himself in Sesqua woodland, walking beneath a twilight of trees. From unseen places he could sense the diminutive things that followed him as he made his way to the place of pale willow branches, and to the clearing beyond. He saw the figure that danced within the clearing, the lithe and enchanting figure to which he drifted. She took him into her embrace. They danced in darkness, surrounded by small shaggy forms that pranced around them. Around they whirled, until they fell, laughing, onto the ground. They wound their limbs together and he kissed her pallid mask, then gazed beyond her into the obscurity of a haunted heaven. She bent her straddling body to him and breathed into his ear.

"Do you see it, cousin, the dark star of Hastur? Oh, call it, dear one; summon it with the yellow sign." Her too-soft fingers took hold of his hand, his hand into which had been etched a symbol of flowing fire. Together, they raised his hand to the sky, and he roared as his hand separated from his wrist and sailed above him. He watched it transform, enlarge with mutation, heave and expand into an opaque star that blistered with black fire. This flame transformed, turned into melted gold, a blinding radiance that formed a living emblem. Thoby felt that symbol burn into his eyes and find the essence of his soul. It found his tongue and shaped his mouth. He spoke the unknowable name.

He awakened with blood on his hand. Bringing his finger to his mouth, he sucked at the re-opened pinprick. Below, thoughtfully sipping hot almond milk, his sisters spoke in hushed voices. "Fate is so curious, so utterly inescapable," Virginia intoned. "We felt influenced—nay, compelled—to invite Thoby to the valley. We are puppets in the paws of ancient beings. Our heritage is branded, forever."

Vanessa lightly laughed. "And we thought we could escape it in our youth when we fled Dunwich. And yet what were we running from?"

"From the squalor that was our upbringing, from the hideous ignorance of others in our clan. From the shame we felt for our backward mother and her superstitious ways. Oh, what snobs we were. And when Elkin invited us to this valley, we smiled at the memory of his childlike simplicity. How wrong we were! He taught us our true nature. How I wish mother had lived long enough to be here with us."

"And now Thoby, with his visionary ways, of which he has no understanding. How I longed to see what he was witnessing. Oh, I burned! I could sense its power, its longing . . ."

"It dreams beyond the rim, awaiting alignment. We mean nothing to it, really, and yet it seems to hunger for our adoration. Perhaps, puny as we are, we can hurry the time of glorious pandemonium. Thus it sends us dreams."

"I could feel it influencing me to give Thoby the clasp. We be of Whatley blood, no matter where we dwell. Monsters have been our kinfolk, and our birthright calls eternally, never dying, like the Old Ones. And here, in this valley, we've found another brood of creatures. Oh, Ginnie, sometimes when I sink my fingers through their hair and work their scalps, I sense the most extraordinary things. It was not by accident that those Whateleys who fled Dunwich after the horror came to this hidden place."

They silenced at the sound of movement from the room above. As a disheveled Thoby stumbled into the room, they greeted him with magical smiles.

"The bloody finger opened up again. I'm afraid my bedding is rather shocking."

"Not to worry, darling," Virginia cooed. "Sit and have some breakfast."

"I'll eat later. I'm in the mood to enjoy this beautiful fog. Have you looked outside? There's a wonderful kind of mist, almost mauve in shade. It looks entrancing. I'll fix myself a meal when I return."

Not heeding their protests, he went outdoors and found the road that led to town. The thick, moist air swam into his mouth and left water on his brow, which dripped into his eyes. He wiped those eyes and looked around, finding himself near the ancient building he had taken for a church the previous day. As he studied it now he felt an overwhelming urge to enter it. Climbing up its massive stone steps, he pushed at one of the solid and gigantic doors. Passing the threshold, Thoby found himself within a dusky foyer. And then it came to him, from beyond another pair of doors—the sound of eerie music.

He touched one of the doors, which seemed composed of very old wood and had upon its surface a curious design of interlocking images. Silently, he opened one of the doors and peered beyond, into what was a vaulted chamber that did not seem to conform with the building's outer structure. He entered this place of semi-darkness, which seemed to him more like a burial chamber than chapel, and followed the source of fluted music. As his eyes adjusted to the lack of light, he saw before him an oblong block of pitted stone on which there reclined a figure that held a reed-like instrument to its mouth. Thoby frowned as he studied the deformed silhouette of the recumbent figure, for its trunk swelled with peculiar bulk and seemed to subtly shift its shape.

Thoby raised a hand to the thing. "I say," he spoke with quiet voice. The weird bulk on the figure's stomach began to writhe with undulation, then stretched thin wings and drifted into the darkest reaches of the vaulted ceiling. The figure on the slab sat up, and Thoby thought he could discern a pair of silver eyes that peered at him.

"You share your elder sister's face. The valley grows overcrowded with your clan, Mr. Whateley."

"My clan? You make us sound sinister."

"Well, there *is* something slightly sinister in calling daemons from the sky."

"You've been listening to absurd legends."

"They do not seem absurd when one stands among the domed hills of Dunwich, among the curious piles of bones and strange stone altars."

"I haven't visited those hills since the days of my youth. Since you're so informed, you must know that Virginia took us from that town and relocated us . . . ."

"To witch-haunted Arkham."

"You have a curious way of expressing yourself, Mr. . . . ."

"Simon Williams," the fellow answered, holding out a large dark hand. Hesitantly, Thoby approached the fellow and took his hand. He did not like the texture of the other's flesh.

"More curious than your following family tradition and calling to forces in the sky?"

"Someone's been talking. Vanessa, I wouldn't wonder."

"A charming creature. Yet, don't you find it fascinating, your seeming inability to escape cosmic fate?"

"Nonsense. My siblings and I are no common hillfolk. We grew up hearing the stories of the 'horror of 1928,' as it's called. You cannot be a Whateley in Dunwich and not encounter a kind of prejudice that is based entirely on legend and idiotic wives' tales. Pah, the ignorant fools who would surreptitiously make their weird little superstitious hand signals when we passed them by. You can't imagine what a relief it was to leave that stinking hole and move to a real city."

The other shrugged. "I did not mean to conjure forth bad memories. I've known your kin for many decades, and find them delightful, though most are not as educated as you and your sisters. I would say to you that there are diversities of learning, and I would not rashly dismiss the ways of those whom you term ignorant hillfolk."

Feeling a growing irritation at this fellow's talk, Thoby changed the subject. "What is this place?"

"A place of refuge from the world, like unto the valley itself. This tomb on which I sit is the resting place of one of Sesqua's forebears. He built this edifice so as to worship his great Jehovah. We have modified it to our own tastes and inclinations."

"And the music you were playing?"

"Delightful, wasn't it? The music of the spheres, like songs heard in deepest dreaming. Don't you find it interesting, my dear fellow, the things that call to us in dreams? Especially when one is of a sensitive aesthetic caste? This dream you experienced last night, that exotic vision—wasn't it wondrous? They call to us from the unimaginable places, beyond dimensions, and why on earth do they bother? What can we offer them other than absolute acquiescence? And yet there seems to be a link. Something in us allures them. Perhaps the old rumors are true and we were composed of star-stuff brought with them when the world was raw. Perhaps we are kindred, kind calling to kind, grotesque as the idea seems."

"You speak riddles. But I'll leave you to your weird gods. I've tarried here long enough, and find that I grow hungry."

Simon laughed. "Gods, my dear fellow—oh, no! We have no gods in Sesqua Valley—except, perhaps, the mountain. Well, I bid you good day. I suppose you'll be attending the gathering tomorrow evening?"

"This is the first I've heard of it."

"A little gathering of townsfolk," Simon told him, shrugging as if it were not a thing of much importance. "Your sisters will probably inform you of it today, since they are preparing a beverage."

It was odd that his sisters had not mentioned this, but perhaps they had meant to this morning, being prevented from doing so by his abrupt departure. "I'll most likely see you there," Thoby answered, bowing slightly in farewell. As he walked to the doors, he thought he detected a slight rustling in the shadow-hidden eaves, and as he found his way outdoors there came from the building the low sound of fluted music, some aspect of which disconcerted him. Thoughtlessly, he wandered through the still-thick morning mist, and it wasn't until he came upon an extended stretch of cemetery plot that he realised that he was moving in the wrong direction.

He entered the graveyard and examined tombstones, some of which were from the last century, but a surprising number of which were from the past few decades. As he examined the dates, it gradually occurred to him that many, if not most, of these souls had died at an early age. His attention was suddenly caught by a small flame, over which someone knelt and swayed. A homeless person, perhaps, who was trying to stay warm by building a campfire. This was hardly the place for such goings-on, and Thoby slowly walked up to the figure, digging into his pants pocket for some loose bills which he would offer to the hungry soul. See a few twigs on the ground, Thoby loudly stepped on them so as to alert the other of his existence. When the kneeling figure turned to look at him, Thoby gasped at the aspect of the fellow's face.

"Clear off," said the face that was smeared with blood and ash. "Your kind ain't welcome here." Thoby was startled by the voice, for it was that of a young woman. Clearly the creature was mentally ill, judging from the filthy clothes, the irregular cut of the close-cropped hair, and the dangerous aspect of the wild wide eyes.

Thoby stood his ground. "Are you all right? I have some money, if my offering it won't offend you. My name is Thoby Whateley. I'm visiting from out of town."

The kneeling figure examined him with a stern gaze, then suddenly smiled. "Thought you were one of 'em. Shoulda known. They never bother with this place. Couldn't tell in the mist, but now I see you wear a human's face. Whateley, eh? You kin with that pack of snobs? Pity. Take my advice and don't stick around too long."

Thoby cautiously walked a little closer and saw a strange pattern of small bones and stones on the ground. There was a dish of ash, and one of dark liquid. To his horror, he watched as the woman took a small dagger and rapidly worked at a wound on the back of one hand, the blood from which dripped into the dish. He noticed the stains of blood and ash that covered the tombstone before which the woman knelt.

"I say, that can't be sanitary," he said, kneeling next to her, friendly yet chary. "You'll surely get infected. Please come with me. I can dress your wound and give you a good meal. I was just on my way to breakfast. Won't you come?"

The woman loudly chuckled. "Ah, don't stare at me like I'm nuts. I know what goes on. Gotta protect my own, Mister Whateley. My brother lies here, and I'm doing a protective ritual that he taught me before this place drove him to—to the act that sank him six feet beneath this mud."

"From what does he need protection, his being deceased?"

"Lordy, you are an innocent! This stinking mist, that's what! It only gets like this when something big is about to happen. This ain't no usual morning fog, no sir. They're up to something, those devils. Didn't you hear the howling from the mountain last night? Ain't ya had weird dreams? Take my word, sonny, something's going on."

"Something of portent?"

She hooted laughter. "Dang me, you don't look like them, but you sure as hell *talk* like one of 'em."

"I'm sorry. I don't understand you."

"The freakin' spawn of Sesqua Valley! How long ya been here? Haven't you noticed them, their ugly mugs, the way they smell just like the valley, their weird yeller skin?"

"I did meet one rather odd fellow, Simon Williams . . ."

"Sweet Jesus, he's the worst! Stay away from that freak. Better still, get yer ass outa Sesqua Valley, before it gets inside you. You don't wanna end up like my poor old bro. You clear out. No, don't look at me like that, you stupid fool. The valley likes 'em young and fresh like you. Don't linger. Scat!" Her soiled face quavered with wild emotion.

"Well," he sighed, preparing to rise. "I'll not detain you from your ritual. God bless you."

She snorted in response, and then her expression mellowed. "Sorry, that was rude. I just ain't used to kindness. Wait a tic." She closed her eyes and began to whisper in a language he did not recognize. He watched as her finger went into the dish of dark thick blood, then into the dish of ash. stiffened as she brought that finger to his face. "Nah, calm down." Gently, she pressed her finger to his brow and wrote a symbol on his prickling flesh. "There, that may help, if you're fool enough to stick around."

He wanted to thank her, but could not find his voice. Awkwardly, he rose to his feet and, feeling slightly foolish, waved in farewell. Then he turned and found his way to the road that led to home.

III.

The afternoon was spent with Virginia, reading in the living room. When Vanessa returned from work, she promptly declared that Thoby was in need of a haircut, so as to look nice for "the gathering" of the next evening. He didn't know why, but something in that word, "gathering," disturbed him. It was the same word used by that odd Simon fellow.

"And what is this gathering all about?" he asked his younger sister as he sat on a stool in the middle of the kitchen, a towel covering his shoulders.

"Oh, just a community thing, mingling with friends over refreshments," Vanessa replied as she worked tonic into his thick hair. "Remember the picnics we had when we were kids? This will be something like that."

"I hope not, Nessa. Those family get-togethers were not to my liking. I could never understand some of the almost secretive talk. And, dear lord, the rantings of Aunt Ruth, going on and on about Sentinel Hill and calling to the skies. How overjoyed I was when Virginia packed us off to Arkham! A real town, with an educated community. An actual high school and college. No one giving us the evil eye because of our family name. I say, is that stuff you're putting in my hair perfumed? It's giving me the oddest tingling in my scalp."

"It has a slight floral bouquet when first applied, but that will fade. Don't worry, your precious masculinity is not in danger." She snipped and combed his hair until seemingly satisfied, then held a round mirror before his face. The cut was superb, and his hair had a wonderful sheen to it that he quite liked. And then he caught sight of his sister's reflection as she stood beside him, holding the mirror; and something about her expression troubled him. Vanessa was a simple woman, easily understood; but the look in her eyes, an inexplicable blend of rapture and (it almost seemed) fear brought a chill to his flesh. He turned to look into her eyes, and did not believe the authenticity of her sudden smile. Removing the towel from his shoulders, she gently kissed his hair.

The day passed slowly, and Thoby felt queerly fatigued. Retiring early, he was in bed with a volume of Keats when Virginia quietly entered holding a glass of warm almond milk. Her maternal instinct, born when they were motherless children, had always brought him a soothing calmness in time of trial.

He took the warm glass and brought its foamy contents to his lips, then slightly frowned. "You've altered the family recipe, Ginnie. There's a taste I don't recognize."

Sitting next to him, she smoothed his face with a soft hand. "It's probably the nutmeg and some of the local spices that one cannot find in Arkham. Do you not care for it?"

"No, no. It's quite nice." He noticed her looking at the book that he had set beside him on the mat. "My favorite poet, as you know. I never tire of his odes, and since I'm feeling almost audaciously indolent, I felt inspired to read him. It's funny, that particular ode always reminds me of you and Nessa and myself, when we were very young, dancing to the song of wind deep within the Dunwich woodland. Although we never actually wore sandals and white robes. What strange little creatures we were. Something about this valley reminds me of those times."

"Now that is absurd," Virginia protested. "Great heavens, the uneducated dolts of Dunwich. It was like growing up within a community of mongoloids. There were no books! Do you remember the pathetic shack that served as school, where we were crowded in with others of all ages?"

"What I remember is the cruelty I suffered because my name was Whateley. Do you remember the time I came home banged up and bloody, and told you I had fallen while playing on Sentinel Hill? I never told you the real story. I had been followed to the Hill by some of the Frye and Corey clan, to the altar place. They surrounded me, each holding a sturdy branch that they had picked up along the way. They beat me until I fell upon one of those piles of misshapen bones that so oddly litter the place. I picked up something with which to fight back, thinking it was a large stone. Instead it was an extremely distorted skull, disformed as if portions of it had been melted. They stopped as I held it to them. And then the sky above them seemed to darken, and I thought I saw a shadow in the sky that wore a Whateley face. A coldness entered the flesh of the hand that held the skull, a frigidity that spilled into my flesh and found my brain. I began to scream words that I did not understand. The effect was immediate. Those scoundrels dropped their weapons and fled. It has never left me, Ginnie, the hatred on their faces as they surrounded me chanting a mocking song about Wilbur Whateley. It was shortly after that incident that you disappeared for a fortnight. When you came back you had secured a teaching position in Arkham, young as you were. And our lives were forever altered."

"Arkham was wonderful, for a time. But when I came to visit family here, ah, something about this place bewitched me. I'm shocked that you could compare it to Dunwich. This is a society of aesthetic and educated people."

"It's a place of secrets. That's what I meant. Didn't you feel it, as we were growing up, the mysteries and enigmas that surrounded our family history? We heard the stories, whispered to us by older children, and we knew we were not to speak of such things openly, even though everyone seemed to be aware of the Whateley taint. That's the word, sweet heart. This valley is blemished by some invisible wound, some outré stigma that one senses but cannot name. Dunwich had it, too, breathtakingly beautiful as the surrounding hills and woodland were. There was something—not just the degradation of the inbred louts who made up its inhabitants. There was something in the land, in the very air. There were areas in the woods where the trees were of unnatural width, with branches that raked the sod and seemed to trace weird symbols in the dirt."

"This is mad talk, Thoby, if you'll forgive me for so naming it. You're not a fool, you understand the reason that we implored you to visit us in this far-off place. Our younger brother had written some rather frantic epistles. Your behavior since your breakdown . . ."

"Simon Williams is not an aspect of my mental fragility. I've just met him, and I've seen others who share his covert nature and outlandish facial features—although none quite so marked as he, I admit. You cannot call him normal! He has a way of talking that quite bewildered—and, I confess it—it—frightened me. The man is a freak."

"Yes, he is. Simon is extreme. But, Thoby, your talk is beginning to frighten me."

Sighing, he drained the glass of its liquid and handed it to her, then sank back into a pillow. "I sound crazy, I know. God, I'm weary. My head feels so heavy."

Virginia bent to kiss his forehead. "Let Nessa and me take care of you. That is why you came here. Close your eyes, my dear, and let go of the world." To his surprise, she joined him in the bed and wrapped him in her arms. It had been her habit to do so when they were very young and he had been beset by nightmares or brainstorms. How wonderfully safe it felt, in her warm embrace. He closed his eyes. If he dreamt, they were but dim shadows in some mental pocket. At times he sensed Virginia next to him, and at other times he thought, by the scented hair into which he nestled his face, that it was Vanessa who held him.

Vaguely, he was aware of them helping him out of bed and dressing him. Perhaps it was dreaming, this journey out of doors, into woodland, coming at last to the place of pale willows. He was sad to see no kneeling figure; perhaps she would join them later. Others were there, some with Whateley faces, others the children of Sesqua Valley with bright silver eyes. He clapped eyes onto one familiar gargoyle, who smiled at him and raised a black flute to a misshapen mouth. The air was filled with eerie music. It seemed to act as signal, for at its sound small shaggy forms crept forward from the shadowed woods. He wanted to clearly see them, but his vision would not focus. Mutely, he allowed his sisters to lead him to the center of the clearing, to the pattern of peculiar footsteps.

He began to giggle as they began to dance with him in that place where the figure had knelt, that figure with a mask of yellow silk sewn onto its face. He moved with them to the song of music, like the three Graces—or was it the three Fates in Keats' poem. He fell with them as they lowered to their knees. He smiled at Vanessa and wanted to call her name, but could not find the energy with which to open his mouth. Dreamily, he smiled at her as she anxiously scanned the sky.

Virginia petted his hair, and he leaned his head against her shoulder. With half-closed eyes he watched the small shaggy figures that crept toward and encircled them. He liked how these beings watched him with their black shiny eyes. He moaned as one of them moved toward him and touched his face with its soft, soft paw. He giggled as they unfastened Ginnie's hair and let it fall onto her shoulders. How beautiful she looked. Shutting his eyes, he listened to the ancient song that issued as humming from his sister's mouth.

Other voices joined in, chanting the song with words he did not understand, in a language he could not fathom. Half-opening his eyes, he watched others of his distant kinfolk as they gathered around him, swaying and scanning the sky with hungry eyes. How he longed to join in their singing, but his heavy mouth would not open.

With blurring vision he watched as Virginia took his hand and kissed it. He saw the silver needle that glistened in cosmic moonlight, and smiled as his eldest sister pierced it into his palm. There was no pain as she worked the golden thread into his flesh. A mouth kissed his own, and perfumed hair brushed his face. He closed his eyes as Vanessa covered his face with a sheet of soft yellow silk. Slowly, he began to open his numbing mouth as the pallid mask was sewn into his tingling flesh.

How fantastic that, with eyes closed and face covered, he could yet see into the sky that called his name, could detect the distant star of darkness that yearned to kiss the yellow sign. He reached to heaven with a hand as someone pinned an onyx clasp to his lapel. Oh, how he longed to touch that star, to watch the black fire that swirled within its thousand eyes, to feel the flutter of its massive wings. How he hankered to float into that void of sentient darkness, to pulse and hiss in that firmament wherein the One had waited strange aeons for the shifting of dead starlight.

Thoby Whateley, that little mortal, could not close his aching mouth. Its lips stretched outward as at last he heaved the unholy name. It was a name that echoed in the haunted valley, an echo that was answered by snouted things that howled atop a twin-peaked mountain of white stone. It was a wail that was imitated by the dancing folk who moved around him in that place of nameless providence.

The saprophytic fungi

(For Peter Cannon)

> When you are alone with him,
> Sphinx, does he take off his face
> and reveal his mask?
> —*Oscar Wilde*

I.

Ah, kiss me with your teeth, Sardonicus,
Those chilly pearls that gleam so white, so wet.
I know that I should be afraid, and yet
I crave your daemon-passion, succubus.

Stretch for me your mouth, Sardonicus.
I can only play at being brave
As I taste the promise of the grave
On the clean dentition pressed to us.

What is it that flickers in your eyes,
Eyes that hold me in unholy spell,
Eyes that burn with what is spawn'd in Hell,
Eyes that taunt and mock, that appetize?

Weigh your nightmare visage unto me.
Taste with teeth my brief mortality.

II.

Outspread, they pose before me, malignant and unmoving, like some diabolic Harry O. Morris Jr. montage: the masked mannequins. Their arms, so nude and meatless, lift, high and lean, above their heads; sensuously pleachèd; and beneath that skeletal awning of woven artificial limbs I step, solemnly glancing at their emotionless and frigid faces. Ah, that faces should be so expressionless, while uplifted limbs should speak so erotically.

Daintily, I creep beneath the still (so still) webbing of artificial limbs, past the smooth torsos, the perfectly postured legs. Hazily, in the dusky distance, I espy the one who waits. He sits upon a royal chair, and when at last I reach his feet, I kneel to kiss. Between the division of his legs reposes a chalice of dull metal. Delicately, I raise one hand and flick a fingernail against the metal, then listen to the echo of the sound, the ringing that seems to deepen as it rises into highest darkness.

I raise my eyes so as to gaze onto the massive mannequin's golden mask, that thing of silken fabric that seems to watch me, waiting. Bending nearer, I look into the chalice, then pick it up and press it to my mouth. Its liqueur is wretchedly sweet, and thickly it slinks down my throat. I look into the half-drained cup, and see the tiny white things that writhe beneath the remaining liquid; and again I drink, until the cup is drained.

I toss away the goblet and leer at the golden mask, then watch as it slips from his faceless countenance and floats, seductive, and settles beside me. I touch it with one trembling hand, I feel the rose-soft surface ripple at my fingertip caress. My lambent gaze masks emotions, as deftly I fall and press my mouth to the golden lips, those lips from which I taste unwholesome breathing. Ah, soft! Soft is the silken fabric that I press against my face, that I push into my flesh until we are conjoined. Ah, smooth are my motions, as I rise and take my place upon my chair, and wait, and wait, and wait.

III.

I do not know how long it has stood on its plot of earth, but the house was very old and quite decrepit, seeming to sag as an entity of dim antiquity. I feared it as a child, but do not recall ever being told that it was haunted. I knew only by instinct that the place was sinister. A shunned house.

It wasn't until I was much older that I found, in one of my favorite Clark Ashton Smith stories—"Genius Loci"—an exact description of the emotions that were stirred as I looked upon the place. If I may quote Klarkash-Ton, I experienced a "strange evil, a spirit of dispair, malignity, desolation" every time I gazed upon the house, upon the twisted trees in whose everlasting shadow it leaned.

On occasion I would espy the elderly gentleman who rocked on a chair on the front porch, his sad face (crowned with dirty white hair) cradled in his palsied hands. One time only did I obtain a clear view of him. It was on one afternoon when I was walking home late from the rehearsal of a high school play. The sun was just setting, and the sky wore a wondrous violet veneer that seemed curiously unearthly, as if it clothed an atmospheric anomaly. I always passed the old house when walking home from school, for the place fascinated as much as it unnerved. Stopping by the old metal gate, and seeing that (as usual) the gate was unlocked, I felt a sudden, inexplicable desire to enter within the dark confines, to step onto the old cracked path of pavement that led through the yard and to the porch. I saw the smaller trees that stood nearest that porch, trees that seemed like stunted and skeletal remnants of what they should naturally be; things that stretched dead limbs to that black edifice that huddled in constant umbra.

I gazed at that house and wondered why its wood was so absolutely black, from age one would assume, although its surface was quite protected from wind and rain and cosmic glare by the heavy growth of towering arboreal entities that surrounded it. And I felt, as I stared at that black wood, a queer kind of terror, as if the outer structure of the house was but a mask of antique timber that clothed some predatory force.

Suddenly, the heavy silence was haunted by a human sound, a combination of singing and soft sobbing. Mutely, I altered my position on the path, and I saw him through the growth, standing beside a ring of stones that encircled a pool of filthy water. In one hand he held a platter of tarnished silver that was covered with a mess of sustenance, scraps of which, now and then, he tossed into dank water. Quietly, fearfully, I backed away, out of the yard, into a sanity of starlight, and fled the place.

That was many years ago. When I attended college, I moved out of Mother's house; but on those times when I went to visit her I would always pass by the old gentleman's residence, that place that I so often dreamt about. And I felt a kind of panic, one late afternoon, when I saw the "Lot for Sale" sign fastened to the iron gate. I went to place my hands on the cold metal of that gate, then pushed it open and passed through, stepping onto the cracked and broken path of stone that led to the porch. Halfway to the house I glanced at my left, to the ring of stones. Feeling an inescapable lure, I went to peer into the pool of dank unmoving liquid, dimly beholding the pale shapeless doll or whatever it was that beckoned with stunted outstretched limbs.

I felt the pull of antique wood, and thus I returned onto the path and climbed the three steps leading up to the porch. My feet touched its wattled surface and took me to the door that so easily opened to my fondle of its knob. How familiar the place felt upon my eyes! And why not? Had I not walked its haunted rooms in deepest dreaming? Had I not conjured forth the antique air that hovered about me, the age-old furnishings that bespoke of the quiet past? Entering a sitting room, I smiled at the venerable rocking chair that had once been on the porch, that chair on which I found a curiously mottled mask of frail rubber that was crowned with a wig of yellowing white hair. How soft that synthetic flesh felt to my touch, how easily I squeezed my head through the elastic opening. Pressing the false face against my own, I walked to admire myself on the cold surface of a cloudy mirror that, full-length, stood encased within a gilded frame. And it was in that distorted reflection that I saw the small nebulous thing on the doorstep, the drenched and dripping thing that, trembling, reached out to me its soggy appendages.

I turned and noticed the small side table on which there sat a battered silver platter covered with husks of dried flesh. I went to it, and picked it up, and walked out to the dark pool, before which I tilted and into which I tossed bits of dried death. I watched the meat that sank through the filthy water, into the grasp of the ravenous lurker in the depths, that soft wee thing that somehow touched a place in my miserable soul. Parting lips, I tried to utter unto it a lullaby recalled from dim infancy; but something in the torment of memory moved me to tears, and I could not refrain from weeping. Taking up a husk of flesh, I touched it to my teeth as my tears drenched it, softened it, made it easier to chew. Feasting upon meat and misery, I turned to walk toward the skeletal trees that touched their dead branches to the mottled husk that was my face. Sucking in the antique air, I found again my rocking chair, upon which I heavily sat, rocking, rocking, rocking, in solitude and sadness.

IV.

We make love in your gargoyle garden. I feel your tongue between my breasts, your fingers' press on my flesh. I know the devil's kiss. Ah, my sinister sculptor, your left hand is a poem of passion. I watch it explore the landscape of my adoration. I watch it rise and seem to catch the wind, for when your hand is pushed against my ear, it sighs.

We deeply kiss beside your pool of crimson water, where stony Cupid's piss is stained a scarlet hue, where the wicked glee you've sculpted on Cupid's face plays along my panting visage. Ah, my sinister sculptor, how did Cupid's wings find their way upon my shoulders, those heavy granite things that weigh me so wearily to earth? Surely wings should serve some other function.

Ah, the wind calls my name, as your left hand traces consonants on my brow, letters that the wind can never utter. Your sculptor's hands are heavy on my face. Your heavy hand! It molds my features to your heart's desire. The fingers of your left hand wind into my hair and playfully push. Oh, sinister sculptor, my head is forced just above the pool of blood-drenched water, where you have often played this game before. I hear the wind sigh just above the water, the water into which you begin to push my head. The last thing that I behold is the image of my terror. But, oh, my face is one I do not recognize.

V.

I hobble home at last, place you into the white child's coffin, wearily fall to the floor and begin to unscrew my legs. Outside, darkness thickens; inside, shadows gather.

Your tiny voice calls out to me, but I try to ignore it. "Ma chère," you cry. I have shut your lid, but now I see the shadows that gather there, that push. I watch the small lid slowly rise. "Ma chère."

I watch the living shadow flow toward me and sheath my wooden legs. I watch the shadow twist, until my legs fall from me, to the floor, wood on wood. I see the gloomy stuff sift through the air toward you, gather like some skiagram that mocks your clownish image, that beckons me. Thus coaxed, I drag my stunted body to your box.

"Come lie with me, ma chère."

Your voice is cracked, like unto your countenance. I peer into the coffin and see the things that lie beside you, the wooden mallet and the mask.

"Does it call to you, my love?" you whisper. "Does its sleek handle ache to feel your fingers' clasp? With it smoothly in your hand, we can forget today's psychodrama. Great Jesu! What a clown you were today, trying to dance before the ones who gawked and tossed their pittance into your cap. How clumsy you were, mon chère, and how heavily you capsized. They must have thought, judging from their expressions, that you had been imbibing. Thus in disgust they parted, and we are very poor."

I observe your nude wooden torso, badly chipped. I see the rusty joints with which your dainty arms are fastened to your shoulders. I see your pantaloons, the battered slippers that cover wooden feet. I try not to see your face, but how can I withstand its lure? Especially when you whisper my name so seductively.

"Ah, my crippled one," you sigh, in a voice that mocks my own. "You look into my eyes at last. Yes, that one on the left is newly cracked. Do you not remember? Last night when we were dancing in this dusky room. Do you remember how you fell, and how I chuckled? I could not help myself, you looked such a buffoon. Can you not recall how you cursed me, how you found the happy mallet and smashed my face? Oh, what a feeling for you, what a sensation. Violence is so intoxicating. Yes, I sighed when the hammer smashed into me. Your blow was so *passionate!* But you know this, do you not, ma chère?"

I reach into your box of woe and pick up the heavy wooden mask, that badly battered thing that closely resembles your comical countenance. I turn it over and see that the ruddy stains have dried. How smoothly it fits over my face. I fasten the strap that holds the mask in place. I dip my hand into your bed and take up the mallet. Precariously balancing on the stumps that are remnants of lost limbs, I hold the happy hammer before our face. How excitedly we sigh, mon chère, as I smash that implement into our puppet physiognomy.

VI.

They came to me in midnight rain, during an hour of wondrous lunacy. I had read too deeply into the book, had spoken aloud the unmentionable words. For many days, for countless nights, I sat there, within the darkling chamber, the wavering flame of candle casting shadows within my fevered eyes, I watched the awful alphabet with which the words had been secretly formed by the Arab, that mad arcanist.

Ah, those words! How they weirdly wavered on the pages, and how I saw them writhing still when at last I shut mine eyes. I sucked the drool from off my lips, those fleshy lumps that itched to mouth the words aloud once more. I thought, indeed, that some thing was whispering those words, but I think it was merely the wind that blew at my ears, that slipped through the drums and chilled my burning brain.

No, it was not the wind I heard, but some other thing just outside my window. It sang the words that I had read aloud, that I began once more to whisper, half-consciously. I whispered as I peered through that huge window, into eclipsing darkness, wherein I saw revealed the black-winged Ones that swam toward me, at whose touch the windowpane melted. Like dripping shaggy shadows they drifted before me, and the wet flapping of their wings beat in rhythm to my heartbeat.

Smoothly, they drifted to me. Gently, they exhaled onto my eyes. Their shapeless paws played with my hair, tautly.

They seductively fingered my still-whispering lips, then placed exotic flutes to their amorphous mouths. Ah, what strange music! Strange—and yet familiar, like some dim-remembered nightmare. And then the nearest One tore at my mouth with clumsy claws, until it tore open my cavity of screaming. Hotly, my madness pushed into its face as I screeched the words that I had found within the tome, those words now forever stamped onto my buzzing brain. Tearing my eyes from the One before me, I eyed the pages spread open beneath my trembling hands, that parchment on which blackly etched syllables crept off the pages and stained my hands.

Those hands! How savagely they found my face!

The book is before me. I scent the wormy pages whereon the words once lived, those words that ache within me, those signals that reach beyond the rim to where the All-in-One pulses in eternal corruption. As these plucked eyes stain my palms, I hear the beating wings that fan my fevered brain. I heard my name whispered above internal storm. Yuggoth damns my puny soul. I tear into the pages of the book and crawl into it. I taste the aged parchment on moist lips that whisper still the awful alphabet. I scent the wet paws that tautly tug my hair and pull me ever onward, as I limp beyond reason to that nothingness where dwells no masquerade of human hope.

VII.

I have heard it said, Peter, that you have set aside your pen, that your brain has determined to say no more, in fiction or in factual essay. I find this inexplicable. How can the true Lovecraftian dry up? The true Lovecraftian (and none is more authentic than yourself) has a never-ending sacred font in which to ever dip their pen. With Grandpa deeply entrenched into our eyes, our soul, we feel the world anew each day. He is there in the slanting sunbeams that plays on shimmering water, in the drifting moonbeams that play on antient tombstone.

When we are Lovecraftian, we are ourselves—utterly.

I have read that Lovecraft is a mask I wear, that as an author I am not myself. What wondrous idiocy. I am never more "myself" than when I am Lovecraftian, for he has molded what is best within me. I came to him as a child, wide-eyed and ignorant. I am wide-eyed still (but hopefully a wee bit wiser). Through my Lovecraftian vision I have seen the verdant Sesqua Valley, that sequestered place of wonder that exists only as a symbol of Lovecraftian passion. To have found it was a rich reward. At the end of lonely day, I drift in dream to the valley, and there I find the freedom to be myself absolutely.

With Lovecraft I have looked at stars, and beyond them. I have tasted cosmic aether, a heady elixir. With Lovecraft I have crawled into the deepest pit of my skullspace, have found therein the stories and the poems whose expression with pen on paper has given me my greatest joy, my finest therapy.

Look again, my friend, into your Lovecraftian heart. You will be amazed at what you find there. For he is eternal. That is not dead which can eternal lie.

VIII.

He wanders darkness, dreaming strange old dreams.
He sucks the night-air, such rare nourishment.
His shadow'd skullspace knows a calm content.
Into his brain the weird old wonder streams.
He watches shadowplay on moonlit stone
And drinks as wine the necropolis air
And feels a spectral wind weave in his hair
And senses presence, although quite alone.
At times like this the neoteric age
Through which he staggers seems the fantasy;
This haunted darkness is reality.
His book of life beats on this antient page.
    He is a poem to yesterday's quaint space,
    To wondrous dreamland, where he finds his place.

A Phantom of Beguilement

Between the acting of a dreadful thing
And the first motion, all the interim is
Like a phantasm or a hideous dream.
                    —*Shakespeare*

I.

Katherine Winters halted for one moment on the small wooden bridge and watched the movement of water beneath her. Dim October sunlight flickered on the water of Blake's Creek, and the scent of autumn perfumed Kingsport's misty air. Katherine was happy that she had stayed beyond the tourist season, for the old town enchanted her, as did its singular inhabitants. Continuing along Orne Street, she arrived at the quaint shop of curios that was her destination.

After a slight hesitation before the dark wooden door, Katherine entered the dim and chilly place, standing in silence after having closed the door. Then, remembering that which had lured her to the dusky place, she stepped past antique lamps, past twisting towers of musty books, until at last she came upon that which she sought. She reached for the framed piece of art and held it up to the room's indifferent light. Absent-mindedly, she studied the picture, vaguely aware of the scent of lilacs that issued from a presence suddenly behind her.

"Hullo, Miss Winters," a soft voice sighed. "The wee painting continues to captivate, I see."

"It does. Luckily, my mother sent a rather generous check, so I can be extravagant and do some reckless spending."

"The other woman smiled with thick mauve lips and smoothed her scented hair with bulbous fingers. "Mothers are such a lovely invention." Reaching for the small framed picture, she took it from Katherine's grasp and steadily gazed at it. "With exceptions. His didn't understand him at all."

"You told me his name the other day. Jeremy . . .?"

"Aye, Jeremy Blond. Poor sod, such a bundle of nerves, with dark hair and pale haunted eyes. Used to come in looking for queer old books. I asked him once what he was researching. 'Just looking for light in darkness, Mrs. Yeats,' he told me."

"And is this the only work of his that you have?"

The elder woman gazed at the picture for a long silent while; then, ignoring Katherine's query, she moved to a spindle of thick brown paper. "I'll just wrap it up as nice as you please, Miss Winters. Such a queer thing, isn't it?"

"It's rather strange, I admit. Almost like an experimental photograph, so indistinct and surreal. Is it a woman on a raft, surrounded by shadow and mists of eerie light? And those things that float above her, like a flock of primeval psychopomps preying on lost souls. Are they gulls; and if so, why so disfigured?" The picture vanished beneath thick paper.

The elder woman faintly smiled. "The way you talk, Miss Winters! I can tell that you're a poet. He talked exactly the same way. He was very young when he left us, was Jeremy. But then, he was never really 'with' us, being such a dreamer, as most of you's arty types will be." Again, the wee smile. "Something in them queer books turned his mind, I think. Not a wholesome thing, them books; and we certainly seem to have our share of them in this old seaport. Aye, bad things, some books. Too, he associated with bad types. Spent many an evening drinking with that lout what camps about the old cottage where the terrible old man used to dwell."

"Occult, were they—these books you spoke of?"

"Hmm? Oh, aye. We get a lot of queer lore from them what's been at Miskatonic. But, do you know, Miss Winters, I don't believe it was them books that did him most harm; it were his dreams. Bad things, dreams." Again, the little knowing smile, and she handed Katherine the wrapped book. The young poet gave the other woman money, held her prize to her breast, and vacated the dreary place. Outside, in gathering dusk, she found the lane that led her homeward, followed by vague shadows in the sky.

II.

She danced upon dark water, as above her loomed the craggy silhouette of Kingsport's ancient cliffs. Above her, in misty air, she could almost distinguish the forms of fantastic things. She cried out, wanting so to see the pallid faces of strange winged beasts. The surrounding mist began to eerily spill its essence into her gasping mouth, an essence that (finding her soul) transformed her into a thing of spreading aether.

When she awakened, it was to the sound of the north wind shaking at the bedroom window. Katherine moaned, not wanting to awaken, longing to return to dreamland. But the wind would not be still, seemed somehow to beckon her, and thus she crawled out of bed and staggered to the window, before which she knelt.

Legend-haunted old Kingsport spread before her, unto which she had come as a poet working on a new sonnet cycle. Here she had discovered a rich artistic community of which she had grown increasingly fond.

One of its rich characters was the "lout" spoken of by Mrs. Yeats, one Winfield Scot, a fellow poet. She had met him in the public library, where he spent much of his time reading and pretending to write (he had not produced new work for many years). His nights were spent at a vacant centuried cottage, famous among the townsfolk as the former home of a curious fellow always referred to as "the terrible old man." This gentleman was said to have been a sea captain, and was at the time of his mysterious death of an incredibly ancient age. It was whispered that he had learned strange rites and secret ceremonies during his sea journeys, and people did not like the large, oddly-painted stones that leaned in the tall grass of his yard, stones that were positioned in esoteric groupings, reminding Katherine of prehistoric idols she had seen in photographs.

Winfield Scot was not liked by the people of Kingsport, for he slept in the place that was shunned by all reasonable persons. His monthly check kept him in good supply of alcohol, of which he was inordinately fond. Katherine had taken a part-time position in a small café, and it was her habit to pack a small evening meal after her work shift, which she would take to the lonely poet. She found his conversation pleasant, and noted an aesthetic intellect that was belied by his disheveled appearance.

So, Winfield had known the young artist who had so queerly disappeared. She rose and walked to the bed, above which she had hung the picture. Kneeling on her bed, Katherine ran her finger over the indistinct figure on the raft. She studied the strands of hair that flowed from the ghostly dome. But was it hair, or a garland of fluid vines; or rags; or, perhaps, shredded seaweed? She looked at the flock of spectral things that hovered in the foggy air. How strange that they never seemed to take on solid form. Were they contorted gulls, or large mutated bats? Surely bats did not have such pale faces. Katherine could never satisfactorily count their number: at times she found seven, or ten. Jeremy Blond had captured their ethereal grace, their uncanny beguilement. Gazing at them almost brought a fever to her pulse, a hunger to be numbered among them.

Katherine studied the curious raft. Was it composed of rotted wood bound by rope; or was it a network of large stood at the very edge of the craft, wrapped in a robe of sparkling mist and inky shadow?

She turned away from the picture, entered the kitchen and brewed coffee, then prepared for the day. The morning had been sunny but blessed with cool autumn chill. Having dressed, she stepped outside and headed for the antediluvian cottage on Water Street, slowing her process as she approached a gathering of small children who were playing at tableau. Each held a thin wooden wand to which had been fastened a pale papier-mâché mask. Katherine lightly laughed as the wee ones danced and frolicked, then froze into elegant living pictures. When the young ones heard the woman's laughter, they held out to her their tiny arms, and she (beguiled by innocence) momentarily joined in their pantomimic play, daintily dancing and then gracefully falling to her knees. Pale paper faces formed above her. Katherine raised her arms as if they were wings, and as she did so the anxious wind blew under her, like some daemonic force that would release her from her prison of gravity. One of the children bent and kissed Katherine's neck, and then the little ones all fled, laughing.

She came at last to the bent and crumbling cottage, and gazed before entering the yard at the curiously painted stones that were grouped in tall yellow grass. The sight of them always momentarily disconcerted her, for the manner in which they were grouped seemed somehow slightly sinister. It was the stones, and the way that shadow and light played upon them, that had kept people from bothering the old man when he had lived; and it was they that kept people from trespassing the property after the old man's rumored death. (There was no recollection of burial—suddenly the old man was no longer seen around town.) Strangely, a subtle but increasing sense of alarm had seized the innocent seafolk of Kingsport after the old man's mysterious disappearance, for now there was no one to control the cosmic influence of the disquieting stones.

Katherine walked past the high iron gate, into the yard. Smiling at her from the gathering shadows of a long porch, whiskey bottle in hand, was Winfield Scot.

"Ah, sweet Kate, come to keep an old man company."

Sitting next to him, she reached into her knapsack and produced a paper bag in which she had packed sandwiches and apples. Showing gratitude, Scot playfully offered her his bottle of booze. Katherine momentarily frowned, then took the bottle and brought it to her mouth. When she began to choke and cough, her companion happily pounded her back and relieved her hand of the bottle.

"How can you drink that stuff?"

"To one such as I, my dear, alcohol is the dearest of mates. It warms the chill of mortality, and soothes one into a state of blessed forgetfulness."

"It wouldn't do anything for me—except, perhaps, give me bad dreams."

"Ah, it's the stones that give me my dreams, sweet Kate."

"I've actually had a rather weird dream myself," she hesitantly said. "It was inspired by a work of art, a painting by Jeremy Blond."

The fellow at her side sadly smiled and gazed into the night, reflecting on the past. "Yes, his work would do that, poor haunted lad. He was a true Kingsport artist."

"Meaning what?"

"Well, we get our tourists, and we get our student artists who seem little more than tourists at times. They're charmed by this lovely old town, but they never penetrate its magick, never see its soul. They see only the surface, suffused with misty light. They never see the darkness where lies the haunted heart."

She bent to him and kissed his cheek. "I love it when you talk like a poet."

"Yes, I'm like Wilde now, a poet who merely talks, but wonderfully. I live in a world of whispered words, just as Jeremy lived in a world of haunted imagery."

"With what was he obsessed?"

Scot obliquely smiled. "If you've one of his paintings, you know. An image of Death on a raft, sailing down the river Styx, surrounded by harpies. I implied that he had been inspired by the famous work of Joachim Patinir's, but he insisted such was not the case. Such a strange, morbid boy, our Jeremy. Near the end he became very odd. And then he vanished."

"You've misunderstood his work, my dear Win. It isn't Death he envisioned, but something far more beguiling."

"More beguiling than oblivion? You jest!" Then he looked closely at her, and something close to fear kissed his spine with velvet lips. "You've been dreaming of this thing . . .?"

"Yes. Last night. A wonderful vision. Didn't want to wake up." Her voice sounded far away.

Scot was silent for some time, then he opened the paper bag and took out a sandwich. He startled slightly as the woman suddenly shifted and rose.

"I'm restless. Think I'll walk for a while."

Scot's eyes filled with momentary panic, then seemed to dim with a kind of resignation. "Come kiss me, Kate." Bending to him, she did so, oblivious to his troubled expression. Then she turned and departed.

Rather than going straight home, Katherine decided to catch a bus to Central Hill. A vigorous North wind blew from the harbor, and she pulled her heavy shawl about her as she finally departed the bus and passed through the high iron gates of the Central Hill Cemetery. Most of the tottering and crumbled stones dated to the mid-1600s. She leaned against a tall, ivy-covered marker and stared down the sloping field of death, over the hill's crest, to the sleepy town below. Kingsport was il-lumed with lamplight. A faint fog crept over the sea's dark water, while a heavier cloud enshrouded the fantastic form of Kingsport Head, which rose one thousand feet above the water. How ancient everything seemed, how removed from tedious modernity. Coming to this town had been a sane, a happy decision. She felt that she truly belonged here.

She moved among the relics of the forgotten dead, to one of the willow trees that swayed near the high iron fence. Raising her arms, she danced beneath the streaming vines, felt them twine around her fingers and weave into her hair. She danced until exhausted, then fell upon cold earth. Lifting her eyes to darksome sky, she watched the creature that hovered in the air. Rising, holding the tasseled ends of her shawl, Katherine held out her hands to heaven. She could almost distinguish the pale face of the creature that watched her. A sudden rush of tem-pestuous wind pushed behind her, agitating her sense of balance. Heav-ily, she fell to graveyard ground. When again she gazed into the empyrean of night, she saw misty fog and nothing more.

III.

She waded through the opaque air, relishing the residue of moisture that kissed her face. Some uncanny instinct led her along the winding streets and sidewalks, over worn and weathered antique bridges. She could feel the heavy pulse of Kingsport's psyche, its remnant of dream and darkness. Almost, she could smell the ghostly past, the spectral future. Ah, the muted creaking of doomed ships that had slipped beneath the harbor. Oh, the moaning souls who sighed beneath the sea.

Katherine walked the narrow cobblestone streets of hoary Harborside. Like one lost in fanciful nightmare, she stumbled past the silent buildings that leaned implausibly over the streets. She knew that she was on Foster Street, for she beheld the tall, dilapidated building that had once been Mariner's Church, but was nigh abandoned. Slowly, she moved on, to Water Street, toward the fog-enshrouded piers, taking in the smell of silent sea as she walked the rotted planks of an age-old pier.

Katherine reached the end of the pier and knelt, looked at the water, waiting. Dimly, sailing toward her in the fog, came the hazy silhouettes of winged things. Her lips trembled, aching so to call out to the odd pale faces that watched her from above. Sighing wind rose from water, brought with it the putrid stink of the sea—and of something else, something not of this world.

Some thing glided toward her, out of the fog, over dark water. As it neared the pier, Katherine knew that the young artist's painting had not exaggerated the unearthly nature of the creature on the raft. Rather, he had caught to perfection its essence.

Katherine pressed her palms against the damp wood of the aged pier. She leaned toward the apparition that stopped just inches from the place whereon she knelt. The figure bent to her; its ropy hair writhed and reached for her, weaving into her own. Its spectral hands wrapped around her trembling fingers. The young woman felt a stagnant shadow fill her pores and sink into her being, into the texture of her skin, the quintessence of her soul. Oh, how she shivered and mutated. How she stretched her tingling mouth and whispered the words of wonder that writhed as unholy hymn inside her burning brain, a homage to darkness and decay.

The withered creature moved away from her. Katherine raised her strange pale face the the sky, to those twilight things that watched her. Rapturously, she stretched her wings and floated above dark water, to the flock that awaited her in the filthy air.

stupor mundi

We stood, Phillippe Amarinth and I, in a gallery, looking at renditions of the Christ. I could tell from my friend's expression that he had no especial admiration for the artwork. Phillippe was a connoisseur of death imagery, and he was hoping to find at this particular show a feast of sacred gloom. I turned to gaze at him as he laughed out loud while gawking at one rather shabby attempt at art.

"Here we have the Christ as some sort of Immaculate Masturbator. Really, that heart with its tawdry crown of thrones should be a phallus. Bah! Is that camp expression the face of one who has suffered ultimate indignation and torment? Is there any shadow of awful extinction, any trace of the profound poetry of the Lord's magnificent sacrifice?"

His questions did not seek for answers from myself, and so I remained silent. Leaving the blue light of the main gallery we entered a room that was bathed in a crimson hue. The walls were painted red, and upon one surface there was a mess of painted lines and squiggles, looking as if some infant had gone wild with a can of spray paint. I chuckled at this sorry attempt at art and turned to leave but then I saw my companion's face, the eyes from which a teardrop gently fell.

"This is amazing," he whispered, holding up a hand as if to reach for some sacred object. "Don't you see it, dear boy? Look again."

Sighing, I turned and gazed at the mess on the wall; and slowly I began to discern a design, an image. My friend leaned near me and whispered in my ear.

"Yes, the more deeply one looks, the more he reveals himself. That madness of dripping circles becomes the lowered head, a head weighed by the sins of the world. And those sprays on either side, you see, are nothing less than the outstretched arms of crucifixion. It is almost nothing more than symbolic, and yet he is there in all of his tragic glory. Those drips—you see how they form into pellets of blood? My god—my god."

And then he shuddered—from ecstasy or horror I could not tell— and I followed as he turned and fled from that place, rushing through the main gallery and finding our way outside. Stopping to rest against a wall, Phillippe placed an Egyptian cigarette into his mouth and lit up, ignoring my soft coughing and disapproving frown. It was twilight, and the full moon, tainted orange, sat low and large in the semi-darkness.

Taking one final puff, my friend flicked his cigarette into the gutter, linked his arm with mine, and led me strolling down the sidewalk. "Do you find it sad, Russell, the lack of originality in today's culture, the lack of authenticity? Now, that gallery is reputed to be the showplace of radical Bohemian artwork, but did you see anything really daring? The clientele of cool seem lost in some kind of time warp. Did you notice that pale young child holding tightly to his second-hand copy of Kerouac and dressed in black? What a sad cliché. What a poverty of poetical imagination. The entire scene, from the artists to their art, is merely a copy of something else. That's why I like you, dear boy."

"You like me because I'm very young and very ugly."

"Yes, I see the beauty in your bestial face, the wonder dancing in your wild green eyes. And I see your unaffected devotion to death, and to its manifestations. You were the first child that I ever picked up in a cemetery. I was instantly attracted to your oddness, an allurement that has made you such a hit in that freak show you travel with."

"I find a peacefulness in places of death, and strange joy in images of the tomb. But I have to admit that that spray painting or whatever the hell it was we saw tonight got to me."

"Yes, it was unique. That's what I look for in art, yet seldom find. I saw it in Pilon's tomb for Henry II and his Catherine, in those unpretentious figures of their nude corpses, those recumbent marble *gisants*. I saw it in Friedrich's *Abbey in an Oak Forest*, a work that is the epitome of eternal and melancholy extinction. It's been compared to Ruisdael's *Jewish Cemetery*, but there's no comparison. Ruisdael is all abundant movement, the wind in the trees, the rolling clouds pregnant with electrical life. In Friedrich there is nought but dry and lonely death."

We had continued our stroll, and I saw that we were walking down Half Moon Street, on the deserted edge of the downtown area. The full moon was a little higher in the sky, and far more pale. Finally, we reached the end of pavement, pausing before a field of dirt. A figure sat some distance from us, bent and digging with one finger in the ground. The silent night was haunted by her low, uncanny singing.

We slowly approached her, and my friend leaned to me so as to whisper, "She draws in the dirt, like Christ. Perhaps she is full of parables." When we were three feet from her, Phillipe squatted and smiled. "Good Madonna, we have come to learn our future."

She had not stopped her soft low humming. Glancing at my companion for one moment, she graced him with an uncanny smile, then began to move her finger in the dirt. Phillippe's expression became very serious as he watched the creation of her art, and I moved closer so as to see the moonlit portrait that formed beneath the creature's moving hand. I gasped at the likeness of the portrait: it was my friend's face, formed in simple lines; and yet it was devoid of life. It could have been a death's mask made of dirt. Phillippe's breath issued heavily from his moving mouth. Suddenly, he thrust his hand onto the ground and wiped the face away, then reached into a pocket and brought out a soiled hand full of cash, which he tossed onto the ruined portrait. The woman stopped her humming, gazed at my friend's face, reached for that face with a hand that moved its rough flesh across Phillippe's smooth skin.

She held that hand to the full moon, then offered a ringed finger to the man before her. Tenderly, he moved the scarab ring from her claw and touched it to his lips, then pulled it onto his finger.

I followed him as he rose and walked away, strolling to an alley between what looked like two abandoned factories. Leaning against the old brick of one building, he looked at his new ring for a little while, then reached into a pocket and produced a cigarette. "You look a bit dashed, dear boy," he informed me. "You are like so many youngsters I have known, who profess a romantic and aesthetic appreciation of death, but who become depressed at the idea of their own extinction. I am guessing that that is the origin of your long face and sober expression. But look around you, at this man-made world. How wonderful it will be to escape it, to lie undisturbed in our porphyry tombs, couched in quietude."

"If death is the absolute end . . ."

"Is that what's bothering you? Yes, the idea of life after death is depressing. What could be more damnable than eternal life? But I don't believe in anything beyond the grave, and that is why death's imagery and symbolism is of such comfort. Come, let us walk into this alley and escape the moon."

I had expected, as we entered the alleyway, to be assaulted by the stench of hobo piss; but the only scent that assailed my nostrils was the odor of my companion's exotic cigarette. I watched as the smoke he emitted sailed upward, out of semi-darkness, into dim moonlight, as from the area we had but just vacated there came the sound of low and distant singing, a sound that, queerly, did not seem to be for us, but rather an offering to unknown gods.

We slowly walked between what seemed to be very old brick factories, and I was caught by a sense of isolation that I had never known before. The place seemed unwholesomely lonely. Moonlight filtered down so as to illuminate one slender portion of the alley, shining on a strange lump of what turned out to be discarded clothing. I stepped closer so to examine the bundle of garments and then reached for a shard of shattered wine glass that littered the ground. Rising, I held the shard to moonlight, admiring how its amber surface caught the dead and distant light. And that was when I noticed the writing on the wall.

"What the devil . . .?" Phillippe whispered, gazing at the graffiti. "Good Jesu, it looks like some kind of outlandish foreign alphabet, until you make out the figure in the carpet, if I may be allowed a reference to my favorite author. Look, don't you see it, that circle there, it could be a head heavily bowed with the suffering of the world. And those outstretched squiggles—how similar to that other thing we saw in the galley tonight. But to find it in this desolate place . . ."

I watched as he walked to it and placed a hand upon its surface. Hypnotically, I moved just behind him, listening to his heavy breathing as he sucked in one final puff on his fag and then flicked the butt away. I felt my face flush with outrage; for this seemed a holy place, a sacred ground, and for him to litter it with such nonchalance filled me with sudden fury.

"Look," he whispered, "you can just make it out in this remarkable half-light: a face of some kind, there, hideously stretched and distorted, yet wearing still an expression of bewildered fear and torment. It creeps my flesh, Russell. I've never seen anything like it." Turning to face me, he heavily leaned against the pattern on the wall, raising his face to the iris-blue sky of early twilight, lifting his arms until he looked like some well-fed parody of Crucifixion.

I leaned toward him and kissed his mouth. "Let me complete the picture," I whispered, then brought the shard of glass to one of his hands, over which I quickly ran the edge of broken glass. He hissed in surprise and pain, and then he smiled and called me a perverse child, leaning to me so as to touch his lips once more to mine. I evaded his kiss and slowly ran the dirty shard over the back of his other hand. Flesh parted, and his mortal liquid dripped onto the pattern on the wall.

I knelt before him and brought my prayerful hands together, those hands that were slightly stained by the residue of blood that smeared the shard of glass I held. He foolishly smiled at me, basking in what he took to be my adoration. I could see from his smug smile that to be worshipped was a thing he felt worthy of. But it was not Phillippe Amarinth that I so piously venerated, but rather that pattern on the wall, that outré graffiti that began to subtly ripple and expand. He, the vain fellow, could not see it with his back to the wall, how his blood had not spilled onto the ground but rather was absorbed by the alien substance that hungrily moved behind my companion.

I watched, entranced, as Phillippe suddenly frowned, as he finally turned to look at his hand, that pale white glove of flesh that withered and grew flat, that conjoined with the moving pattern it had pressed against. I watched as the scarab ring fell from the changing flesh, landing with a dull thud onto the bundle of discarded clothing. I watched his wonderful expression of bewildered fear as a cloud of mauve mist began to issue from the moving thing, that thing that sucked the fellow's flesh inexorably into it. I watched as they rose together along the wall, flowed along the wall so as to reach a place of bright moonlight, and I smiled at the almost clownish way that Phillippe's clothing fell as a heap onto the alleyway.

They moved, the alien thing and its new victim, and still I could see a semblance of my friend's face, flattened and stretched, with lunar beams burning in what remained of eyes. Finally, I lowered my gaze, reached for the scarab ring, and slipped it onto a bloodstained hand.

From somewhere in the distance, a madwoman raised her voice in eerie song.

Past the Gate of Deepest Slumber

Yet for each dream these winds to us convey,
A dozen more of ours they sweep away.
—*H. P. Lovecraft*

I.

(Cyrus Lynchwood)

I was awakened by the sound of moaning wind, and as I listened I knew with certainty that the noise came not from outside but from somewhere within the large old house. It sounded not like natural wind, containing as it did some alien aspect that utterly beguiled me. Gingerly, I arose from the comfortable armchair in which, book on lap, I had fallen asleep, and went into the hallway, listening intently to the ghostly sound. Delicately, I began to descend the stairs that led to the main floor, then stopped mid-way as the door to the library was flung violently open. My landlord, Philip Nithon, stood for a frantic moment in the door frame, a bewildered expression twisting his facial features as clutching hands pulled at clumps of white hair. He did not see me as he moved to the front door, opened it, and staggered into the night.

I reached the main floor of the dusty old house and walked to the front door, closing but not locking it. Then I turned and crossed to the library door, moving with faltering steps as I sensed an uncanny alteration of atmosphere. I passed the threshold and entered the large room, then shut my eyes as a dizziness overwhelmed me. Vague images sallied into my mind, blurred shapes that I almost recognized from dim-remembered dreams. And all around me I could hear the dying echo of some distant, unearthly tempest. And then all was silent, my mind cleared, my eyes opened.

Going to his desk, I scanned my landlord's pile of books. The title that lay open was familiar, a rare volume published decades ago by the Onyx Sphinx Press. Glancing at the open page, I recited the familiar lines of verse.

> "And waves of bitter wind deluge my brow
> As shards of cosmic memory split my brain,
> And in the storm before me I behold
> The bat-winged nymphs who frolic in mid-air
> As my ears sense the sound of blasphemy
> That issued from the reed of a crack'd flute
> That (now I find) is clasped in clumsy paw
> And breathed into by some inhuman maw
> That muttered as it bubbled and it blew."

I turned away from the desk and noticed a small object on the floor. Picking it up, I was surprised at how light it felt. My eyes seemed to be playing tricks on me again, for as I tried to examine the object I imagined that it subtly shifted its form. And then I was aware of the person behind me, and I turned as Mr. Nithon spoke my name.

"Cyrus, please, help me to my chair. Yes, slowly. Ah, thank you. Oh, my poor old lungs. I should have known not to wander out on so chill a night. But I had to clear my head! And of course it was just as strange outside; of course it was, and why not? That devil wind! I thought it followed me, and then I knew that some portion of it was inside me! Great God in Heaven. Gods, rather." He violently shook his head, as if to dislodge some unwanted memory.

"But you're all right?"

He slanted his eyes at me and cocked his head. "You're the very devil, aren't you, young sir? No, don't look surprised. Ah!" He held out his hand to the object that I held. "I see that you've found my wee friend. I must have dropped it when . . ." He then sat back and closed his eyes, massaging his brow with an ancient hand on which the skin was very delicate and thin. His voice, when he spoke again, was very quiet, very calm. "Of what would you say that little daemon is composed?"

"I would have said some kind of wood, except that it's so light."

"Indeed. And it's smooth, almost silky, like some delicate eggshell or polished bone. Quite intriguing."

We paused in silence, and I could not read his face. "Are you feeling more yourself? Shall I put on some water for tea? Dear man, you're shivering."

"Not from the chill air, no." He tilted his head and gave me a queer look. "What brought you down, lad?"

"I was awakened by the sound of windstorm."

"And what did you hear beneath the wind?"

"Nothing. I suppose I was distracted by your odd behavior. I was on the stairs when you fled the library and went outside. Your expression . . ."

"No doubt I wore a multitude of expressions, so as to bespeak a multitude of emotions! And I blame you. No, don't look at me with those innocent eyes. We spoke, when first we met and I invited you to rent my spare room, of dreams. You then astonished me by speaking of dreams as gateways to buried memory. Knowing of my intellectual interest in occult matters, you guided me to certain tomes of poetry, which I now suspect are something more than poetry. You encouraged me to chant certain lines of verse as I lay in bed awaiting slumber, assuring me that the spoken verse would, how did you phrase it, 'usher one into a world of vibrant dream as one has never yet experienced.' Well, your sorcery (yes, so I call it) has succeeded, beyond—if I may say so—my wildest dreams."

"I thought perhaps it might."

"Did you, clever boy? And did you also know that it would affect my waking world? Did you know that aspects of life would take on characteristics of dream? I see by your expression that you did. Thus, when I went to visit my friend in New England last month, we discovered a charming old shop of curios, wherein I thought perhaps to find some rare old books of verse. Instead, I found the thing that you hold so firmly in your hand. How oddly familiar it looked, although I could not recall where I might have beheld its image. I suspected I must have seen its likeness in some book—but I was mistaken. And since purchasing it I have felt an odd inclination to conceal it from the eyes of others, yourself included. Strangely, I felt rather criminal in owning it. And since it has come into my custody, I have had the most fantastic dreams, the most vivid of which occurred earlier tonight. Within this vision I beheld that object as a living thing. Its squat form reminded me of a masculine version of the primitive 'Venus' of Willensorf, with which you are familiar." His eyes took on an almost mystic expression as he softly chuckled and shook his head. "It *danced*, this creature, as it played its noxious flute; and as this thing performed I could vaguely sense other beings in the air. And then I felt that something monstrous lingered just beyond my consciousness, and the little daemon offered me its flute, and I brought that instrument to my mouth."

I waited as he seemed to lose himself within a horror of memory. "Wakefulness came as violent shaking," he continued. "Unfathomably, I had been dreaming while standing on my feet! I nearly fell when I finally came to my senses. Cradled in my arm was that crafted beast. In my free hand . . ."

I placed the artifact on the desk, went to my landlord, and pressed one gentle hand upon his breast. Beneath his jacket I could feel an object. Boldly, I dipped my hand into his inner breast pocket and pulled out the thing that had nestled therein: a flute of polished onyx. It was an exact replica of the instrument that was held by the small statue.

"I brought it with me," Philip Nithon whispered, "from beyond the wall of sleep!"

II.

(Sesqua Valley)

The cosmic storm, spawned among dead stars, felt the force of she who called it, the curious she who was a blend of earthly magick and unearthly alchemy. She summoned, and remorselessly it fell to earth. Infected was the ionosphere through which it plunged. It brought with it, this star-wind, the memories of those who, dead-yet-dreaming, sprawled in endless night. At last it reached the supernatural valley to which it had been called, and there it strayed a little among the jagged peaks of a titanic white mountain. It spun toward treetops, until it found the woman who stood atop a gigantic boulder, her sinuous arms outstretched.

This sentient wind fluttered around the paper crown that the black woman wore above her lush red hair. It whispered at her ears, pressed against her mouth, slipped between her lips. Deliciously, she tasted ancient alien dreaming, the wonder of which so shook her that, swaying in ecstasy, she fell from the boulder, arms outstretched. Caught by the summoned wind, she floated slowly to the ground. The paper crown dislodged itself and rolled some few feet from her.

She listened to the singing wind, then heard the other sound. Another occupant of the place bent low and picked up the paper crown, then playfully placed it on his head. Shutting his eyes, he listened to the song of conjured wind. Carefully, he sensed its passion for the sorceress, and bringing his flute to his malformed mouth he mocked with music the language of cosmic aether. As if insulted, the star-wind swirled out of the dreaming woman and dissipated into the stratosphere.

"Selene," the fellow sighed.

Reluctantly, she opened her eyes, and for one brief moment her face blurred so that her countenance was naught but smooth black surface. Then the silver eyes reformed, and the delicate nose pushed through, and a dusky slit transformed into a full and beautiful mouth. She gazed at the beast before her and grinned at the comical way in which he crookedly wore her crown. Breathing deeply, she puckered lips and exhaled. The fellow shuddered at the taste of a residue of alien air that pushed into his face.

"I see that you have summoned the Winds of Yith. Not wise, even for one of your talents. With what enchantment did you call them?"

"Nothing that you will find in your wormy books. I don't need your mumbled incantations, Simon. I merely linked with that part of the outer realm of which I am a portion."

"Yes," the beast conceded, "you are as much the stuff of stars as you are the shadow of this supernal valley. Such a wonderful combination. However, do not put down the ancient lore, for it is wonderful, potent and alive."

"And what is that 'wonderful' book you hold under your arm?"

"Ah," he chuckled, playfully tossing her his flute, which she sensually mouthed. Lifting his arm, he caught the falling book and kissed it. "This," he said as he knelt beside her on the grass, "is a stunning discovery. Do you remember last summer, when Edith and I journeyed to Providence, Rhode Island, so to visit a church that was scheduled for demolition?"

"Yes, the Free Will Church, from which you brought certain moldy books and various discolored window panes. I could smell the residue that stained those black panes, and something in the aroma beguiled me, reminding me of a thing buried deep within my psyche."

"Even so. Well, Edith has kept this book to herself until now. You know how selfish she is when it comes to sharing arcane lore. I finally wrestled it from her, and was astonished to discover that it is an actual *bound* copy of the *Liber Ivonis*. You cannot, because of your inexplicable disinterest in these elder tomes, comprehend how rare a thing this book is. But here is the really remarkable thing. Since studying the text, I have had a series of profound dreams in which I have pierced the deepest veil of slumber and caught sight of the realm where dwells the Boundless One! Yes, I knew that would startle you. This is a realm that you have often sensed yourself, but have never been able to locate in your own dreamland wanderings."

"It is from that dimension that I heard the howling of mine Elder Brother, the faceless one who teases with visions but mistily discerned. He calls, and yet he eludes my beckoning. My arms reach out, but he will not sweep into my aching embrace. And you say that you have met him?"

"An aspect of his thousand forms and faces, mere refractions of his awesome glory. There are very few who have encountered Nyar-lathotep unmasked! I have yet to meet anyone who actually dreamed deeply enough so as to bow before the throne of Azathoth. But now . . . now . . ."

"Inform me."

"You know that the children of Sesqua Valley leave this place when they come of age, so to journey the world of humankind and locate those rare souls who have tasted the dark secrets. Do you remember the young artist, Cyrus, who did that impressive bust of you in cast iron? Of course you do. He has found a most fascinating soul, an elderly poet, an innocent yet potent dreamer who has never sought the dark side, but to whom darkness calls."

"And this elderly man affects me in what way, my dear Simon?"

"I have felt your restlessness, Selene. That part of you that was born of Sesqua's shadow is growing dormant; and that other portion, spawned beyond the cosmic chaos, is flexing its vibrant muscles. The star-stuff that forms so much a part of your being longs for home. It calls to you as you have, just this afternoon, summoned it. You ache to sit with your Elder Sibling beside the entropic throne of Ultimate Disorder. The Boundless One scents you, and calls you. The universe sizzles with the waves of his dreaming. Psychic activity has increased with supernatural alacrity, here in this valley and—I feel it in my old bones—throughout this haunted globe. Why, I haven't felt such unearthly activity since that dead-yet-dreaming deity lumbered in his sunken city six decades ago. Ah, the wonderful dreamers! This acquaintance of young Cyrus may hold a key to your return."

"And you know this because of the dreams that have spilled into your sleeping mind, the visions that have been inspired by your reading of this curious text that you hold in your hand?"

"Yes; but then, you know, I read such books aloud, and so it isn't surprising that such effects are achieved. We leave tomorrow, to find Cyrus and his Philip Nithon. Tonight, my dear Selene, the valley will adore you one last time with nameless festival."

He held his massive paw to her, and she saw how it excitedly trembled. Sucking in enchanted air, she raised her midnight hand and entwined her fingers with his own.

III.

(From the Journal of Philip Nithon)

I don't pretend to understand what is happening, but I certainly like it. I like this new sense of adventure, this feeling that life hasn't passed me by. I've been in such a rut these past two decades, living my quiet life, devoting myself to good food and enchanting literature. It has always been there, lurking in the back of my brain, an especial interest in morbid verse. I never bothered to give it much thought, there never seemed any reason to ask myself *why* I was so enchanted by the weird sisters in *Macbeth,* or why the really outré stories of Henry James enthralled me far more than his baggy social novels. I had a thing for the macabre—that was my explanation, and it seemed enough.

I had an inkling, of course, that it was a strange and unusual interest, because I knew of no one else who shared it. I think that was the beginning of my eremitic existence. Not finding anyone with whom to share my passion, I delighted in staying home and communing with fellow advocates by way of literature. That was why I was so instantly attracted to Cyrus, when I saw him in the small branch library that, being but three blocks from my house, is a constant haunt. There he sat, reading a wee paperback edition of the best fantastic poems of Clark Ashton Smith that had been published by some newly spawned New York publisher. Well, old habits die hard, and there has always been that part of me that is (how to phrase it?) dramatic. And so I stood a little way from his table and quietly declaimed some lines from "The Eldritch Dark," thus:

> "A wizard wind goes crying eerily,
> And on the wold misshapen shadows crawl,
> Miming the trees, whose voices climb and fall . . ."

The frowning librarian shushed me, but the boy broadly smiled and invited me to sit. Our fascinating conversation ended with my inviting him to my home for supper and a look through my own extensive library. And when I learned that he was seeking inexpensive accommodations, I shocked myself by inviting him to rent, for a pittance, my attic bedroom.

Isn't it interesting, how one can be lonely for so many years and not realise it until some charming personality enters into life and reveals one's desolation? It was like finding a portion of lost youth, having him here, sharing meals and quiet evenings in the library, the silent companionship of reading. It has become a delightful Platonic relationship.

Last night, however, something happened that gave me pause, that moved me to wonder. And now I am certain that the hand of fate has brought this lad into my life. We took a taxi to a rather squalid part of downtown. It was late afternoon, and the place was alive with human activity. The noise was quite appalling, as was the smell. It was a shock to my reclusive system, to be out in such a scene, to witness the race from which I had sequestered myself so efficiently. Ugh! The loonies who had victimized themselves with abuse of drugs and alcohol!

Is there anything more ugly than a loathsome human being, a filth-encrusted sputtering freak who leers at one with naked hatred when its pleas for help are ignored? But *just* as annoying were the rushing business people with blank faces. I don't know, it all seemed so sordid and meaningless, and it triggered a ferocious misanthropy that I didn't really know I had.

All this annoyance lasted but a few minutes, as Cyrus led me from the cab to a high metal gate beyond which I saw a narrow cobblestone lane between two tall brick buildings. Taking hold of my hand, Cyrus pushed open one of the gates and led me through the inconspicuous threshold, quietly closing the gate behind us. I was led down the narrow lane to a cement stairway that descended into a place I took to be a sequestered speakeasy.

"Why don't you sit at this table, Phil, and I'll order us some coffee?" I sat and watched as he went to a window in a wall, gave someone a bit of cash, then returned to join me. I looked around and was pleasantly surprised by the change in atmosphere from what I had only just experienced on the street above. Here I beheld people of various ages, sitting at tables, in quiet discourse, lounging on huge sofas that sat near a wall of bookcases, or roaming the room studying the pieces of art upon the walls. It was deliciously quiet. When the lights flickered off and on three times, Cyrus smiled and leaned to whisper, "It's time for the readings."

A modern bohemian type, a white boy with nappy hair, dressed in black, went to one of the bookshelves and selected a volume, then approached a spotlit area and opened his book. "A poem by Samuel Loveman," he announced, then proceeded to read a lovely piece about a dead poet, Thomas Holley Chivers. There was no applause as he returned the book to the shelf and resumed his seat. Next an elderly woman rose and read from a collection of verse by the strangely fascinating New England poet, Edward Derby. I watched as Cyrus walked to the place of performance, took a small book from his coat pocket and read two sonnets by the unfamiliar William Davis Manly.

I was trying to decide if I should stand and recite from memory one of my favorite pieces by Poe when, from a darkened corner, something emerged with aching deliberation. I watched as the obese creature slowly maneuvered its wheelchair to the area that was illumined by pale spotlight. Cyrus leaned toward me and excitedly whispered, "It's Kyle Gnoph, the blind poet. This is brilliant! He rarely reads." But I could not help my feelings of revulsion as the shapeless mass of distended flesh. I had never before seen such arms, the ponderous skin of which heavily drooped as those arms lifted so that the piece of parchment held in greasy hands could be read. One hand carefully smoothed the paper's surface, as if its language was composed of Braille. The pathetic man sluggishly lifted his heavy head, and I could barely discern the ruined remnants of what had once been living eyes. The awful flabby lips parted, releasing a string of thick drool. With uncouth enunciation the mouth began to warble.

"The lost song of the Mad Arab, from his book of dark dreaming, unpublished and recently discovered. In my own simple translation." I found his voice difficult to understand, but as he tried to speak I felt, not pity, but a warming of the heart. I seemed to know instinctively that a poet was encased within that mound of mortality. Idiotically, Kyle Gnoph smiled at nothing, and then continued.

"Nyarlathotep is his revelation,
All-seeing eye that crawls the quaking auroras,
Among the seven suns."

He stopped as if to catch his breath, and then began to mutter to himself, in a language I could not understand. His gibbering lips gnawed hungrily at the air, as if in search of language. There was something in the sight that, revolting as it was, broke my heart. Before I was fully aware of my actions, I reached into my inner pocket and produced the flute that I had found beyond the realm of slumber. Rising, I went to the stuttering poet and sat before him. Bringing the flute to my mouth, I began to play a song that echoed deep inside my skull. The mass of shuddering flesh before me stretched its maw and began to eerily howl. A hand slapped his face and pierced a ragged fingernail into his forehead, where it etched some kind of symbol.

"In self-mutation we find eternal birth," he hollered.

His blood-smeared hand reached toward me, and I lifted myself to my knees so as to meet it. With wet red gore he marked my forehead, and I saw on his little finger a ring that resembled a small mutated skull. Then, swiftly, as if in contempt, Kyle Gnoph raised his bare and massive foot and savagely smashed it against my head.

When consciousness was regained I found myself at home, in bed, with a prize headache. Cyrus was sitting next tome, singing softly to himself, with candlelight glimmering in his unusually pale, his almost-silver eyes. In his hand he held the carven figure that I had found in New England, which he gently stroked as if it were some familiar. I studied that shapeless chiseled oddity in candlelight, astonished at how much, in my delirium, it resembled the blind idiot poet that had assailed me.

IV.

(Sesqua Valley)

Bathed in silver moonlight, the trees of Sesqua Valley danced their slow dance to gentle windsong. There was a beast somewhere on the twin-peaked mountain who watched the moon, who opened its jaws in praise of lunar light. From beneath her naked feet, Selene could feel the phantom beat that was the valley's pulse, a rhythm of which she was less and less a part. There was another vibration that summoned her, a calling from the cosmos, and it would soon be answered.

She stepped slowly through the grove as the trees reached for her flowing hair with lowered branches. Behind her she could sense those others, the children borne of Sesqua Valley's supernatural shadow, those beasts of adoration whose silver eyes beamed at her ebony flesh, her beautiful blackness. Their swaying motion, was a danse that moved

to Sesqua's subtle pulse, that measured throbbing that matched the dia-
stolic movement of their matchless hearts.

The majestic woman raised her arms to the mist that flowed from
the mountain rock, the thickening mist that moved toward her. She
smiled at the indistinct figure who moved within that bank of brume,
the tall fellow whose lean body was sheathed within a gown as red as
sunset, whose massive hands were encased in gloves as shiny black as
her own flesh, whose face was masked by a net of dark material. She
bowed her head to the triple crown of white gold that he wore upon his
dome. Behind him, in the hazy air, she saw the seven alabaster globes
that burned like newborn suns. Her eyes gleamed as those spheres began to darken and turn black, as they gracefully spread their wings and
soared to her. One of them hovered before her, wrapped its talons into
her billowing red hair, and she could smell upon the faceless thing the
remnant of the dreamland from which it had escaped.

The masked one was before her, clutching her arms, moving his
body with her own. Behind them, crawling through grass and weed and
sifting soil, were the worshipping ones who hummed magical syllables
to sod and starlight. The dancers stopped, and Selene fastened her
mouth to the blank web that masked Simon's face, this fellow who
stood as proxy for that avatar who would soon embrace her, who
would guide her beyond the rim to their place of origin beside the
acidic throne of the Boundless One.

V.

(From the Journal of Philip Nithon)

We sat in the quiet corner of an almost deserted café, sipping beverages
and speaking softly. I casually studied my tenant's friends, these creatures from an unknown town. The black woman especially fascinated
me; for although she was as black as midnight, her features were not
African. There was a hint of something noble and exotic in her sculpted
features, and her silver eyes were like none I had hitherto gazed into.
Her companion was a lean fellow with sallow flesh, excessively wide
shoulders and large hands, who hid his face beneath the brim of a wide
hat. I could not clearly see his eyes, but his oddly formed mouth moved
with much personality. Although his clothes looked new, they were of a
fashion decades past.

"You realise," the fantastic gentleman informed, "that most of these alien creatures of whom one reads in moldering tomes and brittle manuscripts are little more than the mad conjurations of mortal dreaming. The human brain, much as I deride it, is capable of potent performance, although such activity is usually the merest accident, unintended and chaotic, the product of magnificent delirium. Alhazred was such a one. More than half of *Al Azif* is but a record of those daemons that he fashioned in fevered dreaming."

This fellow's language bothered me. For one thing, he spoke of the human race as if it was a thing from which he stood apart. And the incidental manner in which he spoke of the black arts reminded me that I had entered a world of weirdness that I could not really fathom. Indeed, it was as though I had walked into a dream world. Was I truly awake? Looking at Cyrus, I saw in his eyes a keen excitement as his listened to this Simon fellow speak, absolutely entranced.

"Take, for example, They from the Air, of whom you've read, Philip, in Derby's verse. He writes that they are assembled from the chanting of the Dho formula, and that they cannot assist without the aid of human blood, from which they take bodily form. Pah! Would extraterrestrial deity, born in the millennial epochs that predate the dreary period from whence humanity slithered from its sea-bed slime, require such mortal assistance? The idea makes one gag. And yet we have serious 'scholars' who believe such rot. I've met a few at Miskatonic. And yet—there *are* entities born of diseased dreaming, spawned within the cracked skulls of lunatics, forces as deadly as Einstein's nuclear nightmare." He chortled. "What a daemon that was! The human brain, which can create its own reality, that pulsing piece of muscle that can cause and cure disease, delirium and death, may under a variety of circumstances conjure forth a very plethora of gods and devils, creatures spawned in potent lunatic vision. And then the 'legends' of these beasts are recorded in the texts of countless necromantic tomes. It's all so very quaint."

I cleared my throat. "And where do you place me, Mr. Williams?"

"You are an authentic outsider, my good sir, a conduit to the deepest realm. You have not called forth your own created entities. You have been summoned by those from Outside, a pawn in their provocative play."

"How helpless you make me feel," I muttered.

The silent woman suddenly moved and slowly brought her hand to my face. I could smell the earthy redolence that I had vaguely noticed when Cyrus was around (I supposed that it was his after-shave or some such tonic). The smell, which was rather sweet and not offensive, emanated most powerfully from Simon Williams. But there was another aroma, one that reminded me of something that I had vaguely recalled from those times I had awakened from deep dreaming. The woman, Selene, touched her cool hand to my forehead, and I gasped as vision clouded.

"Your soul," she cooed, "has touched the outer place, where dwells the Boundless One, he for whom my Elder Brother serves as avatar. You will please help me to cross the cosmic threshold." And then she dropped her hand and placed it over my own. Blurry eyesight cleared, and I peered into her lovely face.

I deeply sensed that these beings—for what else could I call them?—contained within their make-up an awesome power. And yet they seemed authentically to require my help! For all of Simon's talk of 'absurd' humanity, he required from me a pathway that I had found in deepest slumber, a service that I did not understand, but which I was anxious to offer them. To her.

Gently, I brought her magnificent hand to my lips, and she sighed at my kiss. As I peered into her silver eyes, I thought that I could detect in them a galaxy of emotion.

VI.

(Cyrus Lynchwood)

I stood in the library, looking at titles and sipping my third whiskey. My lightheadedness did nothing whatsoever to tame my growing excitement. Glancing at my elderly landlord, I saw that he, too, was quivering with nervous excitement. Of course, he tried to look cool and collected as he sat at his desk and fondled with nervous fingers the small cedar box into which he had placed the outré flute. Finally, he could no longer contain his mounting emotion.

"Where the devil are they?" he demanded.

"They're preparing themselves. Cool down, Mr. Nithon. Simon likes to make a dramatic occasion out of everything."

No sooner had I said this when Simon Gregory Williams almost floated into the room on a cloud of glee. He was not wearing his hat, and he hadn't bothered to disguise his true features, the eerie countenance that is our heritage. I couldn't help grinning as I watched Mr. Nithon's startled face, and going to where he sat, I put a reassuring hand on his shoulder.

"Yes!" Simon exclaimed, roaming the room with his wide dark hands raised before him, as if he could feel the haunted atmosphere. "This is indeed a portal! Rarely have I felt such *presence*. What we have here is one of those outlandish earthly spots where the realms ooze one into the other. You remember, Cyrus, when I spoke to you of the Rue d'Auseil, of the gateway that I discovered there? Pure accident, or rather pure instinct, led me there. I could *smell* the uncanny aether above the stench of dark river water. There were dilapidated factories whose gray smoke perpetually shut out the light of day. In that smog I could bloody smell the residue of past dreamers, those rare souls who had been lured to the unhallowed spot. This is such a place. When we have concluded, Philip, you must tell me the history of this family habitat. Have you any queer biographies in your family tree? But more of that anon. For now we shall begin our preludial sorcery." Hungrily, he eyed the cedar box. "But, pray, what hast thou there?"

"Something wonderful," the old gentleman assured him, cautiously opening the box and taking from it the onyx flute.

"Oh! Oh!" And the beast of Sesqua Valley took hold of the instrument and scanned it with his awesome eyes. "Clearly a piece of otherworldly work. But it's *magnificent!*" He placed it under my nose. "You remember, lad, when I took you to Miskatonic University and showed you that statuette that had been fashioned by a psychically hypersensitive youth named Wilcox. What a superb piece it was, and containing such an obvious unearthly force. And yet it was composed of human hands. Now, this—"

Gingerly, he brought it to his lips. Gently, he exhaled. A low sound issued from the flute, and the room subtly darkened. Through a doorway a figure entered. She wore a gown of yellow silk that clung to the contours of her sumptuous body. The luxurious red hair, falling almost to her ankles, shone in the glow of many flickering candles that Simon had instructed to be lit. Seductively, she sauntered to where Mr. Nithon sat and bent close, kissing his forehead. "We owe you our deepest gratitude, Philip. You are a rare dreamer." Her mouth found his, and I saw that he could not close his startled eyes. From his expression I took it that he had never tasted such a kiss.

Simon pushed hot living air through the instrument at his mouth. No longer able to contain myself, I let my human mask fade from my face, slowly allowing my Sesquan features to reveal themselves. My landlord, freed from Selene's kiss, gaped at my true self. Smiling, I winked at him. Then I shut my silver eyes and listened to the song of music, and I heard beneath it another sound—of alien winds. It was a noise that I had heard before, as had my landlord.

The majestic woman had moved away from us, and I watched as she lifted her arms, as if in greeting. Eyesight began to blur, and the room grew weirdly less physical. Man, it was so freaking awesome! A figure began to form, an indistinct and shifting thing that held a cracked flute in clumsy paw. Above it I could sense more than see the bat-like creatures that moved in adoration of the Boundless One, that daemon of ultimate chaos. I knew that I was looking on something that should never be seen, and my face burned and pulsed as if its features were being grotesquely mutilated. From the corner of my eye I saw Philip Nithon cover his eyes and cower in his chair. At the old one's feet I saw two other beings, amorphous just like that wee statue that the old man had shown me on the night that this mad adventure had begun for me.

The room was alive with crazy piping that reached its crescendo as another figure emerged from cosmic shadow. It was a faceless thing of smooth blackness, and on its head it wore a triple crown. Singing, Selene rushed to it, knelt before it, howled as the being wound its talons into her flowing hair. The room was alive with noise, and with the movement of unearthly wind. I felt as though that hungry wind would pull the flesh from my rippling face. Still I could not take my eyes from those two black being, the one that savagely pulled at the others hair. The goddess arose, no longer adorned with human mask. Her visage was a wonder of living shadow wherein there smoldered ebony points of midnight starlight. Her Elder Brother took from his dome the triple crown of alabaster gold and thrust it upon her own.

I turned to the sound of joyous screeching, and turned to see Simon, whose face was encased within a mask of smoke, throw the enchanted flute to Mr. Nithon, who had looked up at the sound of Simon's exhilaration. Suddenly Simon was upon me, kissing my shifting face and pulling me toward Selene. The demoniac wind was screaming in our ears, and as it flowed into our pores we tasted the memories of that with which it had been composed, the dead-yet-dreaming memories of the Old Ones beyond the rim of sane reality. God, it was delicious! Ferociously, we snapped our jaws and twisted our limbs. Transfigured, we knelt as pure beasts before the deity of otherwhere. I laughed as one bat-like entity flew to Mr. Nithon and snatched from his hand the onyx flute. I watched as that creature hovered before his face, then touched with one thin claw the old man's forehead. I watched the mark that formed as torn flesh bathed in thick slow-dripping blood. I laughed as the old gentleman fell to his knees, a trickle of crimson mortality slipping into his mouth. The expression on his aged features matched my own sense of ecstatic anarchy.

Simon Gregory Williams raised his bestial mug and yowled. Stretching my jaws, I joined him in unholy howling. That which had been Selene, which now conjoined with her supernal sibling, flowed to us like some dream-wrought succubus and touched our fevered faces with ethereal hands. Happily, our tongues paid homage to her palms.

His Splintered Kiss

I entered the place of sanctity. With faltering footsteps I passed through the corridor that glowed in golden candlelight. At last I reached the stained glass window that had become my obsession. I knelt upon black tile and gazed in rapture at the image I could not keep from my mind since first I beheld it. Oh, his satanic beauty! How it beguiled my senses. How it called to me in deepest slumber. How I longed to join him, surrounded by such jeweled loveliness.

But it was he who completely captivated. His sleek black hair, his dark cunning eyes, his lissome limbs (so ready to leap from the glass of which he was composed). One dainty arm, as silver-white as lithium, was outstretched, and upon its palm were beads of blood, composed of small crimson gems. They sparkled in the shifting light of the setting sun.

The approaching twilight subtly altered his beautifully grotesque face; and the shadowed eyes (set deep within his impious visage) watched me. I moved nearer to the window and thoughtfully considered the thick mound from which his crystal prick subtly peeked.

Evening windsong hummed through the cracks that marred his crystal mouth. Why had the damage not been repaired? It made me feel forlorn to see those sensual lips so shattered. It was his only flaw. Raising on tiptoe, I pressed my mouth to his oxiodic lips, then gasped in pleasure as a splinter of glass pierced my mouth. I pressed my liquid lips to his for many moments, then pushed myself away.

Dim candleshine illuminated the smear of blood that stained his gem-like lips. Thick warm liquid bubbled on my own lips, and slipped into my mouth. I felt a bit light-headed. Something in his blurring image disconcerted me. Oh, the pain in my head. Sinking to my knees I shut my eyes; yet even with eyelids closed I could see the shifting colored lights that whirled about me, dancing to the song of rising wind, the sound of tinkling glass.

My eyes opened. He stood directly before me. His silver-white flesh rippled with ungodly sentience. I could smell his sacrilegious essence. I succumbed unto it. Bending to his outstretched hand, I kissed the proffered palm. His mark of blood was on it, darkly. That ruddy liqueur instilled within my weary soul a voracious passion. I tried to sip the blood, but he moved his hand away, held it before his mouth, kissed his stigmatic stain. I shuddered at the mirthless smile he cruelly bestowed upon me and shivered as his mouth mocked me with a smooth and chilly kiss upon my forehead.

The wet red lips pressed against my burning brow for an eternity, and when at last he pulled away I knew with certainty that I would never leave that place. And nigh I watch with gem-like eyes the dim candlelight that filters through this corridor. I watch the lost, the lonely, who come in search of sanctity. Christ bless their lost pathetic souls. I see them make obeisance before me, and watch as they listen to the night wind that whispers through the cracks that mar my crystal mouth. It is a mouth that feels for an eternity the heartless ecstasy of his daemoniac kiss.

oh, Baleful Theophany

(For Robert M. Price)

I.

Two figures frequented the fragrant room, the dimly-lit chamber that
was haunted by beautiful music. The elderly fellow at the piano moved
like some fantastic marionette, his pale and emaciated body a frantic
silhouette jerking over the keyboard as his shock of white hair spread
over his dome. His frenzied hands flew over the keys as he played a
piece of music that conveyed in its chaotic chords a kind of sublime
madness. His performance was watched by another fellow—sallow, tall,
lean—who stood near to the partially parted French windows and
basked in the perfumed air that billowed inward from an immense garden. Glancing outside, he watched for a moment the clouds that
clothed the moon, then turned his attention to his friend as the music
reached a climax.

The clamor ceased, and Simon Gregory Williams sighed. "Really,
Vombic, that was magnificent. I could feel the flow of chilly starlight,
those dead orbs that crawl across the sky and ache to assemble as signal
to the dead-yet-dreaming. Why, I could *almost* sense the Haunter of the
Dark fumble across the void in answer to your playing. (Music, you
may know—or maybe not, you being so adverse to such things—can
influence they who lurk at the dimensional rim. There is a place in
France where the chords of a viol once . . . Ah, but you don't care to
hear of such things, do you?)" He crossed to the piano and playfully
ran his fingers over the keys as he peered at the sheets of music from
which the elderly gentleman was performing. "Your brother was a genius, and you have beautifully executed this final piece of his. Bravo."

Thaddaeus Vombic's hands had stayed unmoving upon the keys,
and they trembled slightly at the emotion stirred by the performing of
his sibling's composition. "Thank you, Simon," he quietly replied; and

then his bird-like gaze grew startled as he saw the shadow that sallied through the garden to the French windows. He watched the limb that painfully rose and pushed at one of the delicate doors, and he moaned as the figure crept into the room on hunkered limbs. He rose on shaky limbs as the woman fell sideways onto the polished floor and struggled out of the heavy pack fastened to her back. He started to go to her but was stopped by Simon's large hand on his chest. They watched the wretched creature, freed from her bondage of gear, pull herself to them, rise to her knees and place her stiff hands over Simon's feet.

"Well," said Simon in his low clear voice, "our little bantam returns to us at last. A little worse for wear from when we saw thee last." He placed prehensile talons to the chin of the lowered head and tugged. Allowing her head to lift, she stared at the Beast as the light of a candelabrum bathed her face, one half of which was still smooth and lovely, the other half of which was mutilated with ragged disfigurement. Simon's finger touched one scar and followed it upward, to the place where once she had wore an eye; and he hissed as the candle's flame played upon the thing that nestled in the socket. The poor old fellow beside Simon cried out, stepped forward, and went to caress the injured face with his soft old hand; yet when that hand touched the weirdly *chilly* texture of that ruined flesh, he cried once more and yanked his hand away.

"Do stop that pathetic noise," Simon told the old man. "This moment is too magical for your human caterwauling." Once more he placed his fingers beneath the woman's chin and tugged. She rose before him on uncertain legs. "Now, Molly Noble, tell us the tale of your curiously lengthy absence from the valley. And explain to me this thing that is so daemonically embedded within your socket."

Miss Noble slightly shuddered, then sucked in the perfumed air, which seemed somehow to impart some vigor into her frail form. "I went away, as you know," she spoke in a voice that sounded as wounded as her face. "I left, because I am a child of Sesqua Valley, although not shadow-born, as you are, Beast. My mother gave birth to me in the human way, and I have never known another environment. I was raised in valley ways, and so when I came of age, I wanted to journey out into the world, to find the other places of supernatural wonder that pocket this dismal globe. You, Simon, had tutored me with those tomes kept in the tower, that elder lore that you cherish more than any other thing, excepting the magick that they provoke. Ah, you smile."

She began to quietly laugh, then suddenly closed her eyes and tilted toward them. Together, the human and the beast took hold of an arm and led the young woman to a large sofa. Thaddaeus produced a large yellow handkerchief, with which he dabbed at the streaks of perspiration that trickled down the woman's face. "Really, Simon, this is too insane, to force her to talk when she needs rest. No, I'm taking her to a room on the second floor. Your rabid curiosity can be *monstrous* at times!"

Simon's large hand flew to Vombic's face, and one razor-sharp talon delicately pierced the skin just beneath the old man's left eye. "Silence, or you will discover exactly what a monster I can be." Suffering an uneasy combination of anger and fear, Vombic swatting Simon's hand from his face, then went to a small table on which there sat a decanter and two crystal eucharistic cups. Pouring pale liquid into each chalice, he offered one to the weary woman, then swiftly drained the other himself. Miss Noble gratefully sipped, then leaned back her head upon an extremely soft cushion. As she did so, moonbeams drifting into the room from a high window fell upon her proxy eye, and Simon Williams moaned at the sight of it.

"It drives you mad, doesn't it, Simon, not to know whence the jewel came?" Lightly, she laughed. "I didn't want to seek after anything obvious. I like to be original. And so I determined to find N'kai, that lair of the forsaken god. You told me of it, do you remember, sweet Beast, during the autumn long ago when we studied Eibon? You were rather glib about it all, but I was fascinated. I studied on my own, when you were away on your countless excursions. I used the money Mother left me and journeyed to Germany and Asia, the usual places. I won't tell you where I finally found the dismal cavern, for I like having secrets of my own. Oh, how anxious I became when I scented that I was close to success! Alas, in the town where I had asked some rather indiscreet questions I aroused suspicion. I was observed, and followed; and being too intent on my quest, I ignored the inner warnings. Yes, I felt it, Beast, that sharp hunger born of supernatural quest. (I should have learned from all those years of observing you, mad one.) The two thieves who followed me were probably the offspring of the amorphous servitors of the toad-god. They were ugly enough to be so, and savage enough. You see what they did to me. But during our battle, something spooked them. Some racial memory, perhaps, reawakened by the cavern in which they found themselves. They fled before they had finished with me. I was weak with blood loss, and of course I couldn't see well. I reached to clear the gore from my face, and thus I discovered that one of the villain's knives had torn out my eye." She paused, shuddering.

"That's enough, my dear."

"No, Thaddaeus, let me continue. I'm near the end. I crawled on the ground among the litter of skeletal remains, none of which were human. It was weird, how all of these animal skeletons faced the dais on which I found nothing but a dark stain of ancient liquid—or perhaps it was the reptilian shadow of that which had sat upon the dais for centuries, awaiting a renewal of worship that never materialized. How lonely to be a forgotten god. I struggled to that dais and lifted myself upon it. I found some gems, and taking one of them I intoned a prayer to the Old One, as you had shown me, Simon, when we studied briefly the *Book of Eibon*. And I sensed, subtly, that I was not alone, but queerly so. I sensed an uncanny occupancy in the dusky chamber. And I imagined that my vision had inexplicably improved, for the cavern seemed suddenly to glow, to burn with a blue-litten phosphorescence. And in that unearthly light I gazed onto the gem held in my hand, that outré chalcedony on which I detected a curious cloud-like effect, a moving shadow. And when that shadow strangely parted, I beheld at last the wondrous thing that had held the jewel in its paw as it hungered so insidiously for veneration."

Molly's body suddenly jerked spasmodically, like one cursed with epilepsy, and the gentlemen were too slow to catch her as she hurled herself off the sofa onto the floor, upon which she crawled to her backpack. Saliva moistened her mumbling mouth as she clumsily worked to open a zipper. "They filtered through dead starlight when the world was raw." Her voice was deeply guttural, so unlike her natural tone. "They brought their images with them. But, oh, the raw world cooled and altered, and in the riot of modification they lost their awesome foothold. In agony they uttered the signals that melted limpid dimensional space, portals into which they could ooze so as to dwell between the spaces. Yet they were confined, until the stars came rightly and they at last remembered the potent syllables."

The beast went to her, knelt beside her, pushed away her useless fingers and opened a zipper. Swiftly, he reached into the pack and produced from it a squat and heavy object. "It's beautiful," he sighed, holding it up to moonlight. Beside him, the young woman shuddered, then tried to contain herself. When again she spoke, it was with her natural voice.

"There were others on the floor, mingling with the debris of death; but this one called to me. I could *feel* it so heavily reflected on the gem that I held in my hand." She winced as Simon touched a talon to her false eye. "I know an alchemical surgeon in Prague, and with his skill we fit the jewel into place within my ruined socket. It's weird, Beast, but at times I can *see* with it. Not the natural world. I see between the realms, and some thing sees me in return. It cries to me, hungered for sacrifice. It gazes on this jewel and seems to remember it. And why not, for hadn't it held this gem within its paw for nameless aeons? And gazed and gazed, thus implanting thereon its supernal likeness?"

Vombic floated to them and leaned to kiss the ruined flesh of the savaged face. He leaned so as to gaze closely at the moonlit surface of the blue gem that sat inside the girl's eye-socket. Peering at it, he watched its surface grow cloudy with pulsing shadow. He watched as a blacker form pushed through that veil of velvet darkness, a form that monstrously blinked at him. Shrieking, he flew away from the others and fell upon the sofa. The woman tilted her head and grinned at him. Her human eye was enlarged with veneration as she spoke the ancient, the unhallowed name.

"Tsathoggua."

II.

Molly Noble sat in candlelight on the round wooden floor of Sesqua Valley's old brick tower, an edifice in which the valley (or, to be precise, Simon Gregory Williams) kept an astonishing library of occult works and artifacts. She sat beside an old oak table, her dark hair encircled with a nimbus of soft flickering light from the candlestick that sat above her on the book-littered table. Before her, on the chilly floor, lay a dubious edition of the Pnakotic Fragments; and as she studied them she fancied that another psyche inhabited the room with her, and she guessed that this unseen wraith was what legend called the Fragments' Guardian. Touching a hand to the pages of old parchment, feeling the slightly embossed lettering that had been etched by hand in thick sable ink, the brutalized woman summoned the wisdom of the book. With her free hand she raised a leather pouch filled with white sand and poured its contents beside her on the floor. She turned her face toward candlelight, the flickering cadence of which scintillated on her eyes, the one that lived and the one that was lifeless. Without watching, she poked a finger into the debris of sand and drew in reverse the Pnakotic Pentagon, an ancient symbol used in elder aeons so as to seal the tombs of wizards and thus prevent their restlessness after earthly death. Reversed, it opened gates through which the dead-yet-dreaming could inculcate influence. Softly, she whispered her toadish deity's name, summoning any portion that might still be receptive to veneration.

Something fumbled in a darkened corner. Molly turned her eyes toward it, then smiled as a figure timidly approached. "What are you doing here? Sorcery was never an interest of yours."

The elderly human hesitated, then spoke with faltering tongue. "I . . . wanted to see it . . . once more. Oh, the sad and loathsome thing! I thought . . . I thought I could *feel* it call my name."

"And so we did, Thaddaeus."

He wrinkled his brow. "We?"

Abnormally, the candlelight subdued. "We knew thy brother, and smelt his intoxicated blood in the hour of his extinction. And we scented thee, Thaddaeus Vombic, the one who fears the darkness out of time. Yet in thy fear we sense a spark of enticement. We felt it othernight as you performed the musical piece that Ephraim composed as latria to we dwellers in darkness. Oh, Thaddaeus, your Ephraim saw in dreaming our burrowing through dimensional aether." She stopped speaking in her deeply altered voice as the old man began to shake with weeping. Clumsily, she grabbed at the table and pulled herself to a standing position, then moved with faltering footsteps into the weeping man's embrace. When again she spoke, the voice was one he recognized.

"Oh, Thaddaeus, it hungers, and you have felt its awful ravishment. I, too, know as intimate torment its miserable pangs. I can feel its slothful movement on this gem that sits in proxy for mine eye. Ah, the ghastly jewel! It shoots roots of memory to my brain, and coats my tongue with the taste of awful slaughter. We are linked. And yet I cannot catch hold of him and lead him earthward, through the curves of vaulted nebulae. Oh, Vombic, be like unto thy sibling and help us. Mine ancient friend."

One violated portion of his seething brain wanted to hurl her from him. Yet this was Molly, the girl he had know when she was a wee lass who wandered wide-eyed in his garden. This was the young girl who had comforted him in his hour of tragedy. How could he push her away? Nay, he would press her close, this wretched young woman who had met with torment of her own. Taking her face into his hands, he smiled at her. He watched the dim flow of shadow that tainted the artificial eye. "What must I do?"

Her smile was a sinister thing, as was the oblique kiss that touched the tender skin just beneath one eye. Her voice, when she spoke, was weirdly echoed, as if by an undertone of alien vocal cords. "Speak with us," came her breathy voice, which seemed to purl about his fevered head, which seemed to softly reverberate in surrounding shadow. Her mouth was very close to his. Gently, she touched his lips with hers as she began to phonate incredible language. Yet it was not wholly alien to him, this sound. He had heard its like once before. At first sound of it his entire being shuddered with revulsion. But as he continued listening to it, and as the young woman's lips and tongue vibrated on his dry mouth, he began to feel seduced. There *was* something wondrous about this language, and the power it evoked. Feebly, he moved his lips, trying to echo her sound. Yet it proved impossible, and tears of frustration filled his eyes. Her moving mouth kissed the salty streams that trickled down his face. They found his eye, which they erotically mouthed. Roughly, they sucked. Seized with sudden terror, he pushed away from the panting woman.

Outside the tower, the wind arose as a thing of fury that howled through the small squares that served as windows in the ancient edifice. From somewhere on the white mountain an emotional beast yowled to dead starlight. "Oh!" Molly Noble screamed above the tumult. "I see! Ah, the long flight between spaces of the void. We scent the raw new sphere of chaos. I see, Thaddaeus! With a sense that mimics sight! I am it and it is I! *Iä!* I am claimed as amah! It melds with me and infiltrates my tiny soul. Thaddaeus!"

He watched in horror the agitated shadow on her cloudy non-human eye, and shrank as that blackness seeped onto her ecstatic countenance. He moaned as her visage subtly rippled. He watched as she lifted to him her hands, hands of mutating shape, paws that began to spout bristles of coarse black hair. He screeched as those paws flew to him and wound into his shock of hair, that pulled his fearful face once more to hers. Upon the cloudy eye he saw the amorphous outline that watched him with a mixture of desiderium and detestation. And then her mouth fastened once more onto his eye and savagely sucked.

Just outside the tower, glorying in the supernatural tempest that whirled about him like a thing of abomination, the beast of Sesqua Valley swayed and sniggered, then yelled the formulae that the woman had just momentarily shrieked. Simon knew (too well) the intoxicating kiss of preternatural frenzy, had tasted it oh so often. Beneath his padded feet he could feel the crazy throbbing of Sesqua Valley's unholy heart. The wind, that unearthly pneuma, filled his mouth and sang with him the calling to the Old One. He accompanied the baying of the children who dwelt atop the twin-peaked mountain. Tilting back his head, he chortled at the echoes of Vombic's crazy terror.

III.

(From yᵉ Journal of Simon Gregory Williams, Esq.)

I entered Innsmouth as the sun was sinking, and thus beheld the antient seaport silhouetted in shades of red and orange and violet. I confess to a dislike of Innsmouth's *stink*, but I adore its ambiance, that pervading sense of foreboding. I found, in Old Town Square, a rather marvelous thing. It was a statue, rather new I thought, of a deity that I took to be a representation of Dagon. Below this delightful fellow, on what looked like a plaque of gold, were inscribed the words "To That Which Shall Not Be Denied." Yah!

A vigorous breeze pushed the harbor stink into my agitated nostrils, and so I hurried onward, to Main Street. And I smiled as I beheld the faded sign still in the front window of the tottering old residence that was my destination. The letters, sun-bleached, were quite faded, yet could I just make them out. "Henry J. Waite III, Musicologist." As I began to climb the sagging porch steps leading to the front entranceway, I detected the vibrations of song from within. Without pausing to knock, I stepped through the threshold and to the door of what I knew to be the library. It was from behind that door that the delicious vocalizing issued, accompanied by piano. Quietly, I pushed open the door, and the singing ceased as two startled faces looked my way.

I confess that I wanted to dance when I beheld the alteration in Henry's physique, the inhuman hands that rested on the keyboard, hands that were dark-toned, mottled, webbed. His torso had thickened with mutation, glorified to an almost amorphous proportion. But it was the splendid *face* that made me shout with glee, for it signaled the final stages of his transition, the purging of detestable humanity, the revelation of his relationship to an Elder Race and their sunken master. Well, a pox of restraining myself! I did dance, to them, the bent old monster who gradually broke into pharyngeal laughter as he recognized me, and to the tall beauty at his side. Oh, she was exquisite! She was obviously a youngster of Henry's clan, and reminded me of an Innsmouth lass I once courted, Asenath; except that this young woman was quite tall whereas Asenath had been smallish. Of course this girl looked taller than usual due to the tiara with which she had been crowned, that work of perfection cast in gold (but gold that seemed unearthly, as if the material had fallen earthward from another sphere, or had escaped into our realm from some other dimension). The thing's contours had been fashioned quite specifically for an Innsmouth dome, and the designs moulded in high relief on its surface reminded me of an elder populace beneath the waves.

Smiling, I slightly bowed and made to her the Elder Sign. Oh, how those lovely overprotuberant eyes sparkled.

"That will be all, my dear. And remember! You have been chosen as Sacred Rites Priestess of the Esoteric Order! Remember the one in whose honor you warble!" Graciously, the beauty bowed to her master, smiled to me, and was gone. "My dear Simon," Henry chuckled, the feelers on his face happily writhing. "How long it has been since last you frequented us. Come, sit in that chair there, and I'll turned down this lamp. We must not agitate your sensitive Sesquan eyes."

"You are looking well," I said as I sat.

"Yes, yes," he mumbled as he made himself comfortable in an oversized chair. "I shed the final vestiges of loathsome humanity. What a weight off my shoulders."

"I'm rather surprised to find you still here—although delighted, of course, that you are. But I would have thought you were anxious to dwell in your final home beneath the waves."

"Soon, old fellow, soon. I have much to do before then. These youngsters need to be coached, and coaxed. It's amazing how the human taint stays so potent in some of them, retarding their inescapable nature. Bah, humanity. Yet, I am astonished, sir, that *you* are still crawling on this plain. Hasn't your precious realm of misty shadow called you home? Why do you linger so?"

"Oh, I'm having too much fun to return just yet."

"Really? And how long do you plan to wait?"

"Oh, until the end of mortal time."

"Ah, that's all right, then. You haven't long to wait." We shared in diabolic laughter. "Well, what dark matter brings you to Innsmouth?"

Rising, I sauntered to a nearby bookshelf and removed from it a heavy tome. "I desire some technical edification," I told him as I turned pages until finding the diagram I sought. I placed the grimoire onto his lap and tapped the page as his mouth folded with frowning.

"Dear me, the toad-god. Whatever do you want with such a dry old deity?"

"I want to assist a friend, Henry. I've been trying to summon forth the twin tones that reawaken this particular dead-yet-dreaming."

The other leaned anxiously forward. "Not with your enchanted flute, I hope!"

"I was tempted to, yes; but I do upon occasion heed my sense of precaution, faint though it be. I also tried raising windsong, then mutating it so as to hum a semblance of the tones; but Sesqua wind is too wise for such tomfoolery."

Waite shook his head. "You have always been too rash," he scolded. "This is potent stuff, even for a wizard of your abilities. You *do not* assemble any semblance of this song until you absolutely need to use it. You Sesquans! How addicted you are to reckless magick! You rush into it without thought, especially you. You think yourself impervious."

"Such is my nature, to which I am absolutely true." Cryptically, I grinned at him. "But you don't fool me, old fellow. I can taste your anxious interest in this affair. Your surface is calm water, but beneath it breaks the waves of adventurous expectancy. And so!"

Stepping to a small window, I opened it. Outside, darkness had fallen, and the evening air was laced with salty harbor fog. I sat once more and switched off the old lamp, and in that velvet realm of Stygian gloom I summoned alchemy. The sound of wind sailed through the opened window, gliding on misty aether. It formed itself musically as I esoterically moved my hands, and my companion moaned at the baleful melancholy of the noise. Pushing his aching limbs from out the chair, heavy tome in hand, he shuffled to the piano and placed webbed hands onto the lower keys, all the while piercing the book's diagram with pensive eye-beams. I listened to the malformed wind and lowly whispered its ghostly melody. Quietly, Henry began to play an alternate tone in weird accompaniment. Yah! The wretched *loneliness* conveyed by those discordant chords! Oh, the aching of a neglected god. I listened, and I memorized. And when at last the miserable noise ended, we sat there, my friend and I, very still, our eyes dim with silent tears.

Henry shifted his bulk and slowly rose. "And we think that we are patient. How long they have awaited the clearing off, when they can return this globe to its wonderful rawness, sans mortality. What will become of us then, Simon?"

"What can it possibly matter? This sphere is theirs, ultimately and absolutely."

We stepped outside, into nigrescent night. Henry led me to a place where we could see the low, distant line of Devil Reef showing just above dark water. I saw, now and again, the nude forms of they who swam the midnight waters.

"Does the government still oppress this place, Henry?"

"Not at all," he answered, smiling. "We give them Innsmouth gold."

Absent-mindedly, I began to whistle, and his webbed hand shot swiftly to my mouth. "You *will* be forever foolish! Do *not* articulate the song of the toad-god until you are absolutely prepared to summon!"

Complacently, I shrugged; and then I smiled and began to softly sing:

"Eh——Ahhh—Ah. E'yhaa-n'gai,
Ph'nglui—Cthulhu—fhtagn."

Sighing, my companion bent to kiss my throat with thick lips. Shutting my eyes, I listened as he disrobed. From the distant reef I could faintly hear the echo of my song issuing from other voices, with a clear nonhuman pronunciation that put mine (yea, even mine) to shame. I heard the plash of nearby water, felt the stinking breeze that soared off that salty stuff. When at last I reopened my eyes, I was alone.

IV.

It summoned her, the slothful thing that had fallen out of starlight, to its hypogeal lair. In dream she located the dusky place, and thus she joined the inhuman throng. They welcomed her as kindred, these servants who (through occult self-mutilation) had implanted within themselves the hoary artifacts that contaminated their mutation of flesh and psyche.

It summoned her, to its antediluvian throne, before which she knelt, ritual dagger in hand. With the knife's point she etched into her palm an antiquated symbol, then held her gory appendage to the creature before her. It smiled, and so did she, with a mouth that oddly stretched. Behind her, the servitors chorused in alien homage to their deity, and she closed her enlarging eyes to the sound of veneration, that song that found its way onto her tongue.

When again she opened her eyes she was in the dark and spacious guest bedroom in Vombic's massive home. Her bed was near a window through which the glow of moonlight bathed her hand, that bleeding hand on which her fingernail had carved in sleep a monstrous sign. Molly brought the wounded palm to her mouth and tasted sweet thick blood. From outside her window there came, in the yard below, a replication of the chanting that she had heard in dreaming. It sailed through evening's air, to her. She pushed her aching limbs out of bed, onto the cold wooden floor, and crawled to the window, which was slightly open. On the ground below were the singing things, those curious amphibious children that are especial to Sesqua Valley, those wee frog-like things that wear the faces of human infants. They gazed up to her with wide unblinking eyes (in shape and hue like unto what her living eye was becoming), and they sang to her with slitted orifices. She listened, resting her hands on the window sill, turning over her wounded hand so as to study its symbolic sore.

Some thing cried to her from Mount Selta, and beneath that mournful noise she could sense the dull pounding that was the valley's heartbeat, that pulse that called to her from deep beneath the sod. She felt her own pulse decrease until it echoed in her ears in exact unison with the valley's throb. Without thought, she arose. Without sight, she found her way outside, through the shadowed woodland, into the cloud of mauve mist that was the spectral spirit of the valley, from which the children of the valley are born and into which they must, in time, return. It coaxed her, this mist, into its embrace, and some portion of her dreaming brain took in the nebulous forms that looked like trees but were not. Hazily, she almost made out the shaggy beasts who hid their petite forms behind the trunks of the creeping, swaying entities. Molly Noble lifted her dreaming eyes to the white mountain, and saw that the titanic behemoth wore a crimson taint as it stretched its wings over its demesne.

The windsong in this haunted realm was a siren song, a hymn unto itself, full of dulcet magick. It called to her twin psyches, to the woman she had been, to the creature she was becoming. And beneath the wind there was another sound, and she turned to gaze upon the beast who pranced in moving darkness, a flute at his mouth. She listened to his music, and something deep within her fumbled. Mutely, the small amphibians with semi-human faces turned to follow Simon, and she moved into their throng. Behind, she heard those other things, those tree-like beings who dragged their roots through valley dirt as they waved their limbs of twig to the majestic mountain. They moved alongside the rushing Quamish River, until they came to the abandoned, crumbling covered bridge that crossed the swift river water. Simon stopped at the mouth of the dilapidated structure. Still playing on his flute, he motioned to one of the dendroid dwellers of the valley's shadowrealm. The creature stalked to him, twitching. From a pocket Simon produced an aged ritual implement, the blade of which he stabbed into the tree-thing's trunk. From another pocket Simon took out a bottle of salve, and into its viscous substance he dipped a finger. The woman watched as that finger smeared the bottle's contents into the symbol that had been carved into the creature's trunk; and then she groaned as the beast produced a flint, onto which he scratched a thick talon until sparks danced onto the swaying entity. The symbol burst into flames, a golden signal that Molly had beheld in nightmare and had etched onto her palm. The valley rumbled at the sound that issued from her spreading mouth as she stared in rapture at that incinerating sign. Sluggishly, she moved to the being whose entire form began to catch fire, that thing that reached a trembling limb to her face and stroked her jeweled eye. Shuddering, the entity lifted flaming branches to the mountain, quivering in ecstasy until, at last, it collapsed into a hump of smoky ash.

One of the small shaggy creatures came to that heap of friable soot and placed into it the heavy idol that Molly had stolen from a secret place, that age-old effigy that represented hoary Tsathoggua. Tenderly, that which was still mostly of human origin reached so as to stroke the idol; but then she ceased movement as she beheld the flesh of her distorted and extended hand, that hand that was dark with fine black hairs. Then, as the race of shaggy beings encircled her with dancing, Molly Noble crawled into the bed of ash and cradled the idol to her breasts, as Simon played twin tones upon his flute, a sound that made the wind to shriek, the river to run backwards.

V.

Thaddaeus Vombic sat before his piano and tried to put his emotions to intimate music; but it was not possible, for these emotions were unlike any he had hitherto experienced. He had touched his fingers to the young woman's face, had felt the fabric of the ruined flesh around the thing that nestled in an eye's socket. He had witnessed in vision the shapeless one that had manifested itself to him. Half-consciously, he touched the keyboard. His music was an awful thing of godless beauty, a torment of cosmic solitude.

Cool air brushed his dreaming face, and he opened entranced eyes. The beast of Sesqua Valley stood at the French windows, stepped through them, quietly closed them behind him. Tenderly, he glided to the piano and sat beside the ancient man. "Pray, don't cease. You've never played more beautifully."

Soft light from an ornate candelabrum lighted Simon's monstrous face, the wide nostrils and wolfish lips, the mercury eyes. Having been raised as a boy in this haunted region, Vombic was accustomed to those creatures who were its especial children. But it had been his brother who had easily befriended these strange folk, who had been persuaded in their uncanny ways. Thaddaeus had always been a cautious lad, and he was not easily swayed by tricks of alchemy. He was too aware of how absolutely removed the shadow-children were from his own human race. The beast before him was most extreme, and yet, over time, they had formed an uneasy bond.

Placing a hand on Simon's shoulder, Vombic pushed off the piano bench and walked to the French window, passing beyond the threshold of wood and glass, stepping into the garden's fragrant air. He had never told Simon the true nature of this garden, how it clothed the curiously sweet aether of Sesqua Valley, that somehow the plethora of flowers and budding vines and blossoming trees had altered the atmosphere near Vombic's dwelling. It was as close to personal sorcery as he had ever dared to sojourn. His companion's bestial aura could at times be unsettling, and so he felt the need for the psychological comfort of his floriculture. Yet even here he could not but help to be reminded of the valley's unnatural aura, especially when starlight soaked the twin-peaked mountain.

Cool breath bathed the back of his neck. "You are so very close, Vombic, nearer than you have ever been."

"To what?" the old man scoffed. "Your way of existence? Pah, I've seen what that can lead to."

"Will you forever blame yourself for his demise?"

Vombic watched the shadows on the moon, how they seemed to form a face of mockery that winked at him. "I never told you the entire story of his death. I have never mentioned those final horrific moments that have altered forever my life. It is *you* whom I blame. Yes, blast your seditious soul! Oh, you are seductive, and he was enthralled. You taught him to read by the books in your blasted tower, and he would come home and show me his newest tricks of alchemy. It was you, beast, that took him to Dunwich, to those domed hills whereon he found the molten thing that I thought at first was a human skull, that remnant of bone that was so oddly deliquesced. How obsessed he became with it, taking it to his bed and placing it beneath his pillow. And why? 'Because it makes me dream, my brother.' Was it those dreams, beast, that filled his head with mania? Was it within their realm that he first heard the fatal promise of Yog-So . . .'"

Simon swiftly placed a large sallow hand against the old man's mouth. "I have told you *never* to utter that name."

Furiously, Vombic swatted the hand from his grimacing mouth. "Pah! Don't lecture caution to me, hypocrite! I was there, Simon. I found him, in that awful tower, clasping a dreadful book to his chest. A book from which he learned behavior under your ghoulish guidance. Listen to me, now, beast. He still lived when I discovered him. Yes, and still muttering that godless name, there in the muck that had spilled from where he had plucked out his eyes. No, don't turn away, fiend. Hear the entire tale of one who faltered under your pernicious influence. And not the first, by god! And not the last, you devil!"

Thaddaeus choked back strangled sobbing. The air was very still, and Simon stood unmoving, gazing at the moon without expression.

"He lived, only just. In madness he mumbled still to 'the Lurker between the spheres' or whatever the hell you call it. He called to darkness, and darkness answered him. I saw the shadow that formed above Ephraim's ruined face, that shadow out of time and dimensional space to which he had been calling. I watched that shadow kiss my brother's face, his face that folded in upon itself and then was no more. And I made a *vow*, Simon, never to participate in the madness that stole from me the sweetest soul that I have ever loved."

Without a hint of anger, the beast answered in an oleaginous voice.

"Am I hypocrite, old man? Yet wasn't it you, just now, who sat in that room and summoned with music a nameless thing? Unlike you, I have never pretended to virtue that I lack. No, I am the thing I am, happily and wholly. You cannot blame me for Ephraim's addiction. The addict alone is responsible for his fate. You disagree? Then who is accountable for this alteration within thyself? Nay, I have never tempted you toward sorcery, nor ever shall I. And yet here I find you, enthralled, calling out to a Great Old One with *enchanting* threnody."

He watched Thaddaeus quiver, then winced as Vombic swiftly turned to him and grabbed hold of his lapel. Up close, Simon could see the bruised area around one of the old man's eyes. "I saw it . . . on the surface of that agate eye . . . it called my name . . . Great Jesu! It is a grim, an unwholesome monstrosity; so uninviting . . . and yet . . . and yet . . ."

"And yet you were seduced—yea, even thee," Simon softly intoned, gently pushing the old man's hands from him. "No, do not feel ashamed and hang your head. Fate has found you, as she always will. Did you imagine that you could dwell forever in this valley and not be kissed by alchemy? Ah, no."

Vombic shook his head. "This has nothing to do with magick, Simon. This creature is a cosmic entity that has somehow found its way onto our sphere of temporary dust. What you call its 'alchemy' is naught but the non-terrestrial laws by which it exists. It is real, not spectral. I am not smug enough to believe that this planet is the only one capable of sustaining life. There are galaxies beyond our own, and realities that would scorch our tiny minds with terrible wonder if we only knew of them. And from some place in our ever-expanding universe this creature has come, to us. Why I cannot fathom. It fell to this sphere of dust, and it was worshipped as deity by humanity's ancestors. Oh, the grim and violent veneration that it has enjoyed, from a sick, a cruel, an over-imaginative race of pigmies. Aeons passed, and its adoring rabble died away. Thus in dark and lonely solitude it dwelt, remembering in dream the clumsy and uncouth veneration of clowns. How lonely it has been since then. How it has called out for those dreaming souls who would find once again its effigies, its hidden totems of slate, the small crude idols that mimic its image. A terrible and yet a wondrous thing. I saw it, on her cloudy eye, and I heard it call my name. Oh, Simon, I would kneel before it if I could, on mine ancient aching knees."

"That's easy enough. It's priestess awaits you, inside the old ruined bridge that spans the Quamish." He tenderly touched the bruised area around the fellow's eye. "Her kiss you have already experienced. You will find her generous in assisting your veneration for Sadoqua. Get thee hence."

Vombic hesitated for a moment, and then fled. The beast reached into a jacket pocket and produced his ebony flute. He kissed the instrument, then held it to the moon, that globe of dead refraction, whose waves of lunar light seemed to sway in following the signals formed by the talons of Simon's free hand.

VI.

(From the Notes of Thaddaeus Vombic)

I fled that place and from my home, and led by moonlight I reached the river. I have always loved the Quamish, for it seemed one of the only things in Sesqua Valley that was truly *natural.* There was nothing weird about it (as I had learned what weirdness was from the times I escaped the valley and observed the outside world). And so I followed the river as it rushed past meadow, alongside railroad tracks, to the rarely used road that led to the old covered bridge. I marvel, actually, that the bridge still stands—or, rather, sags; for it was ancient in those days of my youth when I would play beside it. Like so many things in the valley, it has its mysteries, its secrets. We children were warned not to enter it (because it was unsound, we were told, and we might injure ourselves by falling through its floor into the water), and for the most part we weren't tempted to enter its confines. One learns at an early age to heed such warning pertaining to certain sections of the valley, especially those regions that feel too deeply Selta's shadow. I never entered the bridge, but there were times as I played near it when I would *listen* to that which dwelt inside it—to the scampering footfalls, the hushed tittering.

I finally came to the place where the road ends into a steep decline along the river's edge. The moon seemed awfully bright, and I hesitated so to study it. And some queer emotion made me fall to my knees and prepare to pray, as father had taught me. But, wasn't it funny, the way I couldn't find the words of prayer, or the image of whatever I was supposed to pray to? All I could see when I shut my eyes was the image on Molly's jeweled eye—and I still wasn't certain that I wanted to pray to *that!* So I raised my bowed head and simply stayed there on my knees, listening to the valley's quiet. Oh, it was so silent, as if Sesqua Valley was holding its breath.

Well, I stayed there on my knees, listening and watching the weird trees gently moving in the wind. (Was there a wind?) I couldn't remember those trees being there before, but it had been a long while since I had last visited the spot, since in my old age I've found that I like to simply stay at home and read from my vast library—or eat—or take naps. I adore taking naps! Suddenly, a sound came to me, from within the entrance of the bridge. It was chanting, soft and low, a common enough sound in the valley; but this was even more peculiar than the usual thing. Can't quite explain it. The quiet voices were far more genteel than the normal howling of queer phrases that one is wont to hear from places in the woods. I felt a kind of enchantment, really, as I listened to it, and so I picked myself up and took my arthritic limbs to the bridge, stepping over a small mound of ash on my way to the covered entrance.

Well, I stepped onto the wooden planks that are the structure's floor, and at first I couldn't see much. Something flopped near my shoes, one of those large frogs or toads that one sees near the swamp. I'd never really seen one up close before, because I avoid the swamp like the plague; and I was rather taken aback by the aspect of the creature's odd smiling face. Why, it looked just like a wrinkled new-born babe who seemed very pleased with having had escaped the womb. And then the ugly slit that was its mouth parted, and it made a whispered sound; and I swear that the noise it made was the faint murmuring of my name! Confused, I bent down next to it and was about to pet the damn thing when it bounced away so to caper with a crowd of its kindred that were softly chanting before the shapeless bulk that nestled in deep darkness.

I took out my pocket torch and lit it up, and the huddled figure raised one hand to the crystal blue eye set deep within its dark shifting face. The thing called my name, in a voice I thought I recognized.

"Molly?"

"We are here, Thaddaeus, ever pleased with thy company. Come close, that we may kiss thee."

I stalked to her, and my eyes began to sort of adjust to the darkness. I saw her, that poor malformed girl. In one extended arm she cradled the ancient idol that she had found in whatever region she had wandered to. How pecular it was, that the longer I looked at her, the easier it was to see her spreading bulk, the undulating face, the gem that gleamed in her eye-socket. Why, was it from that piece of jeweled rock that a faint blue phosphorescence filtered, subtly illuminating the place? So it seems in memory. I could not take my eyes from that gem.

"It is wonderful, is it not, Thaddaeus? I have admired its luster for an eternity, have gazed at it for so long a time that I have burned the core of my essence onto the smooth cold surface. It has been admired by many, and knelt before in veneration. The wizard who penned Y^e *Livre d'Eibon* named it 'the eye of Tsathoggua'—and so it is, for I live in portion upon it. When we had it placed, in Prague, into my human socket, it rooted an influence to mine internal quiddity, as thus we are magnificently transformed. We are wondrous and seductive, and you will adore us."

I could not move as I watched her grope in the dark for something near to her, and I silently watched as her dark inhuman hand took up a ritual dagger.

"Give us thy human hand," she demanded. Hesitantly, I did so, and winced as the blade sliced deep into my palm, forming an odd symbol. Her mouth, so awfully enlarged, opened, and the loathsome appendage that was her transformed tongue touched my hand. And—good Jesu!—I wept; for something in the press of that ghastly muscle against my flesh reminded me of Molly's kiss.

Shifting, she oozed nearer, resting her malformed head in my lap. "The Old One requests new sacrifice, and appoint thee our servitor. No, fear not, nor be amazed. You loved us once, dost thou remember? Love us again, Thaddaeus. We require the scent of human sacrifice, the sweetness of which hath been denied us ever long. Do this as remembrance of our old affection."

One paw brought forth the heavy idol, which was offered me. I took hold of it, the weighty thing, and watched as her head slipped off my lap, onto the floor. I stared at that face, and I wept as it suddenly smiled; for in that smile I saw Molly, the innocent young girl whom I had cherished.

"Do this," she begged. Blinking tears, I lifted the elder idol high above me, then brought it savagely downward, crushing the pleading face. I shall always be haunted by the sound of that destruction. Sobbing, I lifted the gore-stained idol from the mess that once had been a face.

It sifted toward me, the scent of sacrifice, sweet and pungent at the same time. And it glistened in the gore, that rare gem. Oh, it was seductive. I pulled it from the pool of blood and kissed away that crimson liquid with which it had been stained. I gazed unto its surface and saw thereon the outré clouds that parted so as to reveal the supernal countenance that I idolized. I brought that blasphemous jewel to my face, my face that cooled at its touch, with a chilliness like I had felt when I touched the young girl's altered visage. Oh, she had worn it, the sacred gem, within her socket, and it had spawned within her brain the glorious history of the neglected god. She had tasted the sweetness of sacrifice, and had known the secrets spawned in cosmic eternity, an intoxicating wisdom. A wonder that could be mine.

Oh, yes. I began to understand Simon's mania for arcane wonders. I wanted—so—to experience such phenomenon. Thus, with my free hand, I found the ritual dagger with which a potent symbol had been etched into my palm, a carving that called my sorry soul. I picked up the knife and touched my tongue to a residue of my sweet blood. I placed the point's sharp steel beneath my eye, to the place where, recently, the beast of Sesqua Valley had minutely pierced my skin with his talon. I gently pushed the dagger into my bruised skin, that flesh that had experienced Molly's savage kissing. And yet something—some wretched vestige of human weakness—stayed my hand.

I heard behind me the ghostly playing of his daemon-flute. I sensed him kneel beside me. His talons took the dagger from my grasp. "My dear Thaddaeus," the beast whispered, "allow me to assist."

The strange Dark Folk

I.

The darkened woodland was moist with heavy mist, an emanation that seemed born from the very trunks of trees, those moist trunks that now and then he would pause to peer at. The subtle carvings etched on various trunks disturbed him, for he seemed to remember these designs from dim and haunting dreams. Stopping to place a palm against one disfigured trunk, the young creature closed his eyes and saw an image much like the place wherein he wandered; but a place that was curiously altered, as only dreams can transmute.

Something moist clasped against his face. A leaf, soft and scented, that had drifted to him from some unseen limb. Reaching for it, he wiped its essence into his skin, then pushed away from where he stood so as to continue his journey. Beyond, in the heavily misted places he could not see, he sensed other beings that stealthily watched his progress. Indeed, the entire woodland seemed a magnificently sentient thing, a beast composed of myriad components of beings, separate creatures that shared one single soul. It was a soul that he could almost feel as he placed his feet one after the other on a ground that was littered with nature's fragrant debris.

Stepping out of the woods, he encountered hazy daylight. Although the sun was hidden behind an expanse of crawling clouds, the small lake's water sparkled at its very surface, while beneath that surface he seemed to detect moving shadow, shapeless and indistinct. The two-story cabin stood just beyond the lake, and he gazed for a long time at the yellow wood with which the structure had been crafted. In front of it stood three totems, two of which were slanted at such precarious tilts that the lad was amazed they had not toppled to the ground. The third totem, close to the cabin and standing thirty feet, looked very strange; and as he walked nearer he saw that it was in fact an amazing statue of a lean seraph, with two wings covering its face, two wings covering genitalia, and two wings spread outward as if the beast were preparing to take flight.

From inside the cabin he could hear the sound of chanting. Creeping closer to a window, he looked into a room weirdly lit with greenish illumination. Dimly, he could see the figure seated on the floor, rocking to and fro, a figure that seemed suddenly to sense that he was watching. She turned her large face to his, smiled, and with waving hand motioned for him to enter her abode. The cabin door, which he was certain had been shut, now stood slightly open, and after a moment's hesitation he stepped to it and pushed at it. Gingerly, he entered the large room and stood for a moment to allow his eyes to grow accustomed to the aura of this outré habitation. Deeply, he breathed, drinking in the spiced air.

The woman turned her eyes to him, and for a moment he was blinded by a piercing light that emanated from the woman's face. When at last he removed his hand from his eyes, he discovered that he was somehow nearer to the person who sat on the floor before a glowing candle. Slowly, he knelt before the candle, watching its green flame.

"Are you the witch Marianne Snyde?" he whispered. In answer the woman reached for the candle's flame, a flame that hopped onto her fingers, fingers that moved to his mouth, that mouth that opened and ate fire. He shivered.

"You're with that traveling troupe of carnies, yes?"

"We're not carnies," he spoke, feeling the essence of what he had swallowed seep into his mortal liquid and flow within his veins. "We're a sideshow of human curiosities."

She smiled as she studied the gnome before her, the shaggy beast with black eyes. "You're not human," she indifferently replied. "You're a creature of this valley, long lost and now returned unto us." Confusion clouded his colorless eyes. "What brings you to Sesqua Valley?"

"I suggested it. I found a map on one of the letters my father wrote to my mother."

"Your father?"

"Yes. William Davis Manly."

It was the woman's turn to shiver. She watched as the one who knelt before her reached into his tote bag and pulled from it a bundle of letters that had been bound together with a piece of mauve ribbon. Without asking, she grabbed the packet of epistles and slipped one from the others, removed it from its tattered envelope and read. "Why do you call the poet your sire?"

"I asked mom once who these letters were from, and she said they came from the one from whom I was born."

Excitedly, the witch rose and glided to the window, where she examined the epistle in muted sunlight. "And your mother was Rachel Kemp?"

"Yes, and you knew her, because she and dad wrote about you in some of those letters."

"So they did," she chuckled. "But these were written long ago. You've taken your time in locating us."

He was silent for some minutes, turning his eyes to the window by which she stood. "I was afraid, because of dreams. Mom would sometimes draw pictures of the valley, and in some of them there would be this weird red daemon that really terrified me! I had the most awful nightmares about it. It was weird finally to come to this place and see a version of that daemon, in the form of a white mountain with twin peaks! Dad wrote about that mountain in some of the poems he sent to mom, but he always called it by some goofy name—Khroyd'hon."

"Yes, he referred to Selta by its dream name, always." She narrowed her eyes at him. "You have *poems* by William Davis Manly?"

"Oh, yeah," the lad said, reaching into his bag and taking from it a cardboard folder. "Mom kept them in this."

Marianne carefully leafed through the pages of yellowing lined paper, stopping only when she came upon a piece of free verse that spoke in a language with which she had been intimately familiar by way of constant reading of a volume of poems. She spoke a few lines aloud:

> "And that which thou hast stolen must return,
> Return to danse upon death's chilly ground,
> The hungry ground beneath which fitfully
> It dreams . . ."

The shaggy young beast smiled. "I always liked that one. Sometimes, when I was alone on one of my walks, I would read it and dance on the ground to imaginary music. Mom caught me at it once, and she gave me such a weird look that I thought she was angry with me for sneaking into her stuff and taking the poem; but instead of yelling at me she came and danced with me, humming a really strange little tune." He closed his eyes, trying to remember. A few notes of whispered song emerged from his mouth. Smiling, Marianne joined in his humming, and he ceased his song, amazed that this stranger knew the dimly remembered tune. Grinning, she skipped to him, took hold of his hands, and began to dance.

Suddenly, the witch stood still, gazing intently at her young companion. "There is a place I want you to see, and a person to whom I want you to show these poems. Will you come with me?"

"Certainly," he replied.

The woman wrapped a shawl around her shoulders, yet kept her naked feet unshod. Taking his hand, she led him outdoors, into gathering darkness. A faint mist was rising from the lake, and a darker haze hugged the woodland into which they wandered. The lad's keen ears were alert for any sound or sign of life, but the one sound was that of soft wind sighing through the trees.

"And what do you call yourself, Master Kemp?"

"Huh? Oh, I'm Victor. Victor Manly Kemp."

A tall dark bulk appeared, and Victor gazed in wonder at the old round tower of ancient brick. "Go ahead of me, Master Kemp. There's something I need to perform before entering. Climb the winding steps until you reach the topmost platform. I'll join you momentarily."

He hesitated, suddenly unsure, slightly fearful. Smiling, the woman knelt before him, dug her fingers into the ground, brought up a handful of dirt which she sprinkled over his head. He listened to her whispered words, and closed his eyes as her sullied hand pressed against his face and seemed to write upon it. "Go," she commanded, then poked a finger into the ground and began to write into it.

Timidly, he entered through the arched threshold and began to climb the winding steps. At one point he came upon an opening in the surface of the wall, a cavity of blackness into which he tried to peer. A musty scent came from the place of darkness, a smell that somehow seemed familiar, like a memory of childhood. Carefully, he crept through the hole, into the unseen space.

He didn't venture far into the place, for a sense of caution gave him pause; and when something soft and padded touched his face, Victor yelped and backed away, out of the hole, climbing on hands and knees up the remaining steps, until he reached a wooden circular floor.

Victor heard the other before he saw him, a faint humming and sighing of an alien tongue. And then a face that wore an outlandish strangeness turned and gazed at him with gleaming silver eyes. "What the devil do you want? And why are you so absurdly attired? You're a strange wee one."

The lad tried to speak, but it came out weirdly. "Excuse me, sir."

"Good Yuggoth, it speaks." The figure slowly rose and sauntered to the edge of the steps up which Victor had crept. Curiosity and confusion mingled in the wondrous eyes. "Who are you, sirrah? And why do you reek of witch-fire? Are you some familiar of that Snyde hag?"

Candlelight and shadow formed on the floor from behind the cowering lad, and a friendly hand patted Victor's hair and reached under an arm, helping the boy to his feet. Victor leaned against the warm form of the woman who held a candlestick. Reaching into his shoulder bag, he produced the Manly poems and offered them to the tall lean beast. "I'm supposed to show you these." He watched, slightly smiling, as the grotesque face curled in confusion, and he wanted to laugh when the wide bestial mouth gasped in perplexity.

"Explain this, hag," said Simon Gregory Williams.

"Certainly, beast," Marianne complacently replied. "This young fellow is Victor Manly Kemp, a member of the sideshow that is taking a rest stop in the meadow. His mother was Rachel Kemp."

"A pox on her name," Simon subtly snarled. "So, this is the piece of valley that she stole when she left us, is it?"

"Even so. And the poems, he believes, are the work of his sire, William Davis Manly. You'll remember that she and Manly were intimate friends. No doubt they corresponded after she left the valley."

"I have some of my father's letters."

Simon's eyes glowed with emotion. He held out a palm, and Victor placed a letter into it. "Yes, it's his hand. Undated, as was his manner. Listen to this, hag. 'The dark one whom thou hath taken will slumber for three years, during which time you will whisper the ritual that will feed its dreams. When it awakens there will be no remembrance of what it is or from whence it hath been born. But the valley will call to it in deepest dream, and it cannot choose but eventually find its way homeward. You are mortal, sweet heart, and one day will expire. If you are kind, you will return the dark one to us before such an event occurs. But kindness was ne'er one of your features, alas. I will come to you in autumn, and together we will discuss this further.'" Simon looked at Victor with slanted eyes. "What became of your mammy?"

"She fell to her death from a mountain's cliff," Victor quietly replied. "We miss her horribly."

"We?" Simon asked.

"The troupe. She was our soothsayer."

"How apropos," Simon sneered. "You taught her well, hag."

"She had a natural gift."

"Well," the tall creature sighed. "I'll take these poems and that parcel of epistles. Manly's reputation has already brought more than enough trouble to this town, ever since that fool Nathan published that collection of poetry shortly after Manly vanished."

"You can't take my stuff. He was my father. These belong to me."

"He was not your sire. The children of Sesqua Valley do not procreate. Haven't you explained his origin?"

Victor glanced at Marianne. "She said some crazy stuff about my not being human, that I belonged to the valley or some such thing."

"Victor, what is your role in this sideshow? What is your billing?"

"I'm kind of a missing link, because of my features, the fur and all that."

"How old are you?"

Sadly, he lowered his head. "I don't know. I was never told. Mom and I never celebrated things like birthdays or other holidays. Useless twaddle, she called it."

Simon knelt before him and leaned so that his face was almost touching Victor's. "You were stolen from us in 1947. In 1951, William Davis Manly disappeared, although the date has been altered in various accounts, for reasons of our own. Manly did not return unto the valley's shadow, as is our wont. He vanished, as you did. Unlike you, he has never returned. He was a special son, and his absence has left a bruise on Sesqua's heart, that heart that is buried beneath the place of human death, that place where your kind dance at moonglow so as to soothe the valley's ache." Victor frowned in utter confusion at this outlandish babble. "I am not certain that you and Rachel are connected to William's mysterious fate; but I find it curious, this sudden revelation of their prolonged intimacy. I shall study these poems and epistles with great care for some clue."

"Well, I want them back before we leave. The sideshow has a gig in Seattle in three days."

Simon lifted his eyes to Marianne's, and they shared a cryptic smile. Gently, Simon raised a large sallow hand and placed it over Victor's face. There came from the strange beast's flesh a potent scent, a smell that was the essence of Sesqua Valley. Breathing deeply, Victor brought forth two tiny paws, clasping them over Simon's hand. The young one drank in the heady odor, that fragrance that suddenly smelled like home.

II.

He shifted in his bed of straw, stretching out of somnolence. And then he stilled; for outside his barred wagon there came an unfamiliar sound, the prancing of tiny feet. The sound surrounded him, moving around the ancient circus wagon that was his home, his stage. The valley air, so sweet, so curiously weighty in his mouth, moved over his face, like a hand's caress. From the corner of his vision he could see the twin peaks of the white mountain, that mountain that seemed to drink the moonlight and sparkle in ecstasy. And then the sky darkened, and the sound of dancing fled at the fall of a heavier foot. The sinister painted face blocked the mountain from Victor's view.

"You were late getting back," said Gregory's low voice, his dark eyes almost hidden by the black greasepaint that encircled them. "Where were you all day?"

"I met an old friend," Victor lied, "and spent the day with her."

The sardonic clown slightly sneered. "Huh. Is that why you insisted we camp in this forgotten hole, some old girlfriend? I thought you were up to something."

"Don't be stupid," came the youth's defensive reply. "She was pals with my mother, way back. I wasn't even sure if this was where she lived. We had to stop somewhere, what's wrong with here?" He watched as the clown produced a pack of cigarettes and lit up one slim cylinder.

"This is a queer place. That crowd tonight—phew! Some of those mugs were uglier than yours. That tall skinny guy, did you see his face? Ugh! When he took out that flute and started to serenade you I wanted to sock him, he looked so superior and pleased with himself." Gregory smiled with rather heartless mirth. "That was, comical, you trying to dance to his stupid music. Fumbling around on your bed of straw."

"It was a weird rhythm. I couldn't find my way into it. But I liked it, his music."

"Did you notice the way some of those freaks were looking at you? Flipping weird."

"People are always looking at me, Greg. That's why you hired me."

"Nah, this was different, weird." He sucked on his fag, then loudly exhaled a cloud of smoke. "I was watching them. Some of those freaks would stare at you, then turn to each other and nod, like they were in on some joke or something. Didn't like it, not one bit." He took a final drag on his cigarette, then tossed the butt to the ground, where it looked offensively out of place. The mirthless man crushed the butt with an oversized shoe, then paused and examined more carefully the ground. "Dude, have you been jogging around your wagon?"

"What?" Victor laughed.

"Check it out," the clown said, bending low. "Your footprints are all over the place, like you've been hopping around your wagon."

"They're not mine . . ."

"Don't be stupid. Who else leaves footprints like that? Maybe you've been dancing in your sleep?"

"Don't you be crazy," Victor replied, frowning at the indentations in the dirt.

"Whatever. I gotta go remove my face and get some shut-eye. We move out early in the morning." The fellow foolishly yawned, then danced mockingly away, winking and waving. Victor opened the panel that served as door and leapt out of his wagon, onto soft sod. Falling to his knees, he placed a hand into one of the shallows in the ground. From somewhere high on the white mountain, a creature sang to darkness. The wind came suddenly up, seeming to lift the lad to his feet and push him into the dense woodland. Victor listened as the wind—and something else—moved through the tops of trees. He followed a path that led to a clump of extremely soft moss, a sweet-smelling bed onto which he stretched, strangely drowsy. The windsong was a soothing *berceuse,* beneath which he fancied that he could faintly hear his mother's voice. Thus lulled by enchantment, he shut his eyes. Had those eyes stayed opened, they would have imagined that the lowest boughs moved as if to touch his sleeping face.

From somewhere close at hand there came a song of fluted music, from one who leaned against a tree. The silver eyes watched as a mauve mist slid closer, finally enveloping the sleeping youth. In slumber, the small mouth sucked in the tainted air.

The beast who played the fluted tones set his ebony instrument upon a thick low branch, then bent beside the boy and touched talons to the sleeping eyes. The gnome awoke, startled, and stared into the moving vapor that poured from trees, from earth, from sky. He watched as she came to him in that brume, the woman of enchantment. Without pause she reached and pulled him up by the hair of his head, and together they floated in undulating shadow, stopping only when they came to a small circular clearing of perfect symmetry. Tenderly,

Marianne guided Victor to the center of the clearing and knelt with him before the squat red stump of a felled spruce. This shattered vestige was of shocking hue, the likes of which he had never seen. Encircling it were the dry dead remnants of what had once been fleshy mushrooms. From out the middle of the residual of wood there issued a growth of sickly yellow leaves and small black blossoms, florets whose petals were stained with wet red dew.

The witch stroked one blossom with a pale hand, and the boy saw that hand come away stained with crimson. He watched that hand swim toward him through the foggy air, then shut his eyes to the touch of cool rough flesh and soft warm liquid. The heavy stuff was on his face; it wormed over his features and sank beneath his pores. As Marianne kept her hand upon him, Victor could hear the sound that surrounded them, the soft dancing of padded feet that moved to the enchantment of the beast who had once more picked up his flute, the music that his mother had hummed as cradlesong.

He opened his eyes, but the mist was so close and so heavy that all he could discern were the small dark shapes that pranced just outside the circle of dead mushrooms in which he and the woman knelt. But then a place in the foggy air seemed to clear, and Victor watched the shape that achingly crawled toward them, the misshapen bulk that seemed to be composed of vines, leaves, bark, sod, of all the elements with which the valley had been formed. It clumsily entered the circle, and a withered paw reached into the clump of leaves and blossoms. The boy watched as that awful appendage reached for his face and smeared the crimson liquid just above his eyes. He felt that thick liquid spill slowly to his eyes, those eyes that began to blur as he tried to stare at the creature's face, that visage composed of Sesqua Valley. And then the face smiled at him, and as he recognized that smile, his tears mingled with tiny streams of blood.

III.

Gregory slammed shut the door to Victor's wagon and turned to face the Lizard. One would have thought, to look at him, that Gregory wore his makeup still; but then one realised that the chalky pallor of his face was its natural complexion, that the dark hollows into which his eyes were sunk was not an effect of paint and powder. The frizzy red hair, so wild and unkempt, could have been mistaken for a zany wig, and when one observed the bare feet, one knew that the absurdly oversized shoes that seemed part of a clown's costume served a necessary function. "Where the hell is he, Krug? He's riding with you to Seattle."

The Lizard shrugged. "Ain't seen him since yesterday."

"Screw this!" Gregory thundered. "He knew we'd be leaving at first light. Fine, let him walk to Seattle, we're moving out." Kicking a wagon wheel and then wincing in pain, the boss man pushed the other gentleman out of his way. Shrugging, the Lizard shut and locked the wagon door, then sauntered to a small crowd of silent on-lookers of fellow freaks. An hour later the wagons, caravans and pick-up truck departed the scene, and Sesqua Valley seemed to sigh with relief.

Victor awoke in an attic room in Marianne's cottage, to breakfast smells. He was, in fact, quite hungry, and so he hopped into his clothes and cautiously climbed down the ladder-like steps to the lower region. His new friend smiled at him and motioned toward a table that was littered with food, the likes of which he had never seen. From the look of it, others had earlier breakfasted, leaving empty plates and bowls. Victor ate the oddly-shaped rolls and dipped a wooden spoon into a bowl of purple gruel.

Having eaten his fill, the youngster sat on a sunny spot on the soft wooden floor, fingering titles on the lower shelf of a bookcase. Pulling out a volume bound in purple cloth, he opened it and saw that it was a collection of poetry and sketches by William Davis Manly, published in 1955. "Tell me about my father," he said to Marianne.

"William Davis Manly was not your father, Victor," she informed him, smiling at his sudden frown. "He was your brother of the valley."

"I don't know what that means."

"You will, in time. You were stolen from us, by Rachel Kemp, who was not born of Sesqua's shadow, but had been adopted by the valley. She was one of our wild ones, and thought that she could bend rules. An altercation with Simon caused her to act foolishly. And so she left us, and took you with her when you were but newly-spawned. You say that she is dead."

"She fell off a cliff. We found her clothing at the edge, but her body was never found. She was cool. She could read palms, but her specialty was reading eyes. I miss her. I had the weirdest dream about her last night. She came back to me, but she looked all distorted, like she was composed of vines and mud and stuff. Weird."

Marianne shut her eyes and tilted her head. "She had a wonderful gift, and was much in the company of our beloved poet, Manly. We never understood their relationship. He tried his best to convince her to return, and when he left us, we took for granted that he went to seek her. Yet he never returned."

"So they both vanished. Wish I could have known him. I see him sometimes in my dreams, but his face is always kind of blurry. It's frustrating, because I feel this deep affection for him, although I never knew him, and I want to see his face." She watched as he gazed into space, and knew that he was day-dreaming, seeking in memory for Manly's face.

"Come," she said, standing and reaching for his hand. Rising, he followed her out of the lakeside cottage, through the woods to the center of town. They entered the old cemetery, and Marianne took him to a statue. Victor looked at the name etched upon the base: "William Davis Manly, Poet and Brother." Pregnant with sudden emotion, Victor went to the statue and reverently put his hand to its stone.

"What are you doing there?" came Simon's deep voice.

Victor turned and waved. "It's William Davis Manly. He kind of looks like you, Simon. Come on." And he held to the tall lean fellow a beckoning paw.

"He won't enter," Marianne softly informed him. "There are two places where the children of Sesqua Valley do not feel comfortable. The mountain is one such place; this is another."

"But I'm a child of Sesqua Valley," Victor protested. "I don't feel weird being here." Then he turned and shouted, "Come on, Simon, don't be a wuss."

Marianne softly laughed. "Yes, Simon, don't be a wuss."

"Go to oblivion, hag," the beast retorted. And then he stood very still as Victor began to dance around the statue, whistling a haunting tune. Marianne watched with wonder gleaming in her eyes, and then she too began to dance and whistle. Simon watched, and felt a strange aching in his stubborn soul. He felt the valley wind push to him and echo the tune at his large ears. He felt it coax him onto the forbidden sod. Feeling a multitude of queer emotions, the beast hesitantly joined in the danse, bringing forth his ebony flute and playing upon it the wondrous melody. Beneath them, they could feel the heartbeat of Sesqua Valley, pulsing in time to their danse.

IV.

An evening came when Simon watched a pick-up trunk enter town and stop in front of the building that served as hotel and general store. He watched the fellow who vacated the vehicle and scanned the area. Subtly growling, the beast casually walked to the place where the other stood and nodded to him.

"I'm looking for a pal of mine," Gregory said. "Small hairy kid, name of Victor Kemp. He was with us a couple weeks ago, when our company was parked in your meadow yonder."

"Ah, yes, young Victor, Rachel's boy."

"You knew Rachel?"

Simon shrugged. "Many years ago, when she resided here. If you're looking for Victor, you might try the old cemetery down that road. Do you know it?"

"I kind of remember it. Is that where he hangs out? Freaking morbid, that kid. We want him to go with us to Oregon, to a gig in Portland. He was a main attraction, people love to watch him dance on his bed of straw. They think he's really some kind of missing link, something close to our hairy old ancestors. Funny what people want to believe. Where is this graveyard, then?"

"Come, sirrah. I'll show you."

"Thanks," said the clown man. "Weird, I had the hardest time remembering this place; then I came on some sketches I had made of that damn mountain, and all of a sudden I remembered how to get here. I've had some freaking weird dreams about that mountain, I can tell you."

"Really?" Simon casually replied. "Well, you were fated to find us. Here we are." And yet he hesitated, not certain that he could stepped onto the hallowed sod without the support of others of his kind. But when he looked into the smug face of the fellow at his side, he knew his course. He knew what was expected of him by Sesqua Valley.

"I don't see him," Gregory said.

"He sometimes naps nearby that mound, the one from which that curious pillar extends. Do you see it? Yes, it is a queer kind of marker. It's said to be the burial place of one of the first white men to enter the valley, one of those pioneers who recklessly ignored their dark dreams and settled here, and thus began to stir things up."

"What the hell are you yammering about?" Gregory snarled, looking around and only half-listening to his host.

Ignoring the other, Simon sat upon the mound and gazed reverently at the ancient stone pillar, upon which had been etched a series of
odd figures that looked like some sort of alien alphabet. "That's when I
awoke, you see, and slithered forth from the shadowed realm. My, how
long ago it was."

"You're a weird cuss," Gregory sneered, mocking the beast. "Look,
he ain't here, and I ain't got time to listen to your tales. I need to find
that lout and take him with me."

"Oh, surely you have time to rest after your long journey. Come,
recline upon this soft, soft sod. There, isn't it rather comfortable?
Doesn't it relax? And doesn't it smell good? Say, why don't we climb to
the top. Perhaps from there we'll be able to see that little imp of yours."

Something in Simon's tone soothed Gregory's violent brain, and
the villain followed as Simon climbed up to the stone pillar, against
which he leaned his head. Gregory ran a ragged hand over the pillar's
surface, and shivered. "Damn thing feels really cold. It looks freakin'
ancient, don't it?"

"Freakin' ancient," Simon agreed. "The story is that if you place
your head against its surface, it makes you dream. Of what do you
dream, sirrah?"

Gregory lustfully smiled. "Of the day when my ship comes in.
Someday, I'm gonna make real money. Oh, we make good with our gig,
especially when the p. c. crowd come and boycott us. That's always
good for business."

"You said earlier that you dreamt of our mountain."

Lazily, Gregory leaned his large head against the pillar, and his eyes
observed the mountain's white surface against a sky that began to darken.
"Yeah. It kinda fascinates. I wish I had a camera. I made some sketches
of it when we was here earlier. It almost looks alive, don't it, dude?"

"Almost," the beast acquiesced.

"Man, this dirt is soft. Must be some sand in it." He pushed his
hand into the mound, and was amazed at how deeply it sank. Then he
went to pull it free, and became alarmed when something, some force,
tugged him deeper. "What the hell . . .?"

"Peculiar, isn't it?" Simon ventured, digging into the soft stuff and
bringing up a handful, which he gracefully spilled through his fingers.
"It almost feels hungry, this place. As if it would devour one. Don't you
find?"

Ignoring Simon, the outsider got onto his knees and tried to push free of the force that held him, only to feel his other hand sink easily into the mound. Softly, the dirt on which he knelt began to shift, to sift, to spill over him as he slowly began to sink into the moving surface. Simon smiled as the outsider's foolish face glared at him in alarm. Bringing lips together, Simon whistled an ancient tune, and as the place grew darker, Gregory turned to watch the small figures that suddenly surrounded the mound, those small shaggy things, one of which gleamed at him with eyes that were familiar. The outsider tried to shout at Victor, but was utterly ignored, and soon he was so deeply embedded into the sifting stuff that the taste of dirt violated his mouth.

He sank, pulled by the hungry place, that place that weirdly pulsed with ancient heartbeat as it fed. His last sight was of Simon's mocking face, and of the mountain behind the beast.

V.

Victor followed his friends into the woodland, into the moving mist that came to meet them. Memory was returning, of his previous existence in this supernatural place. He knew that this mauve mist would usher him into the shadowed realm of Sesqua Valley, that realm from which he had been born. It welcomed him, this dreamland, where nature was transmuted and glorified. He stared at the dream aspect of Mount Selta, at the stone that was no longer sparkling white but red. He watched the twin peaks that subtly moved against a haunted sky.

Victor watched the hazy figures that slowly approached him from the shadowed mist. Marianne was beautifully nude, and she beautifully smiled as Victor recognized the creature at her side, the mortal who had been adopted by the valley, who had recklessly wandered from these magical confines, who had stolen one of the valley's strange dark children. Victor danced to that creature, that woman who had returned unto the valley, who now wore aspects of the valley's sinister essence. He laughed as the creature brought a hand to his face, a hand composed of transformed flesh, of vines and living mud. He happily howled as the petals that were lips kissed his brow, as all around him his kindred dansed to the song of Simon's flute.

Above them, a mountain walked.

Your Metamorphic Moon

Fear not, for you shall find your fate anon,
Beneath the arch'd peaks of antique Khroyd'hon.
—*William Davis Manly*

I.

The goth/punk girl, just turned twenty-one, entered Sesqua Valley a little before sunset, fatigued from hours on the road. As promised, her mother had given her $20,000 of "coming of age" money (hoping, her daughter was certain, that the money would be spent so as to procure a new, "less morbid" wardrobe, to attain maturity by shearing the black dreadlocks—into which petite porcelain skulls had been braided—so as to return the hair to its natural blonde shade). Instead, Aubrey Brood had borrowed her boyfriend's band touring van and set off on a little tour of small-town Amerika. It charmed the hard-edge city girl in her to come across one of those small towns that scattered the Northwest, to shop in the wee stores and eat delicious home-style cooking. And although not an exhibitionist, it amused her to see the reactions to her plastic mini-skirts and bondage gear as she sat sipping coffee with a bunch of mumbling lumberjacks.

It was growing late as the van entered into the valley, and she was weary at the wheel. She knew (dimly) where she was, but when she parked alongside the road and checked her map, she could find no indication of the valley she had entered or the small town spread before her. She pushed open the van's door and moaned at the tension in her muscles as she climbed out onto the rocky road. She paused momentarily as she inhaled the valley air, puzzled by its cloying heaviness, its unnatural surfeit of sweetness that was, at first, difficult to breathe in. Instinctively, she reached into her skull-bag and brought out an inhaler—just in case she needed it.

She scanned the ground for some specimens of rocks, for it had become a hobby of hers, amateur sculptor that she was, to carve weird faces and daemons (and, yes, skulls) out of the more interestingly shaded and shaped stones that she found on her journey. This was a habit she started while in her early teens, having been inspired by the jacket of an old book from the 1940s in her mom's personal collection of supernatural fiction. She was squatting among the rocks when she heard the curious wailing sound that issued from somewhere on the white mountain that she had vaguely noticed when entering the valley. Now she looked steadily at that twin-peaked titan, and something in its nature so stunned her that, gasping, she lost her balance and fell among the stones. The inhaler that was still in her hand found its way to her mouth, and she gulped two sprays of its contents.

Aubrey concentrated on calming her breathing, then reached into her bag for her photo-phone. How could she not have noticed this magnificent mountain straightaway? The longer she looked at it, the more fantastic a thing it appeared to her. At this angle it almost seemed, to her over-imaginative mind, a hunkering daemon, slumbering, with the two arched peaks seeming like the tips of folded wings on the behemoth's shoulders. Aiming her phone and peering through the camera lens, she took a photo, then looked at the phone's diminutive screen; and she frowned at the indistinct blur that was the image she had photographed.

"Hell, this sucks," she grumbled, smacking the phone against one palm, then aiming it once more at the mountain—and shrieking at the ogre that she unexpectedly found standing in the way.

"Are you quite all right?" asked the goblin, not moving.

"Dude, you scared the living piss outa me!" And then she began to laugh heartily and struggled to raise herself from the stony ground (not easily accomplished in stiletto heels). Aubrey watched the fellow cautiously approach her, and hesitated before accepting the proffered hand. (How smooth was his sallow flesh to the touch, more like the hide of a beast than the flesh of a human hand.)

"And what is that interesting gadget in your hand?"

"My phone? It's one of those photo-phones that have become so popular. Smile." And before he understood her intention, Aubrey brought the gadget to her eye, aimed, and took a photo. Smiling, she showed the gentleman his image on the phone's tiny screen, wondering at the disconcerting grimace on the fellow's odd face. "Don't like having your photo taken, huh?"

"I have never had my picture 'taken,' as you say. I am merely a bit uneasy at the idea of it." And yet, she noticed, he seemed rather fascinated with his peculiar image, unable to take his eyes from it.

"Like those tribes in Africa, who fear that a part of their soul is stolen whenever they're photographed?"

"Oh, that's not a worry," he assured her, gazing into her wide green eyes. "I have no soul to speak of." And then he smiled, and so did she, taking his comment as an odd attempt at humor. "I'm Simon Gregory Williams," he informed her.

"Aubrey Brood," she said. "So, what is this place? I didn't see a sign or anything."

"You have entered the Sesqua Valley."

"Ah," she said, nodding. "I couldn't find it named on the map." She watched the sky begin to darken. "Well, I've traveled enough for one day. Is there a motel or something down there, in town?"

"There's a hotel of sorts, but I believe it lacks vacancies. There is a rather delightful break-and-breakfast establishment conjoined with the old curiosity shop."

"That sounds cool. Can I give you a lift?"

Simon squinted at the van, then shook his head. "Thank you, no. I'm walking in an opposite direction. But do tell Mr. Creighton that Simon Williams sent you." And winking at her in a friendly, non-flirtatious way, Simon Williams turned away and began to walk toward the thick growth of nearby woodland.

"Thank you, Mister Freakoid," she whispered to herself, then returned to the van and drove it into town. The main avenue was of black pitch, and as she parked along the sidewalk it amazed her that the walkway was made of even planks of wood rather than cement. There were few people about, but one of them pointed her to the Old Curiosity Shop, and in the establishment's front window was a sign that read "Bed & Breakfast." A bell softly sounded as she opened the door and entered in, and she smiled at the sight before her. The large dimly-lit room was crammed with antiques of every kind. Near to her was an old nickelodeon, and dropping a nickel into its slot, she pressed her face to the viewer as the thing's gears began to click and grind. The image seemed like some very early bit of cinema, and she could not ascertain if it was an early movie or some kind of dated documentary. The camera showed an expanse of meadow on which there stood a tall monument or pillar of black stone. Some distance from the monolith there stood a fellow clad in 1930s fashion who was playing a flute, and around the tower of stone there danced a circle of children or dwarves who were swathed in dark shaggy costumes. The man who played the flute approached the camera, smiling and waving; and Aubrey was amazed at how much the fellow's features resembled those of Simon Gregory Williams. Then the screen went black and the machine stilled its activity.

"May I assist you?"

Aubrey turned and almost laughed out loud at the figure who stood within a darkened doorway. The man was delicious, and she wanted to hail him as Gothic Brother, despite what she took to be his great age, judging from the shock of matted ivory hair that framed his deathly-white face. The face was fabulous, containing a kind of wicked cunning in the curve of the sardonic lips. At first she thought that he wore a thick black kimono, but then realised that he was clad in some kind of caped coat. Atop his head was a slick beaver hat, and she wondered if the felted fur was authentic or false.

"Hi. I'm looking for a room for the night." She noticed the way he regarded her own unique attire, and so she added, "Simon Williams recommended you."

At this his smile widened, and she saw the twin rows of serrated teeth. Maybe he *was* seriously gothic and filed his teeth, she marveled. "Ah, you are acquainted with Simon. Excellent. Yes, I have a room. For one night?"

"Probably. I don't have any definite plans. I'm doing a little tour of the state, checking out small towns and things. Kind of a vacation. Do I pay in advance?"

He waved away her query and reached for an antique lantern. A tiny ember flamed beneath the protective case of cloudy glass, and the fellow turned a wee knob so that the flame grew brighter. "This way, Miss."

Aubrey followed him through the doorway and up a small dark stairway and down a narrow hallway. Opening a door, he entered a spacious room and switched on an overhead light that filled the room with dull illumination. She nodded approvingly as she looked about the quaintly-decorated chamber. "This is wonderful."

He waved a white hand toward the various candelabra. "Some find artificial light too severe, although the bulbs are of a very low wattage." He examined her once more, and smiled. "I am Leonidas Creighton,"

he informed, but did not move so as to touch hands. Aubrey introduced herself. "And are you an artist, Miss Brood? Young people of
your sartorial persuasion often are, I have found."

"Yeah, I like to sculpt."

Creighton beamed. "Ah, we have many such in the valley. You are
among aesthetic kindred." Turning, he began to close the door, then
paused. "The shop will be opened for another two hours, and then the
door is locked. There is a back entrance near to the stairway below, for
after hours activity."

Thank you, Leonidas," she said, loving the sound of his name on
her lips. His bizarre countenance regarded her familiar addressing of
him with a briefly quizzical expression; then he bowed and shut the
door.

She looked around the room, touching some of the charming (and
obviously antique) furnishings. "This is so bad ass," she quietly exclaimed, then went to the door and down the dark stairway, finding the
other door that took her outside. A tiny café reminded her of hunger,
and so she sat in solitude and ate an excellent repast, after which she
got supplies from the van, returned to her room and washed up.
Checking her watch, she saw that there was still time to investigate the
shop's museum of antiquities and curios, and so she found her way
through the dusky hallway, to the barely lit stairway (Mr. Creighton was
certainly saving money on electricity), and finally to the chamber of the
past. She found the room warmly lit by various antique lamps, beautifully preserved. The proprietor was nowhere at hand, and she was the
room's sole occupant; and this rather surprised her, for certainly the
room's contents must be worth a fortune. How could Creighton leave
such a cornucopia of valuable relics unattended?

She found a low table that was covered with cloth of black velvet,
upon which there sat a plethora of religious icons. She recognized Gan-
esha, but found this rendition of him rather diabolic, with ears absurdly
elongated and trunks looking especially wicked. Aubrey carefully reached
down to stroke a very androgynous replication of Shiva (the deity of
skulls, one of her absolute favorites), then touched an equally epicene six-
winged Seraph. She frowned at a rather crudely carved Thanatos, then
sighed in ecstasy at the image of a faceless god that wore a triple crown,
the entire figure beautifully chiseled from a piece of smooth obsidian.
Next to this, in perfect contrast, was a small semblance of the valley's
white mountain, sculpted from a chunk of pure crystal.

Wanting to gaze upon the actual peaks once more, she went to the shop's door and out into the night. There was no moon, but the heavens twinkled with countless stars, more than she remembered ever seeing. The mountain was a dark behemoth that towered above the valley. It wouldn't take long to drive to it, if the roads were easily managed. To climb it, with her troublesome asthma, was out of the question; but she knew she had to investigate the lower region, to touch the white stone with her naked hand.

She looked around and wondered where everyone was, for the town-center was empty of residents. Not much night life in Sesqua Valley she thought, sniggering to herself. And yet, how peaceful it was, standing in this dark and silent place. What a relaxing contrast to her usual chaotic night-life of loud music and inebriated comrades. Yes, after a while the dullness of the place would drive her crazy; but for a day or two it would be really nice. This was exactly what she had been seeking in her little tour of backwater Amerika—an absolute alternative to the world with which she was familiar. Winking at the shadowed mountain, she returned to her room and, suddenly exhausted, fell into a dreamless sleep, a void of slumber.

II.

Breakfast that next morning was served in a smallish dining room adjacent to an equally small kitchen. A husky, normal-looking woman served her own home-style cooking, and it was excellent. Aubrey's companion at the table was a rather frail young man a few years her junior, who introduced himself as Klarkson Ash, poet. She liked his auburn hair and very pale face, upon which, above a beautiful mouth, he was attempting a first mustache.

"So what brings you to the valley?" he inquired, delicately buttering a slice of toast.

"Oh, I just happened on it. I'm doing a little tour of small towns in the region, kind of a vacation. And you?"

"I'm visiting friends, and working on some new poetry inspired by the valley." He stopped and gave her a quizzical look. "So you came here by happenstance? And you actually stopped in town? That's rare."

"Really?"

"Oh, yes; the valley doesn't like to be noticed by outsiders. One usually drives straight through without having noticed the place, their mind a mental fog. It's very rare for the uninvited to stop."

"Huh. Actually, I was going to drive on through, but I stopped to collect some stones. I like to carve images on rocks, just a little hobby of mine."

"Aha, so you *are* an artist! I suspected as much. People like you usually are."

"People like . . .?"

"You punker types."

She laughed. "That's bullshit. Most of the punks I know are into wild noise and getting drunk."

"Yes, but you have more of an aesthetic sense than most of the ratty street freaks I've encountered. And you obviously spend a lot of money on your delicious attire."

Recognizing the leer in his eyes, Aubrey sneered. "Damn, and I thought you were gay, with your exquisite little moustache and femmy hands."

Slightly irritated, Ash blew out air. "I'm *quite* hetero, I assure you. I'm merely delicate, cursed with fragile health. Well, I apologise if I sounded a snob. I merely speak from personal urban experience. The image I have of your kind is of dancing in black light and writing morbid verse in moonlit cemeteries."

"I adore cemeteries."

"Well, there you are. The stereotype contains a grain of truth. I thought as much."

"For a kid of seventeen, you sure talk grand."

Ash shrugged. "I'm a wealthy woman's son, private education and all that. Queerly brilliant, a phenomenal child scholar who was writing somber verse of a fantastic nature at age seven. Accepted into Miskatonic University at age fifteen, blab blah blah."

"How boring for you," Aubrey cynically replied.

"Not at all. Such mental expediency gives one a freedom of maturity at an age when one still enjoys the pleasures of childhood. Brilliant as I am, I'm still *very* much a child. I like having fun, although of an outré nature. That's why Sesqua Valley is so appealing."

"And what's so 'outré' about Sesqua Valley?"

"Damn, you're clueless. How long have you been here? Hasn't anything *struck* you about the place? Of course, if it hasn't, I really shouldn't be bringing it up."

"What the hell are you talking about? Yeah, some of the people seem kind of weird. And that mountain!"

"Ah, you've notice Selta. Very good. But, listen, I'm done here, and in the mood for a stroll. You said that you adore cemeteries. Let me shew you an exemplar of the species."

"Coolness. Let's split."

Thus they arose and went outside, into crisp morning air and softly tinted sunlight. After a ten-minute walk, they came upon the resting place of those who were outsiders to the valley, and Aubrey moaned at the sight.

"Rather splendid, isn't it?" Ash asked, pleased with her expression of awe.

"Hell, yes. Not one of these tombstones is the same. Look at that one, carved in the image of a gargoyle reading an old book. And on the cover of the book is the dude's name and the date of death." Then, as she looked around, the really *odd* nature of the place struck her. "Dude, almost none of these markers have the date of birth. What's up with that?"

"I believe that in most cases the date is unknown, for these are the buried trespassers of the valley. Mostly."

"The what?"

"Those, such as yourself, who 'just happened' upon the valley and were unable to leave. Those who perished in natural fashion, for the most part."

"And the 'other' part?"

"Ah!" And he gazed at her with wide, expressive eyes. And for the first time since entering the valley, Aubrey Brood felt a tinge of unexplainable fear. Suddenly wanting to get away from him, the young woman nonchalantly roamed the graveyard, then stopped before a granite statue that startled her.

"What?" queried her companion.

"It's the dude in the movie."

"What movie?"

"In the curiosity shop. You know, the nickelodeon. He was dancing in a meadow by some black pillar or something, playing a flute." She read the inscription on the statue's base. "William Davis Manly, Poet and Brother."

"There's an image of Manly on *film?* But that is really extraordinary. The children of the valley don't care to be photographed."

"I think I met one of his kin when I first got here, some guy named Simon."

"Ah," said the poet, suddenly somber. "You'll want to stay away from him. The fellow's a bit mad."

"Dude, I'm beginning to think this whole freaking valley is a bit mad."

Obliquely, Klarkson Ash grinned.

"So, where is this meadow? I want to check out the pillar."

"It's out a ways, in the direction of the mountain."

"Groovy, I want to check out the mountain, too."

He looked at her as if she were mad herself. "There's no road to the mountain, my dear Miss Brood. You'll have to trek through the tainted place."

"Huh?"

"The place that feels too deeply Selta's shadow." He ruefully shook his head at her ignorance. "If you're going to the Black Stone, I'd like to accompany you. I was going to visit the site myself this afternoon."

"Screw that, let's go now. I'll probably be leaving this afternoon. We can go in my van. I want to get my sculpting gear and work on a couple rocks."

"Excellent."

They made their way to the vehicle, and Aubrey changed shoes, not wanting to hike in heels. Following Ash's directions, she drove along a narrow road through dark woodland, coming at last to an incline in the roadway that led to a wide expanse of meadow. Parking, Aubrey leapt out and bent to pick up a couple of good-sized stones, then ran through the high grass, toward the Black Stone. Panting, her companion caught up with her.

"Wow, it must be ancient!" she exclaimed, admiring the tall monolith.

"Not at all. It was raised in the late 1920s, by some of the children of the valley. It's a replica of another stone—and one that is indeed ancient—in the town of Stregoicavar. Simon encountered the original on one of his journeys, and was so taken with it that he ordered this replica to be raised here in this meadow."

"You're a bad liar, dude."

"I beg your pardon?"

"Simon couldn't have found anything in the 1920s. He's too young to have lived then."

Secretly, the young man smiled.

"Don't look at me like that. Look." And she produced her photo-phone and found Simon's image. "Is that the face of someone who's lived for a century?" And then she laughed at the expression on the young man's face. "What?"

"You've captured the image of the Beast? You really are remarkable!"

"Yeah, well, I caught him off-guard. You can tell by his expression."

"Yes." And then Ash unexpectedly giggled. "Remarkable!" He leaned toward her. "May I kiss you?"

"No."

"One chaste peck is all I ask."

"Piss off," she yelled.

His face took on a wounded expression, and his eyes were slits that regarded her unhappily. "As you wish, my dear." And before she could reply, he turned and walked away.

"Why are men such pathetic babies?" she asked herself. "But you're not a man," she said in a louder voice to the figure who vanished into the woodland. "You're still a child." Well, let him go; she had other business to attend to. The two stones held precariously in one hand were becoming heavy, and so she returned her phone to her bag and sauntered to the Black Stone and placed the stones she held onto the ground; then knelt and touched one hand to the monolith. It was surprisingly warm, perhaps from the mild mid-morning sunlight. She looked at the grass near to her and noticed how some of it had been trampled. She recalled the old film she had seen in the museum, and the oddly-attired children who had danced around the monolith, so many decades ago. Sitting, she leaned her back against the warm stone, then dug through her bag for some small sculpting implements. Delicately, she began to work on one of the sizable rocks. Digging once more into her bag, she recovered her phone and found Simon's photo. What was it that Klarkson Ash had called him? Ah, yes—the Beast. Quite appropriate, she agreed, considering the fellow's malformed face. And yet the more she studied its miniature reproduction, the less it seemed a face that was disfigured through genetic default. Rather, the face of Simon Gregory Williams seemed that of another race altogether, an alien genotype with which she was unfamiliar. And the man in the film, the poet William Davis Manly, had shared a similar heredity. Obviously the poet was ancestor to the Beast.

Now and then, as she worked on her rock, she felt an overwhelming presence, as if she were under subtle observation. She thought that perhaps Klarkson had secretly returned, but every time she turned around she saw nothing but meadow, forest, and the nearby mountain. Whenever her eyes fell upon that titan of sparkling white stone they did not want to turn away. Everything about it captivated Aubrey: its size, and shape; the nature of the singular material with which it was composed.

Finally, she was finished, and held in her hand a remarkable rock that wore a very close resemblance to Simon Gregory's fantastic face. Stretching, she put her artwork and equipment back into her bag and struggled her numb limbs into a standing position. The afternoon had grown pleasantly warm, and she hummed as, returning to the van, she followed the road in the direction of Mount Selta. The humming turned into cursing as the road became ruinous, when finally it ended. The mountain was very close, easily within walking distance. She would merely have to trek through that stretch of barren ground before her, that gray ground from which sickly yellow shoots of grass reached sequaciously from the ground, where here and there a lifeless-looking tree reached out its withered limbs toward the mountain.

Vacating the van, and placing the strap of her bag over one shoulder, she stepped onto the soft gray ground, remarking to herself about the sudden chilliness in the air. The valley's sweet aether, to which her lungs had grown accustomed, turned rancid, leaving a sour taste in her mouth. A dull weakness weighed her limbs, and for a moment she leaned against one of the few lean trees, the trunk of which was so soft that she fancied herself sinking into its substance. The air about her had grown peculiarly dark, from the bulky shadow of the mountain, no doubt. Glancing at a distant place of gray ground, Aubrey thought she could descry subtle movement beneath it. With renewed determination, she pushed away from the diseased tree and continued her trek to the growth of lush woodland that flourished just below the mountain. Although it seemed to take an eternity, the young woman finally stepped on more solid ground, and once again the air grew sweet. She entered the forest and admired the really wonderful woodland, the magnificent trees that towered above her, the fragrance of the deciduous remnants that covered the path she followed until—at last—she walked in sunlight upon white rock.

A slight incline of mountainous rock became a wall of sparkling stone that towered above her, so high that, gazing upward, she could not see its peaks. Squinting at the brightness of the stone, she leaned very close so as to study its surface; and beneath the almost crystal surface of gleaming white rock she fancied she could detect other faintly glittering shades, flicks of color so unusual that they seemed of some unknown, some unearthly, spectrum. It was hypnotic, and something in her brain seemed to melt in ecstasy to be touching it. Pushing away from the steep wall, Aubrey scanned the surface on which she stood for any remnant of fallen stone; but there was naught but solid stone beneath her, pristine and unbroken.

She had to have a piece of stone, to take with her as souvenir. Absent-mindedly, Aubrey Brood reached into her shoulder bag and brought forth hammer and chisel. She placed the implement's sharp edge against the wall of crystalline brilliance and raised her hammer high, then powerfully struck hammer against chisel, breaking free a chunk of stone.

The sky darkened, and from somewhere high on the mountain a creature raised its snout in a macabre anguish of howling. A moist wind issued from the woodland behind her. Underneath her feet, the mountain trembled.

Looking skyward, Aubrey saw the sky just above Mount Selta grow black with sudden storm. Once more, a wretched wail of baying came from somewhere on the mountain, nearer than it was before. Filled with inexplicable terror, Aubrey bent to grab the detritus of rock that she had broken off the mountain, stuffed it into her bag, and fled. Wet branches scratched against her flesh as she rushed through the shadowed woodland, and when she stepped onto the tainted sod of the diseased place, the sandy ground was difficult to trespass. A miasma of mauve mist rose from that ground, beclouding vision. She wiped at her eyes with frantic motion, but when she tried to peer before her the view was a phantasmagoria of fantastic bizarrerie. Where did all these trees come from? Surely there had not been so many before, pale and ill, twitching pallid branches toward the mountain. The ground beneath her weirdly moved, and from it a flock of flaccid roots wrapped around her feet. Heavily, she fell upon deficient earth, earth that seemed to sift so as to pull her into its depths. Screaming, she tried to free herself from the pull of sod and root, but she could not. Inexorably, she was dragged deeper into the ground, until a sudden pair of large hands found their way under her arms and forcibly freed her from the clutches of decadent dirt.

Her eyesight blurred with streaming, stinging tears, she looked into the face that panted so near to her own, that wild and wolfish countenance in which a pair of silver orbs feverishly flamed.

Then her eyesight faded, and Aubrey became lost within a void of blackness illimitable.

III.

Klarkson Ash moved his feet in what might have been a jig as he peered into a nickelodeon. "Have you seen this?"

"Of course," Leonidas hissed.

"Why have I never been told about it?"

The elder creature shifted noiselessly in his large chair and ran a pallid hand through wild white hair. "Because you are a creature of no consequence. Nor have you ever shown an interest in my collection, except for the library."

"That's because I'm a poet, with a poet's interest in literature."

"Bah."

"And I've been published."

Leonidas sneered. "By the Miskatonic Rhapsodist League, in a chapbook of, what, fifty copies? You are no Rimbaud or Clark Ashton Smith, in whose memory you have altered your name. You are certainly no William Davis Manly."

The image before the lad ceased and darkened, and the antique machine quieted. Backing away from the nickelodeon, Ash moseyed past a row of ancient artifacts, then stopped before a bookcase. Seeing the volume bound in violet cloth, he took it down and carefully flipped through some pages, until he found the poem he sought. His voice, as he read, was low and hushed.

"After midnight, when sanity sleeps,

You rise, with face as dead as moonlight,

With mouth a hungry slit beneath which gleams,

Like daggers of pure pearl,

The ravenous teeth that tear.

After midnight, with rare appetite,

You prowl.

I feel your hunger.

I feel the doom that glints on shadow-eyes.

Help me now, to taste mortality."

Leonidas rocked back and forth in his chair, deeply frowning, saying nothing. Nonchalantly, Ash shut the book and leaned against the oaken case. "A rare honor, to have a Manly poem written about one's self."

"You are overly imaginative if you think that absurdly inscrutable bit of nonsense is about myself. I barely knew the poet."

Ash opened the book's cover and looked at the title page. "And yet the book is inscribed to you. Now that's curious, because *Visions of Khroyd'hon* was published in 1955, and Manly vanished in 1951. How can such a mystery be explained?"

"Ah, what a sorry little simpleton you are, Ash. Nathan Vreeland, who published the volume, worked on it for many years, and he had the poet sign a series of autograph sheets shortly before Manly vanished. There was trouble over the book, as perhaps you know. Simon in particular did not want it published. He feared that the book would bring unwanted attention to the valley, as indeed it has."

"I find that difficult to believe. The legend, as I have come to know it, is that Sesqua Valley cloaks itself from the outside world, that only they who are specifically initiated can find their way into its confines. And of those few, only the very select are invited to stay."

"Such is our wish," the elder one murmured. "But desire if often thwarted by reality. The valley's history is stained by the sad fates of those who have come accidentally, and who have been beguiled by the mind-numbing supernatural wonder that bewitches our sacred region. One need only visit the necropolis where those unhappy souls are buried (those whom we could gather up—for others have not been so fortunate) to see how many of them there are. Such as your mother." Ash looked at him with smouldering eyes. "Yes, it bothers you to hear of it, for the wound is fresh. But tell me, little one, how did you come to know of the valley?"

Solemnly, the young man walked down a dusky aisle between rows on antique furnishings, queer sculptures, treasures of a deathless past. He approached a wall and gazed at an enormous oil painting of Mount Selta. "My grandfather painted that, just before his final madness. We never understood where he disappeared to, those months when he would habitually vanish. Then, one evening, he returned lugging this painting into the library. Mother could tell that his hold on sanity was slipping, but she did not want to face the truth and have him confined. I'd sit with him, sometimes, in the library, as he stared at the painting and mumbled to himself. That's when I first heard of Sesqua Valley, at age nine. Three weeks later I found my grandfather's lifeless body in his leather chair, the wide eyes still fastened onto his reproduction of the mountain."

Queerly, he inclined his head, then raised a hand to the daemonic image and moved his fingers in occult signal. The elder one watched for a while in silence. "I knew your grandfather well," he finally whispered.

The boy turned to him. "You never told me."

"Of course not. You become such an emotional infant at any mention of your doomed family. Your grandsire had had from his youth an interest in the supernatural, but he had never actually encountered it until he discovered Sesqua Valley. And he became acquainted with the valley by way of a chance discovery of a book in a New England bookshop. A book bound in violet cloth. A book in which—stupidly—Nathan Vreeland inserted his name of an invented press!" His eyes flashed with buried fury. Turning away from the painting, Ash opened the book to its title page. At the bottom he read, "Sesqua Valley Press, 1955." Closing the book once more, the young man returned to the ancient movie machine and fished in a pocket for a nickel.

"Shall I continue the history, Klarkson? Speak of how your mother found the valley and of the strain of paternal lunacy that led her to do that which ended with you digging her a ditch in forsaken ground?"

A coin fell into a slot, and tear-stained eyes peered into the viewer as Simon Gregory Williams entered the room. He detected the misery in the air and squinted at the humans in the dimly-lit room. "She's awoken. What's been going on down here?"

"I've been admiring your kindred, Simon," said Ash, in a voice of feigned merriment. He held up the book of poetry. "Listen, when a new edition of Manly's verse is printed, you should stand in proxy for an author's photo, you two look so alike." He lifted his head and seriously frowned. "Ah, but I forgot—your kind doesn't like to be photographed." Then he roguishly smiled and snapped his fingers. "Say! We can use that photo that Aubrey took on her little phone gadget!"

Casually, a strange smile playing on his unmentionable mouth, Simon made his way to the boy. With superb grace he touched a soft inhuman hand to Klarkson's face, then pressed a nail as sharp as needle's point into the tender skin just beside an eye socket. Ash could feel the talon tenderly scrape the surface of an eye, could feel the tiny trickle of blood that began to slowly stream to his nose.

"I fear that your frail attempt at lampoonery is unappreciated, my dear boy. That gadget's extinction has already been accomplished. Now, have you given Cyrus the remnant of stone?" He removed his hand from the young man's troubled face.

"Yes, Simon."

"And instructed him *precisely* as I have told you?"

"I have."

"Excellent." And then he turned his eyes to the woman who appeared at the doorway. "My dear, you shouldn't be up. You've suffered quite a fall."

Tenderly running a hand along one of many bruises and cuts that covered arms and limbs, the outsider shivered. "I need a drink. Do you have any brandy, Leonidas?"

"I'm sorry, I do not."

"They have some excellent brandy at the pub," Ash offered.

"Cool, let's go. Look, I'm sorry I was such a bitch this morning. I don't like unfamiliar guys coming on to me, okay?"

"Okay."

"I made this for you, Simon." She held to him the rock on which she had carved his impious image. Eyes twinkling, Simon took it from her with large soft hands. "I copied your photo from my phone, which I seem to have lost during my . . . accident." She brought a pale hand to her worried forehead. "Damn, I wish I could remember what happened. Guess my brain must have gotten joggled in my tumble." Weakly, she attempted laughter.

"But this is *exquisite*, my dear. You've captured me to the very core," Simon replied as he held the image up to the dim light, examining it from every angle. He then stepped to the low table on which the religious icons sat. "I shall place myself here, among the other gods." Klarkson Ash rolled his eyes and swallowed laughter, then winced in pain and rubbed the wounded place near to his eye.

"What happened to you?" the young woman inquired.

"A foolish accident," Simon answered for the lad. "He'll need to show more caution in the future. As will you, my dear. Do you remember nothing of your contretemps?"

"I don't remember a damn thing." She looked at Ash. "I remember going to look at the Black Stone and being a bitch to you, then I worked on my carving of Simon; and then I drove to where the road ended, because I wanted to investigate the mountain up close. That's when things get murky. I walked across that crazy plot of land, then through a rather wonderful bit of forest. I went to the mountain ... and ... and ..."

"Pray don't tax your brain, Miss Brood," Simon said, still bent over the low table and trying to decide the perfect position for his chiseled image. "You'll remember all in good time, when you least expect it."

Aubrey stretched and moaned in anguish. "Oh, man, I'm stiff and sore all over. My joints really ache."

"You need to return to bed, Miss Brood," said Leonidas.

"Screw that, I need a good drink. Come on, Klarkson, let's go get drunk."

"An excellent idea," the young man said, turning to exchange dark glances with Simon, then vacating the place with Aubrey at his side.

Eventide had fallen, and as Aubrey turned to gaze at Selta's splendor, she saw, just above the peaks, a convex moon. "Ah, there she is."

"Hmm?" asked her companion.

"The moon. I couldn't see her last night. She must have been behind the mountain. Wow, she looks so close! She's never seemed so gigantic in the city, so close that you can almost touch her." Dreamily, she lifted a hand to the sky.

"It is the very error of the moon,
She comes more nearer earth than she was wont
And makes men mad."

Aubrey turned to look at Ash as the poetry was whispered on his lips. "What's that, Shakespeare?"

"How clever of you to know."

"I didn't. You just look like the kind of dude who would quote Shakespeare."

Quizzically, he smiled, uncertain if this was compliment or no. "Here we are," he said, ushering her into a dark saloon. As they entered, Ash was hailed by a couple of young men who sat at a booth, and cautiously touching Aubrey's arm, he guided her to his friends. The two fellows regarded her with especial interest, then shared esoteric expressions with Ash.

"So," Aubrey said, unceremoniously plopping her ass on the wooden seat and looking wide-eyed toward the bar. "Do they have whiskey?"

"Oh, yes," Ash assured her, still standing. "Are you gents drinking Sesqua grog?"

"We are," replied the one called Cyrus.

"What's that?" asked the girl, leaning to a nearly empty glass and sniffing its contents.

"Try it," Cyrus told her. And so she did, bringing the glass to her lips and loudly sipping.

"Holy mama, that's potent," she enthused, rubbing her throat. "Drinks are on me, boys. Let's party."

Klarkson Ash observed her with interest, for Aubrey Brood suddenly seemed an entirely different person, a more comfortable one. This was obviously the kind of scene with which she was familiar. She caught him smiling oddly at her and furrowed her brow, then reached into her skull bag and produced a wad of bills. "Don't stand there gawking, chump. Move your ass."

Ash playfully lowered his head. "I am subject to your dominance."

"Yeah, whatever." And then she groaned and moved her shoulders. "So is this stuff gonna help me sleep?"

The other lad, named Nelson, smiled. "Like the dead."

"Groovy."

Ash leaned against the bar and watched them as he waited for the bartender to take his order. Aubrey was talking a mile a minute, more animated than he had ever witnessed. Her loud voice and laughter filled the room, causing other patrons to glance her way and take in her wild attire. Ash studied the satin top that barely covered the woman's small breasts. She was undeniably sexy. And yet he sensed instinctively that her scanty attire was not meant to send sexual signals, being simply what she was most comfortable wearing. She was a "scene" girl, to the core.

Having given his order, the young man returned to the table, surprised to see his friends shaking with laughter. Aubrey smiled at him as he sat across from her. "I was just telling your mates about Simon's reaction to my taking his picture. So, where's the drinks?"

"On the way."

"So what's the book?" she asked, pointing to the thin volume that Ash had absent-mindedly brought with him from the shop.

"*Visions of Khroyd'hon,* by William Davis Manly," said Nelson. "I'm surprised Leonidas allowed you to steal away with that book. It's his inscribed copy, isn't it?"

"It is. I forgot I had it in hand as we left. Perhaps I had best go and return it . . ."

"Oh, sit still. Here's our brew." And she smiled at the fellow who set the drinks before them and collected the empty glasses. Aubrey picked up one of the mugs of grog and sipped. "Oh, yeah, boys, I feel better already. Here's to Sesqua Valley and her weirdness!" She lifted to them her glass; and after a momentary pause, the others smiled and did likewise, touching glass against glass, spilling liquid.

They drained their drinks and ordered another round. Aubrey grew more loquacious as the hour slipped by; and then she was suddenly silent, her flesh more pale than usual.

"Is something wrong?" asked Cyrus.

"Hmmm? Sorry. I'm not feeling so hot. My joints are stiff, and these bruises itch terribly. And my fingers . . ." Aubrey raised a hand and stiffly moved her fingers in the hazy light. "I don't know, they feel numb and—weird . . ."

"Maybe it's merely the grog. Takes a bit getting used to," Ash suggested.

She tried to smile. "That may be it. I feel light-headed. Can we leave? I feel the need for air." Unsteadily, slightly moaning in discomfort, she rose and stumbled to the door, followed by the lads. They surrounded her outdoors as she stood in the middle of the road and stared at the mountain. "It's so bloody quiet out here." Not too distant she espied the low stone wall that surrounded the old cemetery. Drunkenly, she smiled. "Come, lads, let us pay our respects to your glorious poet. You can read from that book in his honor, Klarkson." Ash glanced at the other gentlemen and winked at the obvious discomfort on their faces. Aubrey, too, was carefully observing those faces, and her smile was slightly odd.

"Certainly," said Ash. "Come on, gents." With the young woman leading the way, they moved as one through darkness, walking down the street until they came to the low stone wall that encircled the place of inhumation. Aubrey waited at the high arched gate of green metal until the others, who had slowed as they neared the site, caught up with her. Once more, she observed the features of Cyrus and Nelson, especially their silver eyes which combined a kind of wistful longing with subtle fear.

The three men stopped at the gate, and only Ash passed through it. "You guys coming?" Aubrey asked the Sesqua boys. Nelson touched the cool metal of the gate and looked as if he were about to pass through until Cyrus placed a hand upon his shoulder. Aubrey was fascinated by their manner, not only the way they gazed into the cemetery, but also the way they seemed to be intently listening.

"We can't join you," Cyrus finally spoke. "But it's been cool getting to know you. I've been working on a little piece that I'd like to present to you before you leave."

"Cool, Cyrus. Thanks." Chivalrously, the young men bowed to her, then nodded to Ash and walked away. "That was kind of freaky. It was as if they were uptight about entering."

"The children of shadow almost never enter this place, except Simon, and that rarely. He'll come and play his flute to the statue. Have you heard him play his wretched flute?"

"No."

"Ah, well, it defines 'freaky,' as you put it."

"Did you notice?" she asked him as they walked upon the burial ground. "Those dudes had the Sesqua look."

Softly, Ash laughed. They approached Manly's statue, and the young man was singularly alert. To be in this place at night was insanity. Beneath him, subtly, Ash could detect the dull regular pounding that was the valley's muted heartbeat. He concentrated on the rhythmic sensation. Deeply inhaling, he swallowed haunted aether. Lifting his eyes to look over the mountain his jellied orbs soaked in chill moonlight that touched his seething brain. His blood, that rich liquid so enamored by this daemonic dirt, coursed thickly through his veins in time to the valley's preternatural pulsation. This it was that the children of the valley evaded, this madness that emanated from beneath the ground and found its way into one's brain, one's soul. The children of shadow felt this lunacy with far more keenness than did their human neighbors. But young poets were especially susceptible to this dangerous dementia.

Klarkson Ash turned his gaze to the stone face of Manly's statue. As a rising wind began to play with his soft fair hair, he began to quietly sing.

> "The sickened thing lies deep beneath the sod,
> The wormwood heart beneath the brackish ground.
> It feeds on salty flesh, on withered blood.
> It holds the human psyche so spellbound.
> Its tethers wrap around the mortal soul.
> Its poison spills into the Sesquan heart.
> It laughs as it unpins sanity's thole,
> And we, unanchor'd, drift and split apart."

The wind had risen in strength as eerie accompaniment to the young man's lullaby. "More Shakespeare?" Aubrey asked, listening to the wind move through the trees above them.

"No. William Davis Manly."

"How in hell can you read in this darkness?"

"I'm quoting from memory. I know most of his stuff by heart, by tender heart." His voice had lowered and grown strange. The young woman came closer to the statue and placed a dainty hand to its chilly stone.

"So is this where Manly is buried?"

He chortled. "The children of the valley aren't buried anywhere, fool. They return unto the shadowed realm in which they were formed."

"Say what?"

He tilted his small body closer to her own and admired the shapely legs that spilled from out the mini-skirt. "Aren't you cold, dressed like that?"

"No."

Casually, he wrapped his small hand around one thigh. Cursing, she pushed him away. "You're a chilly nymph."

"I'm also a lot taller than you, so chill out, asshole."

Yellow moonlight danced within the young man's trembling eyes. Deeply breathing, he sucked in Sesqua's sweetly tainted air. Beneath his heels the valley's heart pumped its influence through his skin, warping his psyche. Aubrey backed away at the sight of his sneering visage.

"Aubrey Brood, you're such a prude," he mockingly sang, in a voice so altered that it seemed to her inhuman. Softly snarling, he lunged at her. Swiftly, her fist cracked against his jaw. Yelping in pain and fury, he fell backward and toppled against Manly's statue. Aubrey stood at combat stance, defiantly. Moonlight glistened on the drool that dropped from the madman's gasping mouth as he pushed away from the statue and hunkered in preparation for another attack.

From some darkened place outside the necropolis, a flute eerily sounded. The boy froze as the weird high-pitched music drifted to them through the scented air. His worried eyes scanned the darkness for the beast he knew was watching them. Something sinister slid from his soul, and he shuddered. "I'm sorry. I've had too much to drink. Please forgive me."

"Leave. Now."

He tossed to her the book of Manly's verse. "Return it, please." Then, nervously glancing into the lightless places surrounding the walled cemetery, he fled.

She watched him take his leave, then turned to face the high statue. Faint moonshine illuminated the features of Manly's face, that face that seemed to her so queerly bestial. As she stood there, staring, she fancied that something stirred beneath her, a rhythmic pulsation that sifted the ground on which she stood. Suddenly fearful, she turned from the statue and rushed out of the graveyard, hugging Manly's book to her chest, not stopping until she reached the steps that led into the quaint curiosity shop's back entrance.

IV.

Sitting in bed, a book in her lap, Aubrey's face was very pale in the soft light of a bedside lamp. Scanning various lines of verse in Manly's book, she deeply frowned. This was obviously where Ash had obtained his bizarre allusions to "shadow children" and other esoteric references to the valley. Manly's poetry was filled with numerous (if oblique) mention of "the wonders of this supernatural vale." She smiled at the idea of Klarkson's troubled mind taking seriously the figments of Manly's poetic fancy. Finally, her eyelids heavy, she shut the thin volume and sank her head onto a mound of pillows. Groaning at the dull pain in her joints, she stretched her aching limbs, wondering if perhaps she had caught a fever and was actually ill. She would heed the advice of Leonidas and rest in bed for a few days. Money and days were hers to waste, and the bed was extremely comfortable, the food exceptionally tasty. Because of their extreme strangeness, the inhabitants of this small neglected town fascinated her. She would certainly not be bored.

Sesqua grog was tasty as well. She liked that the laws here were lax enough so that a minor like Ash could slip into a pub with no problem; she had gotten away with the same thing when she was underage, because of her height. Such were her thoughts as her breathing deepened and slowed, as her eyelids closed. Her dozing mind drifted into the landscape of Manly's dreamy verse, that spectral world of Sesqua Valley's secrets. She was walking on a field of whispering rocks, and when she bent so as to pick up a rock and place it at her ear, the stone whispered what was supposed to be Manly's verse, although the voice was distorted as it often is in dreaming. Above, the sky was enflamed as if by sunset, and Mount Selta caught the reflection of crimson light on its tainted stone.

Her arms, as she lifted them to the mountain, were tinged as well, especially the bruises and scars resulting from her accident. The blemished areas seemed almost to sparkle, like the mountain did when it caught the light of sun or moon. As she examined her skin, the wind awakened, humming through the distant treetops like low fluted music, like the music she had heard when Ash was acting the moron in the cemetery.

She danced to that music, through the wind and beneath the trees, until she came to the moonlit meadow and its black monolith. Here the music was far more clear than it had been elsewhere. Selta was partially hidden in a low and almost-misty cloud. Another cloud, dark and convulsive, swirled like a wraith atop the Black Stone; and from within that midnight undulation there came the high wail of eerie music; and as she kept her eyes upon that place atop the monolith, a humanoid figure began to materialize through the density of darkness. It was, she saw, a child of the valley, and she knew that it was either Simon or William Davis Manly, for there was no mistaking the singular shape of head, or the hands that held a flute to the bestial mouth.

Beneath the daemoniac music of the flute she sensed another sound: the low and heavy pulse that was the valley's heartbeat. She sensed that it came from some place far beneath her; and yet, it seemed also to emanate from the mountain itself. And when she looked at that sparkling titan of majestic rock she saw Selta tremble to the sound of song, to bend toward them and spread its antediluvian wings.

Aubrey awakened to darkness, and knew that she had slept all day. Moaning at the aches in her joints, she pushed out of bed and slipped into some clothes, then grabbed Manly's book of verse and entered the hallway, pausing for a moment at the door of Ash's room before she continued to the stairs and down them. Muffled voices were coming from the museum room, and as she entered the area two strange faces turned to greet her. They sat in a corner that had been given the appearance of a comfortable place beside a hearth. Two small sofas sat against the corner where the walls met, and beside them were short stands that held antique lamps. In front of the sofas were low coffee tables that held various books and cups. Cyrus rose, smiling, and Aubrey returned his smile, even though the shadows in the room seemed to accentuate his odd facial features, which looked in this muted light like an odd combination of frog and wolf.

Leonidas remained seated in one of the sofas, and his fantastic face looked more pale than she had previously noted. The eyes were particularly wide, as if the skin beneath them were being pulled by invisible hooks. He waved a withered hand to her, on which the fingernails looked long and very sharp. Despite what she took to be his great age, there was in his aspect a kind of feline vitality, ever ready to pounce despite a veneer of quietude.

"Are you hungry, my dear?" queried the ancient man. "There are some cold sandwiches in the icebox."

"Not really, but thanks. I'm not feeling so great and don't have much of an appetite. I may have to stay just a bit longer than I anticipated."

"Stay as long as you like," came his friendly return.

"Thank you, Leonidas," she answered, relishing the sound of his name on her lips, then going to him and handing him the book. Taking it, he indicated that she should sit across from him in the other sofa. She did so, and Cyrus sat next to her. "Klarkson accidentally took that with him yesterday, when we went out boozing. Poor guy had a bit too much to drink, I think."

"He tends to let himself go at times," said Cyrus.

Aubrey chuckled. "This is between us, but he's a bit of a nutcase, I think. He's obsessed with that book of Manly's, he's even got most of it memorized."

"A passion for poetry is not 'nutty,' Miss Brood," Leonidas informed her, opening the book and silently admiring a page of poesy.

"He doesn't just eat it up, dude, he *believes* it. Man, the stuff he's been telling me!"

The two gentlemen exchanged saturnine glances. "He's been chattering, has he?" the elder one asked.

"Hell, yes. From the moment we met he's been telling me the weirdest stuff. But it's all from Manly's book. He's totally into it."

"And what kind of—stuff—has he been telling you?" asked Cyrus.

"Oh, let's see. He was surpised I stopped on my way through, because the valley 'doesn't like to be noticed' or some such rot. And then something about the 'shadow children' or 'shadow spawn' or some such thing. But if you've read Manly, you can see where Ash got his ideas. It's all there, in that cool creative world. It *is* intoxicating. I was reading it last night, and man did I have some wild dreams!"

"Yes," Leodinas sighed. "Manly's visions are often a portal to the realm of dreaming."

"You knew him, didn't you?" the girl asked. "The book is signed to you."

"Yes, I knew him, many years ago," the weird one answered.

"How did he die? I mean, he is dead, right?"

"That remains a mystery, my dear. He went away, and has yet to return."

"Was he Simon's uncle or something? They look so much alike, judging from that footage in the machine."

Obliquely, Creighton smiled. "They are kindred."

"I have something for you," Cyrus told her, and her green eyes grew bright as she watched him reach into a deep pocket.

"You found my phone!"

"Ah, no. This is something I've been working on, and I wanted you to have it, as a keepsake of your visit to Sesqua Valley." He pulled the thing from his pocket, and smiled at her expression of joy. Tenderly, she took the proffered necklace and held it up to lamplight, admiring the beauty of the sparkling white stone that had been fastened to a piece of silver link.

"Oh, Cyrus, this is beautiful. I've lost the piece of Selta that I chipped off. Dude, this is awesome, thanks." Unexpectedly, she bent to kiss his face, and as she did so she took in his rare fragrance, a bodily bouquet that resembled the sweet heavy aether of the valley, a perfume to which she had by now grown accustomed. She kept her lips upon his flesh for a long moment, relishing his scent.

"May I put it on you?"

"Yeah, I'd like that, Cyrus." And she watched him as he took the necklace from her and slipped it over her head. His animal face was very close to hers, and she saw the piece of stone reflected on his queer alabaster eyes. She closely examined those eyes, and thought for a moment that she could detect, just beneath the transparent layer that formed the front of that silver cord, a slight gathering of almost undetectable colors, minuscule fragments of light in hues of some otherworldly spectrum.

Suddenly, Aubrey moaned in discomfort. "Sorry," she said, falling back into the sofa. "My body feels rotten. I must be coming down with something. Ugh, it hurts to move. Cyrus, I think a bit of Sesqua grog will make me feel a hell of a lot better. Do you want to accompany me to the pub? I think I need a masculine shoulder to lean on."

"Certainly." And together they rose, she grumbling in discomfort and holding on to him. Nodding their farewell to Leonidas, they departed.

The ancient creature quietly watched them go, then turned to look at the figure who quietly entered the room. Nodding, he smoothly rose.

In his upper room, Klarkson Ash sat in candlelight, putting pen to paper. He so concentrated on his creative effort that he did not hear the opening of his chamber's door. But he saw the shadows on the wall. He turned to face the beast of Sesqua Valley.

Simon raised a large sallow hand. "Pray, don't rise." Slowly, steadily, he advanced toward the boy and looked down at his verse. "Hmm. Mediocre, but it shows promise. You are very young. And like so many of the human young, you are at times excessively foolish."

Leonidas came forward, like a swarm of shadow. "You've been chattering. To the outsider."

Ash felt the velvet kiss of fear. "Not really," he weakly muttered. "Not that it matters. She won't remember anything once she leaves. They rarely do."

"Rarely. There are the exceptions, such as your accursed lineage. You're proving as bothersome as your idiotic mother. Do you wish to join her?"

"I will, eventually. That's where most of us outsiders end up, beneath the hungry place."

Leonidas looked at the piece of paper on which the boy had been scribbling and hissed. "Do you fancy yourself another William Davis Manly, writing poesy about the secrets of the valley?" Savagely, he ripped the paper with his needle-like fingernails. "Were you planning on publishing your own book? Is it not enough to blab to every outsider who finds us? Must you proclaim us to the world?"

"I have more sense than that, Leonidas," said Ash, trying to sound brave and adult.

"Let us hope so. You haven't shown much sense with that young woman. Are you infatuated?"

"I haven't any interest in shallow city girls."

"Excellent," Simon intoned. "We don't want you revealing wonders of the valley to the outsider. We trust that you will cease to do so. But, to make certain, I think—"

The beast was very near the boy, and placed a warm inhuman hand under Ash's chin, then tugged that hand so that the lad rose to face him. Delicately, with seductive touches, Simon smoothed his taloned hand over the boy's moist lips. Breathing deeply through his wolfish nostrils, Simon leaned forward and kissed Klarkson's whimpering lips. He sneered contemptuously at the taste of human flesh, yet relished the savor of mortal terror. Softly, he whispered the boy's name, then brought a wicked-looking talon (oh so deadly sharp) to Ash's mouth.

"The valley's secrets must remain unuttered to those who do not belong, my lovely lad. They are not to be squandered on every pretty young outsider that tickle's one's fancy. The valley is fond of you, Klarkson. It has tasted the mortality of your lunatic lineage, and it relishes your rich madness. Do not betray her, child."

Leonidas came close and watched with hungry eyes as Simon's talon tenderly ripped into the boy's lips. The elder one watched the wet red liquid that began to spill from the weeping mouth, then placed a withered hand over that mouth so as to smother the sound of woe. Blood began to soak the old one's colorless hand. Widely smiling, he flashed his serrated teeth close to Klarkson's face, then blessed that face with diabolic kissing.

V.

It seemed to Aubrey that the pub was especially packed. Looking about her as she stood at the bar and sipped her grog, she detected many locals who had "the look" that seemed so prevalent in this sequestered vale. It must, she thought, be Nostalgia Night, for a bloke was pounding out some killer rag-time on an old piano, and a portion of the floor was taken over by dancing couples. To Aubrey's utter amazement, Simon appeared within the crowd, took from a jacket pocket an old flute, and began to accompany the boogie-woogie. She laughed as he hunkered low and shook his groove-thang with motions that were almost obscene in their wantonness. Something about the sight of him intoxicated her, and despite the dull pain that ached her limbs, she found herself gyrating to the dance area, where the denizens of Sesqua Valley welcomed her with wolfish smiles. Although she had not had much to drink, she found it difficult to fall into the rhythm of the song—something about the meter seemed a bit off kilter.

Trying not to spill her drink, the outsider danced. And as she smiled at them, the children of the valley moved around her, their nickel-hued eyes shimmering in the dusky room. Cyrus appeared before her and clasped his hands around her own. She liked his wild expression as they moved together, and laughed as he led her to the door and out into silky moonlight. Simon was behind them, followed by his claque of fawning admirers. To them he was the Beast of the valley, the first-born spawn of Sesqua Valley's shadowed realm. It was he who found the way into the world of mortality, and through him they were each allowed a little time in the world of material wonder, a world that—in this special region—was tainted by potent magick, by the influence of those who spoke the arcane words, whose talons made the esoteric signs. It was Simon Gregory Williams who intoxicated them with the sound of his flute, with the music of the spheres, those tones that pierced beyond the rim and awakened forces beyond space and time.

Suddenly worn-out, Aubrey paused in her dancing. Her breathing was heavy, and she silently cursed her stupidity in not bringing her asthma inhaler. How exhausted she was. How stiff and sore her joints were, as though she were a woman of seven decades rather than merely two. The piece of stone that hung between her small breasts seemed very cold. Taking hold of it, she raised it so as to study it in moonlight. The thing seemed to catch an essence of that lunar light. It sparkled with unearthly radiance; and as she gazed at it, she saw that the sparkling effect of the stone seemed somehow to spill onto her hand, into her skin, How pale that skin seemed in this uncanny light, lighter than seemed possible.

The strains of Simon's music mellowed, became more eerie. Aubrey thought that the music was echoed by the mouths of those who stood with Simon, that crowd of weird citizens who were watching a certain section of the woodland, who held out hands to the low cloud of mauve mist that began to exude from that place of tree and shadow.

"The shadow of the valley welcomes you, Aubrey Brood," Cyrus whispered in her ear. "It comes to claim you."

The woman watched as the heavy mist met the gathered children of shadow, those offspring from another realm who shuddered in ecstasy as the mist pushed through them. She watched that nameless stuff of aether float to her, felt a wisp of it wind into her braided hair. She moaned as a portion of it found her nose and mouth, entering her. Steadfastly, it moved around and then into her lungs, and when she moaned again it was with a voice that she did not recognize as her own. Although her arms were extremely heavy, she raised them so as to wave the nebulous brume away, only to see it wrapped around her hands, those deadly-pale limbs that grasped into the insubstantial stuff. How strange that this mist seemed to carry with it a kind of luminosity, an almost insubstantial residue that sparkled with colors of an alien spectrum.

Her joints grew more stiff, dull with weight and pain. With great difficulty she turned to try and find Cyrus, to have him take her home. Through the cloud, darkly, she beheld a blurred image coming toward her, an outlandish sight, like something from a dream. The craft resembled a small dogcart, and it was pulled by three small figures, creatures that she had seen on old film stock, dancing in a meadow around a black monolith, accompanied by William Davis Manly. They seemed, these pygmies, not to have faces, but she could see the black eyes that peered at her through matted fur.

Leonidas stood inside the cart, and held to her his withered claw. She tried to protest as Cyrus and the frog-face lad named Nelson took hold of her and began to urge her toward the dogcart, but the only sound to issue through her stiff mouth was a low groan that tingled on the elastic folds of her transmuting vocal cords. When at last they reached the cart, her legs were too stiff to climb up, and so she was lifted up by the two young Sesquans. Leonidas helped Aubrey to grasp onto a railing inside the cart, then leaned against her and wrapped one arm about her waist, steadying her as the cart began to move. Faintly, she could hear his soft high voice singing the melody that issued still from Simon's flute.

Above them, a quartern of moon blended its yellow ambience with the pulsating mist through which the dogcart traversed. Aubrey achingly lowered her eyes from its daemonic light, only to see that dead refraction reflected on the fabric of her translucent skin. She wanted to cry out, but her lips were numb and would not move. The only sound to escape them was a low and almost guttural moan in a voice that could not be her own.

Although her sight was beginning to dim as her eyes slowly lost their color, she could see that they had entered the meadow. The cart drew close unto the Black Stone, then stopped beside it. Simon frantically danced around them and the stone, his music wild with fantastic discord. How such a noise could issue from a single instrument was impossible to fathom. Carefully, Aubrey was lifted out of the cart and leaned against the surface of the Black Stone. Simon's music had become a wail of hideous madness, and she painfully lifted up her arms so as to cover her ears with hands. But this only added to her terror and discomfort; for the texture of her skin had hardened, felt to her, as the hands touched her face, like smooth marble.

A distant figure loped toward her through the heavy mist. Klarkson Ash, small and fragile, limped toward her, and had her inflexible face been capable of expression, she would have winced at the sight of his horrendously flayed lips. Hesitating for one moment, he timidly brought one hand toward her, so as to touch the stone that hung at her slight cleavage. Then the boy brought his tattered mouth close to her own. "I'll kiss you now, Aubrey Brood," he whispered; and so he did, with tender reverence.

The music faltered as Simon tossed his flute to Nelson, who placed it at his thick lips and took up the tune. Raising a large sallow hand to the distant moon, Simon moved his fingers so as to form the Elder Sign. The mist thinned, and through its shifting haze Aubrey could see the majestic twin-peaked mountain. She marveled that stone could so catch moonlight, could capture it so that it seemed to meld with the white rock and alter its character. The mountain sparkled with bewitching scintillation, and Aubrey daemonically moaned as she oh so slowly lifted her arms to Selta. She did not see as Leonidas hopped off the cart with two familiar implements in his hands.

Solemnly, the ancient one moved through the mist, toward Simon. With a gracious yet sardonic bow, he handed the tools to the Beast. Simon held them up to moonglow, the heavy mallet, the lethal-looking chisel. Aubrey dimly watched the Beast approach her, saw him bend to her breasts and kiss the piece of stone that nestled at her bosom. At the touch of his monstrous mouth, the stone grew chilly. He took it in his paw and held it before her frigid eyes, that remnant of Selta that she had ignorantly broken off the mountain. She wanted, so, to push him from her; but she could not move her upraised arms, those limbs that continued to alter, to smooth into stone.

Simon's silver eyes regarded her unemotionally. "You have committed an unpardonable crime, my dear. For this you must suffer an inescapable fate. But, really, 'suffer' isn't quite correct. For is it not a marvelous thing, to become a part of this supernal valley *in perpetuum*? To feel forever on your smooth and graceful form the kiss of lunar luminosity? To hear forever in the concave spaces of your delicate ears the valley's wondrous windsong? And we thought to place you here, beside this magnificent Black Stone, in aesthetic contrast, so to speak. No, do not try to weep or speak, for your fabric of mortality has altered so completely. You can barely utter sound, I know. If only you could see how beautiful you look, your limbs so white and burnished. We should have done something with your hair—something classical. Ah well."

Her hearing was beginning to fade, but she could still make out the song of flute, could sense the throbbing of the valley's maniac heartbeat beneath her unmovable feet. Too, she could hear the weird singing of the creatures that moved around her, the ones engaged in danse around the Black Stone. As her vision began to blur she saw Simon's bestial mouth stretch with singing, uttering a high wail that perfectly matched the sound of flute. She dully felt the chisel that was pressed against her arm, and vaguely saw the shadow of the mallet that crashed against the chisel and broke her limb from off her torso. Once more the mallet was lifted, as the other implement's sleek blade touched her other arm. Somehow, she found one last iota of inner strength. Aubrey Brood lifted her head so as to look away from the mockery that danced within the eyes of the Beast. She could vaguely make out the spectacular image of Mount Selta, that thing to which she was now forever linked. Summoning one final human breath, she uttered sound. It was a low moan, like unto the grinding of heavy stones. It issued through her solid lips as a sound of ecstasy for the mountain, and as elegy for that which had once been her human soul. And then her mouth, which had in life been so vivacious, forever sealed.

Wilum Hopfrog Pugmire is an eccentric recluse who dreams in Seattle, Washington. He is obsessed with H. P. Lovecraft, a madness he hopes never to outgrow. His goal as an author is to dwell forevermore within Lovecraft's titan shadow, and he dedicates his art to his fellow Lovecraftians, the only audience that matters. His books include *Sesqua Valley and Other Haunts*, *Tales of Love and Death*, and *Dreams of Lovecraftian Horror*. He is currently writing a new collection of traditional Mythos fiction for Mythos Books. He is the Queen of Eldritch Horror.